Slippery

By

Kimberly Ann Freel

 Country Messenger Press Publishing Group, LLC
Okanogan, Washington

This novel is a work of fiction. Any similarity to events, places, or people is purely coincidental and beyond the intent of either the author or the publisher.

Copyright ©2009 Kimberly Ann Freel. All rights reserved. No part of this book may be reproduced in any form, by photostat, microfilm, xerography, or any other means, or incorporated into any information retrieval system, electronic or mechanical, without the written permission of the publisher.

All inquiries should be addressed to:

> CMP Publishing Group, LLC
> 27657 Highway 97
> Okanogan, WA 988

Slippery may be ordered from CMP Publishing Group, LLC at the above address and at www.cmppg.com

Slippery is also available at Amazon.com.

Contact Publisher for distributor information.

email: cmppg@cmppg.com
website: www.cmppg.com

ISBN13: 978-098015547-1

Library of Congress Control Number: 2009911083

Dedication

This novel is for my four children who put up with their Mommy, the writer, even when she's brooding over a laptop, or doing dishes or laundry instead of taking them to the swimming pool.

Livia, Emma, Zander, and Ryder—you are the light I look up for when my antagonists steer me toward darkness, and you are the symphony in a house that's never, ever quiet.

I love you all very much.

—*Kimberly Ann Freel*

Slippery

Kimberly Ann Freel

Prologue

Guilt felt like a dozen piranhas in a feeding frenzy on a person's psyche. The perpetrator drove his Toyota 4x4 past The Mercantile for the fiftieth time since the accident. He couldn't drive the car anymore because it would be recognized. But then, he thought, *he* might be recognized too if he kept this drive-by vigil up.

He was pretty sure the young woman had slipped before he hit her and that it was her freakish fall to the ground and his inability to stop that caused him to run over her. He had a niggling sense of guilt anyway, from the moment of impact, and when it came to confessing that he was the driver of the car, he didn't have the courage. He had sulked back to his car and driven discreetly away from the chaos, all the while knowing that what he was doing was wrong, even if he hadn't caused the accident in the first place.

A devout Catholic, he knew that confession was good for the soul, but the nearest Catholic church was in Lewville, thirty miles away, and he felt bad going to confessional when it had been so long since he'd been to mass. He lived alone—there was no one to confide in, but also no one to implicate him.

So the predators—guilt, remorse, regret—kept eating away at his soul. He tried to feed them by repeatedly passing over the place where the young woman had lain so frighteningly still. He hoped that repetition, at least, could erase the bloodstains that remained in his mind's eye long after December snow had washed them away from the street's surface.

Slippery

Kimberly Ann Freel

Chapter One

It started as an ordinary day, without any sign of the upheaval that was to follow. Danica moaned and slammed the snooze button for the third time. She didn't know why it was so darn *hard* to roll out of bed on winter mornings—perhaps it was the dark, perhaps the cold—all she knew was that she wanted to sleep longer.

She stretched quietly, careful not to awake Milo, who laid next to her in the king-sized bed, his full cheeks and heart-shaped lips working a rhythm that suggested he never really quit eating, even when he was soundly asleep. Danica smiled tenderly and placed a lingering kiss on his downy head. He sighed contentedly.

Danica emerged from bed and jolted further awake as her feet hit the frigid hardwood floor. She flipped the switch that turned the alarm clock completely off. She looked past Milo at her husband, Jimmy. She fought a fleeting pang of resentment as he snored his way through another dream. She could wake him later. The kids needed to get up or they would miss the bus. There wasn't alternative transportation—she didn't even know if her old diesel would start on this inclement December morning.

Donning a fuschia fleece robe and leather moccasins, Danica passed the big kids' room and hollered, "Time to get up," on her way by as she headed to the front porch to feed the mutts. Her breath hung on the air, as she filled each dish and picked up the water dish to refill in the utility room.

Returning to the front hallway, she hollered, "Get up, guys, I *mean* it," as she paused at their doorway to find that they hadn't moved since her last trip by.

"I'm tired, Mom," came the voice of seven-year old Lorna from beneath a mammoth daisy-print comforter.

"You don't think I was tired?" Danica replied. "You don't see me lying around in bed, right now, do you? Get up," she repeated.

Seth still hadn't moved on the top bunk. Her nine-year-old was an extraordinarily heavy sleeper and she usually had to use a different tact with him.

"Hit the shower, Lorna. I'll send Seth along in about five minutes, so you need to be quick, 'cause he's next."

"Oh Mom, can't I just take a shower tonight?" Lorna whined.

"If you didn't smell like a dirty old sock, I'd say yes," Danica answered. "Only ten more days until Christmas break and then you can sleep in and stink all you want, I promise. Now scoot."

Danica continued to the kitchen as her sleepy daughter complied. She depressed the switch on the coffee pot, and the gratifying smell of liquid energy infused the air.

She grabbed the stiffened washcloth she'd put in the freezer for Milo—at just six months, he was teething something fierce. The washcloth was going to serve another purpose this morning. Wetting it slightly and ringing it out, she returned to Seth's bunk.

He let out a gasp when the super-cooled cloth was laid gently on his forehead.

"Holy crap, that's cold." He exclaimed.

"Good morning, Seth. It's about time you joined us." Danica took the washcloth back and shuffled back to the utility room to throw it in the laundry.

Seth slept like the dead, but a happier child never existed. Now that he was awake, he popped out of bed cheerfully and yelled to his mom, "Can I have breakfast?"

"Shower first. Lorna, are you done yet?" Danica hollered at the door as steam seeped under the threshold.

"Almost Mom. Just gotta rinse," was Lorna's muffled reply.

"I'll get your robe. Hustle up."

"Can't I eat first, Mom?" Seth was next to Danica, ebony hair sticking straight up, his blue eyes sparkling and clear when he'd been completely asleep only moments before. Danica marveled again at his good nature.

"If you're looking for something to do while you're waiting for the shower, you could get your lunchbox out of your bag for me. I'll make you a sandwich."

"Could I have hot lunch today? It's make-your-own taco day."

"Do you still have a ticket?" Danica quizzed.

"Yep."

"I guess so. I'll make lunch for Lorna, though. She hates the hamburger they put in those tacos."

"Lorna hates everything," Seth muttered.

"Okay. Be nice, mister." Danica ruffled his hair a little more. "She's just kind of picky."

Danica knew this was an understatement. She was pretty sure that her daughter existed on ham and cheese sandwiches and canned peaches. If Danica and Jimmy didn't require that she eat at least five bites of everything at dinner, Danica swore that Lorna would suffer from malnutrition. 'Thank goodness for gummy vitamins,' she thought.

"I need my robe, Mom!" Lorna shouted from the bathroom.

"Coming. Get ready for the shower, Seth."

Seth stripped naked in the hallway, modesty the furthest thing from his mind. He already shared a room with his sister, something Danica and Jimmy hoped to remedy when they remodeled in the spring. There was little to hide, though Lorna was strictly the opposite—she would be mortified if anybody but Danica saw her in the nude.

Danica struggled to see through the fog in the small bathroom as she handed the terrycloth robe to Lorna.

"Can Jimmy take us to school this morning, Mom?" Seth asked.

"Jimmy has to go south for work today. He has a job in Lewville, so he can't drop you off. Sorry."

"That's okay. Maybe tomorrow... Get out, squirt," Seth demanded at the doorway.

"I'm going to. Mom, Seth just called me a name."

Danica was already headed back toward the bedroom to get Lorna some clothes. "Don't wanna hear it," she said.

"Mom." Lorna appeared in the doorway. "I can't wear those pants. They rub me funny on the outsides of my legs."

"You're kidding, right? This embroidery and these rhinestones are all the rage. You insisted that we buy them, so you could be 'stylin',' as you put it."

"I didn't walk in them when I tried them on. I can't wear 'em, Mom. Can you find me something else?" Lorna whined.

"Let me look in the laundry room. You've stained the heck out the rest of the pants in your dresser."

"Can you find me some sweat pants?"

"I'll try, Lorna. Someday, girl, you are going to choose style over comfort, mark my words."

"Maybe I'll be a fashion designer and invent comfortable *and* pretty sweatpants."

Danica smiled ruefully. That was her girl—always

inventive, but never easygoing.

Lorna was in the second grade and Seth in the fourth. They both did well in school, but in completely different ways. Seth was a math and science whiz, but he couldn't spell worth a darn. He was continually frustrated by the English language, but he certainly tried. Lorna was an avid reader. Winter was her favorite time of year because she got to stay inside the house more and spend time reading. Danica struggled to keep enough suitable books around to satisfy Lorna's voracious reading habit. 'Thank goodness for the public library *and* gummy vitamins,' she thought.

"Hurry up in the shower, Seth," Danica called. "I laid your clothes out on Lorna's bed."

"Thanks Mom," Seth called. The mirror slowly cleared as steam escaped through the wide-open door.

She shook her head and smiled. Her children were so different. Lorna's eyes were the same sparkling sapphire blue as her brother's, but her hair was ash blond and much finer. She'd retained some of her baby fat, even though she ate like a bird. Danica called her 'lovably' round, but only if she was out of earshot.

Seth was gangly—all elbows and knees—and he was nearly as tall as Danica was. Since their biological dad was six feet tall, Danica suspected that Lorna would be stretching out in the next few years also.

Aside from appearance, their natures were as different as the sun and the moon. They were both sweet and for most of their young lives, they'd been her whole world, but they had little in common—Seth was neat; Lorna was a slob. Lorna was artistic; Seth couldn't even draw a decent stick figure.

She plopped bowls of instant oatmeal in front of each of them with a glance that brooked no argument over what they were going to have for breakfast. As she filled plastic cups with orange juice, she heard Milo and Jimmy stirring in the bedroom.

"The munchkin is up, Mom," Jimmy hollered sleepily.

"I can hear that. I'll be there in a minute. I just need to throw Lorna's lunch in her bag. Do you think you can take care of blow-drying your own hair, Lorna, so I can feed the baby?"

"Sure, Mom," Lorna muttered as she frowned at her oatmeal.

"Try to eat some, Lorna. You'll need the energy for the rest of the day."

"Mo-oom." Lorna drug the word out in protest.

"No whining," Danica retorted as she headed back to the bedroom.

"Hi, Beautiful," Jimmy's eyes shone appreciatively as he sat propped against his pillow, his knees raised, with Milo grinning and waving his arms upon his daddy's lap.

"Did you change him yet?" Danica kissed her husband and took her hefty baby boy out of his arms.

"Not yet. He was making some noises in that diaper, though."

"I admire your bravery and sense of adventure," Danica deadpanned as she put her son on his changing table.

Jimmy changed the subject. "It's supposed to snow today—first of the season. I'm glad I put those snow tires on over the weekend."

"Me too, but did you know that it's only fifteen degrees outside? Good thing the kids are on time, because I'd never get the diesel started today."

"I plugged it in, 'cause I thought the temperature might drop." Jimmy said.

"I'm grateful you were thinking ahead. It's been such a warm fall. I wasn't sure winter would ever come. Thanks for plugging in the truck, Honey. I need to get milk and bread at the store today. I'm taking Milo with me."

"You be careful if it starts snowing, Danny."

If he didn't call her 'Mom,' she had always been 'Danny' to Jimmy. His nickname for her was just one of the endearing things about her husband of nearly two years. Jimmy worked hard. He was playful and sweet, and he doted on her older kids just as much as she did. As she looked into her youngest son's eyes—chocolate brown and warm as pan-cooked pudding—she saw his daddy. God was never better than the day he sent Jimmy Burdick into her path. She was blessed and having Milo only made it better.

"We'll be careful, Daddy. No worries." She settled back against her pillow to nurse her son. Milo stared greedily at her chest as she readied her breast and he dove in with the same enthusiasm he always had about milk.

Danica relaxed. Perhaps the most rewarding thing about nursing her son was that it forced her to sit down once in a while.

"Little Buddy's hungry, isn't he?" Jimmy commented as he arose from bed and began to put on his work clothes.

"Isn't he always?"

Jimmy smiled and looked around their room. The crib sat beneath the window, forgotten and filled with baby gear, as the two of them learned quickly that, in order to sleep themselves, Milo would require a sleeping place next to his mother. The changing table sat at the foot of the crib. The rest of their furniture—a shabby dresser that Danica had good intentions of restoring, Jimmy's faux maple armoire and their tiny nightstands—were crammed into the remainder of the space around their enormous bed.

"I'm going to make this nice for us this Spring, Danny. I promise."

"I know, Jimmy. Since we sold the car and you started

driving a company rig, we've almost saved enough to do it. That's why I married you. You're a contractor. You're handy and talented and I know you're going to make our home big and beautiful as soon as you're able."

Jimmy grinned devilishly, his white smile a beacon in his olive-toned face. "That's not the only reason you married me, Danny Burdick." He winked.

Danica flushed as Milo continued to suckle away at her breast. "Why I do believe you're right about that, Jimmy Burdick," she feigned a Southern accent.

Then she changed the subject before the heated stare Jimmy was giving her erupted into something else. "You know, Milo's getting bigger, Jimmy. I could go back to work soon if you think it would help us get ahead a little. I'm sure the store could use another hand."

"No way. Your dad is going to have to find another clerk on his own. Our sweet little boy needs his Momma. We talked about this." Jimmy admonished.

"I know, Jimmy. I just feel guilty having you support all of us on your own. I wish I could help out more."

"Danny, you make my world brighter everyday being a good mom to our Milo and to Lorna and Seth. You put a healthy meal on the table every night. You keep our tiny house neat, even when the rugrats threaten to destroy it. Don't even think about messing with that. We're okay, honey. We really are."

"We are, aren't we?" Danica watched Milo tenderly, thanking her lucky stars once again. "Can you do me a favor, Jimmy?"

"Anything."

"Can you make sure Lorna got her hair dry and that they both put on warm coats and decent shoes before they head out to the bus?"

"Sure thing. Then I'm heading out. Have a great day,

honey."

From the bedroom, Danica could almost hear Jimmy ruffling Seth's hair before he stood and ate his cereal at the counter and chatted with Seth. She heard her daughter, her voice muffled as she hugged Jimmy's legs good morning and gabbed her way to the coat tree.

"Bus is here, Hooligans," Jimmy teased. "Better get moving."

"Bye, Mom."

"Bye, Mommy."

"Bye, Danny."

"Goodbye, everyone. I love you," she yelled in reply. Milo paused at her breast and caught her eye. With her nipple still in his mouth, he grinned wholeheartedly.

"And I love you too, little one." Danica smoothed Milo's cap of downy russet hair, her baby molded to her body—nature's perfect fit. She sighed contentedly.

Chapter Two

Danica and Milo drove the two miles to town, braving what was just the beginning of a wet snowstorm. If they finished in town before noon, they could be home again before the worst of the storm hit. She only hoped Jimmy would be careful since he wouldn't be off work until after six. By then it would be dark.

The town of Sibby, Washington, population 552, was best known in the State for its stance on gun laws: If you lived within city limits, you were *required* to own a sidearm. The way the town fathers figured it, one stood more danger of being offed by a rattlesnake or a cougar than by a fellow Sibbian. If the national sentiment was to ban handguns, Sibby's residents were first in line to thumb their noses at such an absurd idea.

Though more diverse commerce could be found ten miles down the road in Rickton or thirty miles South in the larger town of Lewville, there were only three retail establishments in the town of Sibby.

Bob's Hardware occupied the corner of Main and Easy Street. Its stucco façade boasted an emerald green finish and a five foot tall neon sign announcing 'Welcome to Bob's' that could be seen clear from the State highway.

Bob Rickton, a shirttail relative of *the* Ricktons, felt mightily threatened when a nationwide building supply company set-up shop in Lewville. His fears proved unfounded when he learned that his neighbors would not usually sacrifice quality and service for a half-hour drive to traffic lights and chaos. Besides, a surprising number of tourists stopped in at Bob's just because of his sign—a good thing since it had cost him a fortune. Danica waved now to his clerk, Maria, who was dressing the window display.

Wren's Market didn't have the same kind of luck when the big-box grocery store hit Lewville ten years prior. The owner, Glenna Stone, nearly lost the store that had been in her family for three generations. She had to diversify; and her natural foods store and bakery soon became known all over the county for its homey, country décor and unusual organic products. Glenna's daughter, Liz, had been Danica's best friend since preschool. Liz would be working today, so Danica knew she could visit when she went in for milk and bread.

First, Danica needed to go see Mom and Pop at The Mercantile. Pop, a card-toting member of the National Rifle Association, had read about Sibby in an enthusiasts magazine when Danica was three. Her early childhood home west of the Cascades was soon abandoned for the wilds of Eastern Washington. The Blades Mercantile had also been family-owned for three generations, but fast-talking Pop took just a week to coerce the disenchanted heirs into selling. Retail chain stores were imminent at that time, so many of the townsfolk had considered Lloyd "Pop" Dixon a fool when he bought The Mercantile.

The Mercantile was housed in a three-story historic brick building. Mom and Pop and their only child, Danica, converted the upstairs apartments into a two-story home; and Pop, ignoring the trend toward cheaper, poorly-made clothing, decided to eschew fashion trends altogether. Being a cowboy never went out of style, especially in this county, where cattle outnumbered people. The Mercantile was born and was always surprisingly busy, even in tiny Sibby.

For years, it was truly a 'Mom and Pop' business, run by the family; but Pop had been forced recently to hire outside help. Danica felt a stab of guilt and then squashed it. Milo and her family were more important than any store.

The bell over the door sounded her arrival.

"Hey Danica." It was Steve Oaks. Danica had gone to school with Steve. He was a ranch hand ever since then, until now. It still surprised Danica to see him cleaned up, without streaks of dirt on his face. He still wore a western-style flannel with mother of pearl snaps and Wrangler jeans, but his chestnut hair and rugged face were shiny clean, his nails neatly trimmed.

"Gee, Steve. You sure clean up nice."

"You say that every time." Steve looked her over appreciatively. "You're looking good, Danica—especially for a mom of three, with such a cute little baby boy." Steve waved at Milo in his backpack and she could feel Milo wiggle in return.

Danica shrugged off the compliment. Steve was like a brother to her. Danica, Liz, and Steve had run around together since grade school. She was pretty sure Steve finally took the job at The Mercantile so that he could keep tabs on Liz across the street at Wren's Market.

Danica wondered when Liz would stop torturing their good friend, Steve, and finally admit that he was the sauce for her hot wings. Something happened to Liz while she was away at college that made her shirk male attention. After three years, Danica still had not gotten to the bottom of it; but then she'd been mired in her own problems as well.

They were all twenty-five now—old enough to be conquering their demons. Danica felt like she was finally on her way.

Milo started to pump his legs and arms in excitement. Danica looked to her right and laughed. Her mom was playing peek-a-boo with Milo from behind a circular dress rack.

"Hi, Mom."

"Hi, Honey. How's our girl and her brood?"

"Oh, come on now, Marcia, it's not quite a brood yet," Danica's father piped in as he joined them from the stock room. "They need at least two more to qualify as a brood."

Danica balked. "Don't tell Jimmy that. He'll take it to heart. He'd have a dozen kids if I wanted them."

"It is a nice change from the other one, isn't it?" Marcia asked Danica covertly.

"Now don't go bringing that no-good S.O.B. up in my store," Pop boomed. "He's done quite enough to Danica, not to mention Seth and Lorna, to last the rest of my lifetime."

Steve took this as his key to leave the conversation. Any discussion of Danica's ex, Toby Browning, was bound to get ugly, and he didn't want anything to do with it. After all, Pop was mighty good with a rifle; and Steve and Toby had been known to have a beer or two together when Toby was still with Danica.

"I ought to have filled that boy's face with lead shot the last time I saw him. Do you know he actually had the nerve to go into Glenna's place and try to put the moves on Liz? As if he hasn't hurt one of our girls enough already," Pop said.

Danica could see that got Steve's ire up, but he went on hanging new shirts on the sale rack anyway. He obviously thought it best to ignore the entire conversation.

"Oh Dad, it wouldn't be worth it. You'd end up in jail and Toby would have another reason to take me to court to try and get the kids."

"How he gets the money for those lawyers, I just don't know," Marcia put in.

"Well *he* doesn't have it, that's for sure," Danica replied. "I think his Mama does, though."

"You think whatever little business she's got going at the trailer park is paying that much?" Pop asked.

"We don't want to know," the women said in unison. They grinned at each other even as Pop rolled his eyes. He'd always claimed Danica was just a chip off her mother.

"Anyway, I got the best part of him," Danica said. "Those kids are mine and Jimmy's in every way."

"Except for one weekend a month," Pop reminded her.

"Small sacrifice, Dad. I get them the bulk of the time and he weasels out of child support anyway. You'd still like to have Toby hanged for impregnating your only daughter at sixteen."

"And eighteen," her mother added.

"Hanging wasn't what I had in mind, Ladies," Pop said wryly. "All I can say is that he better stay away from Liz. I just wish he'd stay in Rickton and make Sibby a no-fly zone."

"I think he comes here just to raise your blood pressure, Pop," Marcia commented.

"A man's got to buy boots." Danica joked, waiting for Pop's retort.

"Toby Browning will buy boots from me the day he lets me put them on first and kick his butt right on out of here."

"Okay, on that note," Danica changed the subject before Pop really did burst a blood vessel. "I just stopped in to say 'hi.' I've got to get some milk and bread from Wren's while we're in town, and I want to get home before the snow gets bad."

"Why don't you let me spoil Milo while you go, so you and Liz can have a visit?" Marcia offered.

"I don't suppose they'll be very busy with the weather."

"Don't think so," Pop replied. "Steve and I are going to spend the day doing markdowns. The bulk of our customers have to drive to get here, so I don't expect many."

"Okay, Mom," Danica replied, flipping open the latches on the baby backpack. "He's all yours."

"Come here, little man!" Marcia held out her arms as Milo wiggled a happy hello.

"I fed him just before we left, so he should be good to go for a while. Just give me a call at Wren's if he goes ballistic."

"Not going to happen," Pop said smugly. "Your Mom has that baby's number."

"You're not giving him candy yet, right?" Danica joked.

"You'll never know my secrets," Marcia quipped in reply.

"I'll see you in a few." Danica looked over toward the sales rack. "See you, Steve."

Steve mumbled a reply. 'The big chicken,' she thought, 'I oughtta set him up on a blind lunch date with Liz. He wouldn't be able to avoid her then.'

The bell over the door rang again as she jaywalked across the street to see Liz.

Wren's smelled of patchouli and lavender blended with a yeasty invitation from the bakery at the back of the store. Danica could see that Glenna was hard at work through the kitchen window. Liz glanced up from her *People* magazine, her tortoiseshell-framed glasses making her look more like the town librarian than a store clerk. Her corkscrew amber curls were pulled back from her face with a wooly gray scarf that matched her eyes.

Liz greeted Danica with a straight smile—she had earned that smile with three years of braces, years that Steve teased her mercilessly about being a metal-mouth.

"Hi Danica. Where's Milo?"

"Oh sure. We've been friends for over twenty years and you kinda like me, but who you really want to see is my son, am I right?" Danica teased.

"Actually, Seth is the love of my life, but Milo is pretty cute too." Liz came around the counter and enveloped Danica in a fuzzy-sweatered, musky-smelling hug.

"Milo is with Mom."

"I know. I saw you go in with him earlier. I was just making sure you didn't forget him somewhere," Liz said.

"Like I would do that!" Danica laughed.

"You never know. With three whole heads to count, you might lose track of one once in a while. You recall: I was around for the days when you'd leave your math book at home four days in a row and you'd have to call your mom to bring it to you."

"That's true. I hope my inner mother duck has kicked in since then, so that I actually notice how many ducklings are following me!"

"I think your mother duck is probably just fine," Liz admitted. "So what's Jimmy up to today?"

"He had work in Lewville, giving an estimate to some people on restoring one of the Victorians."

"Oooh. That would be a fun job," Liz said wistfully. She had a fondness since her college days in Seattle for historic homes. She'd spent hours on weekends on walking tours of Capitol Hill, admiring the lush greenery and imposing facades of Seattle's finest older homes. She vowed to own a Victorian herself one day.

"Actually, Jimmy would be thrilled to have the job because it would last him well into next spring, but he doesn't relish the thought of driving to Lewville everyday in the snow."

"I don't blame him. I avoid driving altogether this time of year. It's just too dangerous. At least the snow waited awhile this year. Winter won't be as long."

Danica looked outside. The flakes were getting fatter, falling more lazily than they were when she'd walked across the street. The sky was darkening despite the fact that it was morning. They were in for a doozy. She shuddered, refusing to worry about Jimmy and the big kids, though a pressing sense of doom still weighed on her usually agreeable personality.

Liz joined her to gaze out the window. "It's breathtaking, isn't it? Hey, is everything okay, Danica? You look forlorn. I haven't seen that expression since Toby last decided to take you to court."

"Which was only a year ago—the minute he heard I was expecting Milo, he drug me back there. I swear he wanted something bad to happen to me and the baby, and what better way than to stress me out and try to take my kids, again."

"So is he making trouble again?"

"No. Thank God. Other than his once a month visits with the kids, I haven't heard from him in ages," Danica replied.

"So what's the problem, girlfriend?" Liz tucked an arm around Danica's shoulders, tickling Danica's face as her frizzy hair brushed her cheek.

"I just can't seem to shake this feeling that something bad is going to happen. This morning started out so ordinary and I felt happy and carefree. It's like my attitude has gone into the toilet with the weather."

Liz laughed, lightening the mood. "Oh, Danica. This is why you were meant to be an actress, and you would have been if Toby hadn't blown your plans to smithereens. You raised the hair on my arms with your doomsday gloom! Maybe we should see if you can get a part in the Spring musical at the Rickton playhouse."

Danica swatted Liz playfully. "I will be a famous actress someday. I always said I would be. Anyway, Toby wasn't the only one who made those gorgeous kids. They're worth every moment I've missed on stage." She flung her arms in the air dramatically and rolled her eyes, ending with her hands on her hips for added effect.

By now they were both giggling.

"What's up girls?" Glenna asked, emerging from the back with flour spots decorating her navy blue apron. Her hair, a grayer streaked version of Liz's, was pulled back and mostly covered by a chef's bonnet.

"I just came in for milk and a fresh loaf of honey wheat bread. Liz, here, is harassing me."

Liz stuck out her tongue like they were eight again.

"I'll go get your loaf of bread. It's still warm in the back." Glenna volunteered.

Danica's mouth watered. If she got Milo home soon enough, they might be able to slather a piece with butter before it cooled off. He could appreciate it later when he nursed. She was more into instant gratification.

"Do you want two percent or skim?" Liz asked as she headed toward the cooler to get a gallon of organic milk.

"Skim, please."

Danica paid for her purchases as Liz doubled bagged the bread to keep it warm longer. "We'll have to get together Saturday. I bet Steve would enjoy a game of poker at the house, just the four of us."

"Oh no," Liz whined, "Not the 'Steve' thing again!"

"Would it be so bad?" Glenna asked, nudging her daughter gently. As far as Danica knew, Glenna was the only one who knew exactly what Liz had gone through while she was away. It was the reason Liz had returned home with just a bachelor's degree, when she should have been moving forward to medical school.

"Mommy, you know I love Steve and so does Danica, though she'll never admit it. I'm just not ready to go there."

"You know the only reason he took my old job from Pop was so that he could be closer to you everyday?" Danica asked.

"Think so?" Liz wondered. The three of them grew quiet.

"I suppose I ought to retrieve my son from the evil clutches of his grandmother."

"Yeah right," Glenna mused. "She's probably already introducing him to the delightful taste of candy canes, if she's not giving him enough cuddles to sugar him up good for the rest of the day."

"That's what I'm afraid of—that she might be doing both and spoiling Milo irreversibly," Danica laughed.

Danica stepped outside to find that the storm had abated temporarily. The gray cast of the day made The Mercantile window translucent so she could see Pop with Milo on his shoulders, Milo's fists full of Pop's straight black hair. Danica waved enthusiastically at her son.

She could also see herself in the reflection of the solar shades, obviously her father's daughter with thick ebony hair and almond-shaped hazel eyes.

She did look pretty good for a mother of three, she decided, studying her reflection in its crimson wool coat, the bag of bread in her hands, the gallon of milk tucked under the other arm.

Traffic was light, so she decided to jaywalk one more time. She hustled across before the approaching sedan reached her vicinity.

She failed to note, unfortunately, that a layer of ice had formed underneath the falling snow from the colder early morning temperatures. Her haste met with disaster as her boots flew out from beneath her. The rest happened in slow motion:

Danica's gaze tilted from shop window to sky. Milk flew. A brown paper bag skittered across the street's surface. Her head exploded in a white light of pain as it was the first to strike ice and asphalt. Consciousness fled entirely as the driver of the blue sedan laid on its brakes and slid sideways toward her immobile body.

Chapter Three

Pop watched helplessly as his daughter fell and the driver of the sedan tried desperately to avoid her unmoving form. He hefted Milo quickly from his shoulders and clutched him to his chest. He cried out in alarm and abject grief as the car struck and passed over Danica's body.

"Dear God. NO!"

Marcia must have heard his cry from the back office, where she had taken a phone call.

"What is it, Pop?" She yelled, rushing to the front of The Mercantile.

"Steve, take Milo," Pop swung into action, shoving his startled grandson into the clerk's arms. "Mom, you need to get an ambulance here *now*."

Ignoring his coat, he threw the door open. "God, I need you now." Pop mumbled a quick prayer, a devout Christian, never more than right now as his only child lay eerily still on the street in front of him.

By now another driver had stopped to help. Pop rushed to Danica's side. She was breathing, thank the Lord, but only shallowly. Pools of blood were staining the snow beneath her head and her right thigh.

Pop's first-aid training came from his time in the Coast Guard, long before Danica had been a twinkle in his eye. Ironically, this was the first time he'd ever had to use it. Careful not to move her neck, Pop maintained Danica's airway by lifting her jaw carefully forward. A motorist came up and covered Danica with a fleece blanket. The two of them stood by in that position, unable to do anything else to help as a crowd gathered around them.

Glenna and Liz immediately swooped in and grabbed Marcia who rushed out to the street as soon as she called the ambulance. They tucked a coat around her and led her back into Wren's, where Pop spotted her watching in shock. Steve stood in the opposite shop window, in charge of Milo.

All five of these people who loved Danica, each in his or her own way, sent up a simultaneous prayer for her survival. It must have worked because she made it until the ambulance got there fifteen minutes later, and then she made it the ten miles to the nearest hospital in Rickton.

Liz took Milo from Steve and back to Wren's as Marcia and Glenna followed the ambulance in Danica's diesel, the nearest vehicle available to them. The paramedics wheeled Danica, Pop still by her side, into the emergency room. Marcia and Glenna stared on after them.

Glenna broke Marcia's reverie. "Someone needs to call Jimmy."

"I'll do it," said Marcia, as tears finally replaced shock and time suddenly lurched forward again. She let go of Glenna's hand and started toward the admitting clerk. "I need to use your phone."

Jimmy Burdick was making himself an undeniable hit at the stately Victorian on Main and Marble Street in Lewville, Washington. His russet eyes sung his sincerity, making him appear as solid and trustworthy as he was. His ideas for the restoration were fresh and bold, yet he seemed to understand that the owners were working on a budget.

They had come to an agreement on an estimate for time and materials and the handshake was pending when

Jimmy's silenced cell phone suddenly buzzed to life. His first instinct was to ignore it and let voicemail answer. Then he remembered that Danica and Milo had gone to town. He supposed she was calling to see if he needed anything.

He excused himself and answered the phone. "Jimmy Burdick."

"Jimmy, it's Mom."

Jimmy heard the carefully veiled panic in Marcia's voice. "What's happened, Mom?"

"There has been an accident."

Those five words struck the kind of terror a loved one never wanted to feel. His heart now in his toes, Jimmy choked out the next words. "Is it Milo?"

"No, Jimmy. Milo is safe. He's with Liz."

"Danny?" Tears sprung to his eyes, as Jimmy felt the love of his life slipping away from him. He dreaded the words that would come next.

"She's alive," Marcia blurted out, realizing that Jimmy might assume the alternative.

He let out his breath in a whoosh. His clients, noticing his distress, quietly left his vicinity as he focused only on the voice on the other end of the line.

"Where are you?"

"They brought her to Rickton Community, but we don't know how badly she's hurt, Jimmy. They might have to ship her to Spokane if…"

"If she makes it, right Marcia? Is that what you're trying to say?" Jimmy fought rising panic. He needed to get back to Rickton, but it was snowing piles and drifts in Lewville. It would take him at least an hour to get back with the roads looking like they did.

"I'm coming. Tell her to hang on, Mom. Me and the kids need her."

"Be careful, Jimmy. Think of Milo. He can't lose his

daddy…"

The next word remained unspoken—'too.'

Jimmy excused himself, promising his clients he would get back to them later. The owners were gracious, knowing he had pressing business. They wondered at his grief-stricken face as he retreated to his Burdick Building and Contracting truck and rushed away.

Glenna used her cell phone while Marcia called Jimmy.

"Hello?" Liz answered, sounding as frazzled as she felt. Milo was screaming his heartbreak.

"Liz. She made it here."

"Thank God. How are Mom and Pop holding up?" Liz yelled. She could scarcely hear herself over the baby.

"Marcia is calling Jimmy."

Liz stifled a sob. Poor Jimmy. This would crush him.

"I don't need to ask how Milo is doing, do I?" Glenna remarked.

"He's miserable, Mom. I think he's hungry. I don't know what to do with a hungry baby! Whenever he's with Danica, she just latches him on and all is well." Liz was near hysteria between worry for her friend and Milo's obvious distress.

"Give him some of the organic infant formula from aisle three. There should be a glass baby bottle somewhere in that aisle too. You can use the warm water from the sink in the kitchen since it has a filter. Try to get it about body temperature. Milo's not going to like it, honey. He's never had anything but his mommy's milk. But if he gets hungry enough he'll take it from you," Glenna advised.

"What's going to happen to Milo, Mommy, without Danica. She's his whole world."

"No, Liz. Danica was lucky this time. Milo has a real daddy. It's Seth and Lorna that are going to need us, and

Mom, and Pop, as we're all going through this." Liz's mother was wise. She'd been privy to all of the abuse, the tussles, and the just plain meanness of Toby Browning.

"Mommy, do you remember seeing the car that hit Danica after she fell?"

"I saw it briefly, but only after I saw Pop go screaming into the street. It was blue, kind of big, like a boat on wheels."

"Whoever was driving it left the scene by the time the police got here."

"That doesn't make any sense. It was clearly an accident that Danica fell on the ice in front of him," Glenna reasoned.

"They're investigating it as a hit-and-run now. Sheriff Posey himself came and interviewed me, not that he could hear me very well over Milo."

"That's awful," Glenna said. "Maybe the driver will come forward after he realizes that it was wrong to leave."

"The police know that you saw the car," Liz replied.

"Pop got a good look at it too. Marcia says he watched the whole thing happen."

Milo continued to fuss in the background and Liz tried mightily to keep the stress from her voice. They could talk more about the logistics of the accident later. Glenna offered, "You'd better take care of that hungry boy, Liz."

"Can you please keep me up to date on Danica?"

"I'll call you as soon as we know anything," Glenna reassured her.

"Give Jimmy a hug for me when you see him," Liz requested.

"That I'll do, Liz, honey. That I'll certainly do."

Chapter Four

Visibility was low as the world became monochrome, gray over white, white over the increasing black that was enveloping Jimmy as he tiptoed up a highway devoid of center and fog lines. He was making tracks until he got stuck behind a snowplow. At an excruciating thirty-five miles per hour, Jimmy willed his mind to a better place, lest he go insane with worry.

He mentally retreated to one of the happiest moments of his life—when he met Danica Dixon-Browning.

Jimmy moved from a suburb of Yakima, Washington to North Central Washington when he and his brother decided to split their contracting business and take advantage of one of the fastest developing areas of the State.

Burdick Building and Contracting was doing well in Yakima, but his much older brother had a wife and three children in school; and he'd been correct in assuming that they could get more substantial jobs by expanding the business. Besides, he and his brother weren't particularly close. Their similar work ethics made them worthy partners, but they definitely were not friends—just brothers continuing a family tradition.

Jimmy volunteered to move, since he was unattached—footloose, so to speak.

He bought the house outside of Sibby because it was perfect for himself and an occasional guest, plus it was already remodeled. At the time, he'd had no desire to practice his work after hours. Five scenic acres had been cleared of native sagebrush and greasewood and seeded with grass. Jimmy soon built a corral and got a dog and a single horse to keep himself company.

It was common knowledge that Sibby had the best western and tack store in the County, so Jimmy naturally went there to get Laredo, his sorrel gelding, outfitted.

That was the day the sun rose in Jimmy Burdick. Always shy, his dark good looks went mostly unnoticed by women. That didn't mean he was immune to females altogether. At twenty-eight, his family assumed he would stay a bachelor forever; but he secretly longed for a family, someone with whom to share his dreams and thoughts.

One look at Danica told him that she was married. She was all legs in her Wranglers, slender and about five and a half feet tall. Her sleek jet-black hair was cut simply to fall to her shoulders. In a red cowgirl button-up shirt, she was hot, but her demeanor, her ease sung out her unavailability. Plus she had a simple sterling band on her left ring finger to back up his assumption.

She helped him find a halter and saddle blanket for Laredo. His saddle had come with the horse. Before long she was talking him into proper riding boots. He followed her around the store pitifully, just hoping for more glimpses of her hazel-flecked orbs. They glowed like amber cabochons rimmed by lashes of mink.

He felt himself blushing repeatedly as she asked him pointed questions about his mini-ranch and about his job. He didn't know until much, much later that Danica had been scoping him out too.

Sibby is a small town, so it didn't take him long to find out that Danica was divorced—she merely wore the ring to fend off randy tourists. He also heard that she was a fantastic mother to two active children. Jimmy even got the pleasure of meeting Danica's ex, Toby, in the Sibby watering hole. Jimmy cleaned Toby's clock when he started badmouthing Danica.

It took him two months to work up the nerve to ask Danica out and this only after her father hired him to install a closet organizer. Jimmy would never forget that conversation.

They were working together—Pop bringing Jimmy the pieces to the organizer Marcia had insisted on having, Jimmy installing and leveling each shelf and rack. Pop was the first to break their companionable silence.

"So, Jimmy, you don't strike me as the kind of guy who would have a shirt fetish. You seem like me: a man's man, throwing on whatever is closest by."

"I'd say that's mostly true," Jimmy admitted.

"Then why is it that I see you in my shop two, sometimes three times a week, checking out my shirt racks. Now, don't get me wrong. I've noticed that you buy horse treats while you're in and that you're real friendly to my daughter..."

Jimmy reddened clear to the tips of his ears.

"Aaahh," Pop intoned knowingly. "Just as I suspected. You don't really like shirts so much as you like Danica. Well you see, Son, now we have a dilemma."

"How so?" Jimmy was a man of few words.

"The last man who came sniffing around my daughter with any regularity took advantage of her when she wasn't even old enough to drive. Then he impregnated her, married her, cheated on her, broke her son's arm, and *then* proceeded to make her life miserable, in that order. Yep, that about covers it."

"So what you're saying is to stay away from your daughter," Jimmy deduced.

Pop left the room long enough to haul another box from the top of the stairway. He let Jimmy stew on the statement even longer while he removed the contents from the box. Unable to stand the silence any longer, Jimmy tried again. "With all due respect, Sir, I'm nothing like Toby Browning."

"You know Toby Browning? Aren't you new in town?"

"He had the misfortune of meeting me. He and I didn't exactly see eye to eye, especially after I knocked him on his keester," Jimmy said.

Pop chuckled. "I'd have liked to see that. You might be all right, Jimmy. You might be all right."

They finished the job in the late afternoon without broaching the subject of Danica again. Jimmy was packing up his tools and writing a note in his work ledger when Pop approached him once more.

"I'm not sure Danica could take any more heartbreak, Jimmy. You understand?"

"I do."

"But we'll never know what might be if you never have the guts to ask her out," Pop pointed out.

With this, Jimmy felt a glimmer of hope. He wasn't being told to stay away.

"You wouldn't mind if I took her out, Mr. Dixon?"

"Lord, Son. Call me Pop. Everybody else does. No, Jimmy, I don't mind. It is probably about time Danica started to make her way in the world again as more than just a mom and my employee. It would do her good to get out. Besides, I think I like you."

Jimmy flushed again and looked at his shoes. To this, he had no reply. Now he just had to get up the nerve to ask her out.

Jimmy took in a shaky breath now. That was four years

ago. He'd asked her out. He'd fallen head over heels in love with her, and she with him. He'd begun to think of Seth and Lorna as his kids too. And then they had Milo and the world took on a dreamlike quality. Euphoric happiness truly existed in everyday life.

Now this—how could this happen to them? They were young and they had plans. They lived modest, healthy, fulfilling lives. They had a home. They had children.

Danica could be dying. She could die even before he glimpsed her face just one more time. There'd been an accident. Marcia's words reverberated in his mind as he became blind with snow and overwhelming fear. He felt his tires slip again, urging him to pay attention. He struggled to keep his truck on the road. He had to be safe and strong now, for Milo, for Seth and Lorna.

Frustrated tears began to flow as he struggled to remember if he had even kissed Danica goodbye.

Chapter Five

Danica felt pain, excruciating, like nothing she'd ever felt even in birthing three children. Then it melted away. Her body retreated from it like a mouse fleeing from a hawk and finding a tiny vestibule beneath a hay barn. She snugged her mind into this safe haven with her body and allowed it to drift.

Suddenly she was in her wedding dress, the filmy beaded gown she'd worn when she married Jimmy. Her hair was bound in a crown of tiny rosebuds and baby's breath, ringlets tickling her cheeks and neck. She looked to her side to see four-year-old Lorna in her peony pink dress and six-year-old Seth in his handsome cowboy tuxedo, but they weren't there.

A moment later, she was still in her wedding gown, but she was looking at the sky, the clouds as huge as they'd looked on their honeymoon at Glacier National Park—Big Sky Country. They grew larger as she watched. Then she realized she was floating on a lake, her body moving to and fro on lapping waves at the edge of the shore.

The sun grew brighter, beckoning her to touch it, feel its searing heat for herself. Instead she basked in its glow, confused and wanting to know where her children were, and Jimmy, but enjoying the escape from her ravaged body. She decided to stay here for now. Her feet pointed toward the shore, she rode *that wave—back and forth, back and forth.*

Pop stood outside the emergency bay, watching as the doctor and three nurses calmly assessed Danica, inserted a tube down her throat to aid her breathing, stuck two IV's into opposite arms, and started her on a bag of A-negative blood. A portable x-ray machine was wheeled in and personnel were tucked to the side as x-rays were taken of her neck, back, chest, and right leg.

Pop knew, just looking at Danica, that the right leg was horribly broken. What he didn't know and desperately wanted to, was how her brain was. She needed to be much more stable before the ER doctor would allow her to be moved to CAT scan to have her head checked.

Pop stood watching, waiting, until it felt like his knees were wobbling. He felt the familiar weight of Marcia by his side. She motioned to the chairs across the hall from the bay door.

They sat there for what seemed like hours, calm murmurs of the nurses and repetitive, but reassuring beeps from Danica's monitors reaching into their companionable silence.

It was Marcia who broke it. "Do you think she'll be okay, Pop?" She wrung her hands, as if she already knew the answer to her question.

"Oh, Mom," Pop's voice cracked with emotion. "I want to reassure you. I do. And I want to be reassured myself. But that scene just keeps replaying over and over in my head. That car, Mom. It slid sideways, fast, and went right over her like she was a bump in the road. She would have been fine if she had just fallen. But I just don't know now. I don't know."

He hadn't shed tears until now. Just a few escaped his eyes, but he quickly checked them when he saw Jimmy rushing down the hall toward them.

Jimmy looked exhausted, wild with worry, and with grief.

"Where is she?"

Pop nodded toward the door across the hall. Jimmy stood in the doorway, his chest heaving, watching silently. Danica was so still and pale, tubes and wires everywhere. The colored lines and sounds of her monitors told him that she was hanging in there. Though the medical staff appeared to be watching over her carefully, they didn't seem really to be *doing* anything.

He caught the doctor's eye.

"Can I help you?" The young doctor inquired.

"I'm her husband. Can I see her?"

"You can for a second, but I'm afraid you must make it brief. We've finally stabilized her blood pressure enough to take her to CAT scan, so we can see what's going on inside. They'll be here any minute to take her."

Jimmy nodded and entered the room.

He took her hand. It was icy and he winced as he noticed an IV sticking up from the inside of her wrist. Still, he kissed the back of her hand.

"I'm here, Danny," he said simply. Nothing happened. She wasn't there, not really and Jimmy could somehow sense this. He refused to believe that she would slip away forever, though, so he went on holding her hand until the technologists politely asked him to leave so they could gather her up.

As she was wheeled out of the room on a stretcher, he asked the doctor, "How is she?"

"As you could see, she was stable. I'm guessing from her reflexes that she's got a moderately severe brain injury and the CAT scan will tell us what we need to know there. We also need to make sure she's not bleeding internally.

So far we've only needed one unit of blood, so I don't think she's actively bleeding anywhere. She's got a broken femur—that's the upper leg bone—and it will eventually need to be fixed surgically, but we have to resolve the other issues first."

"Is she going to make it?" Jimmy choked out. The doctor answered reluctantly.

"I honestly don't know. She's been injured severely, and there are so many issues to deal with now. It will be mostly up to her. You do need to know that with the extent of her injuries, we might have to ship her to Spokane for more critical care. These tests will tell us everything we need to know."

"Except if she will survive," Jimmy added grimly.

"She's incredibly strong to have survived thus far. I would encourage you to hope, Mr. Burdick, but it would be beyond my scope of practice to do so."

"I understand. Thank you, Doctor."

Mom and Pop stood in the doorway absorbing the conversation. They gathered together again in the hallway, Mom giving Jimmy a reassuring hug.

"You never told me what happened to her, Mom," Jimmy said, wiping tears from his eyes.

"She was crossing the street, coming back for Milo, who was with us. Her feet went out from under her. That's all," Marcia said.

"So she just fell?" Jimmy asked, disbelieving.

"Except that she fell when a car was approaching," Pop added gently.

"Oh, God. Did it hit her? Did Danny get run over by a car too?"

"I'm afraid so, Son. I watched it and I'd tell you the grisly details, but you simply don't want to know, Jimmy; and I don't want to talk about it."

Jimmy laid a reassuring hand on Pop's shoulder. The facts could come out in time, but for now they had both had enough trauma to last a good long while.

"Where's Milo?" Jimmy needed to know that he was safe, at least.

"He's with Liz at Wren's Market," said Pop.

"He needs his Momma and me, but I suppose Liz is the next best thing," Jimmy nodded, thinking of his little man. How would Milo ever survive without Danny? He willed his thoughts quickly away from that possibility. Truth was, none of them could live without her, so she just had to be okay.

They sat again in silence for nearly a half hour when realization dawned on Marcia.

"What time is it?"

"Almost two," Pop replied, examining his diver's watch. Time had really flown while they were waiting for news.

"Somebody needs to get Lorna and Seth from school. They don't know what's happened yet," Marcia said.

"I could send Glenna. I think she's still waiting in the admitting area. I need to fill her in anyway," Pop offered.

"No way, Pop," Jimmy objected. "They're as much mine as they are Danny's. I'm their dad in all the ways that count. I need to tell them."

Pop nodded solemnly. It wasn't a job he wanted, that's for sure.

"I'll fill Glenna in on the way out," Jimmy said, pulling out his keys and cell phone and heading down the hallway.

Mom and Pop watched him go—a dear, forlorn man listing along in a sea of emotion—and they stopped thinking about their daughter long enough to feel raw sorrow for their relatively new son.

Chapter Six

The grade school in Sibby, a square, utilitarian building older even than Bob's Hardware, housed an office, a small gym, and three classrooms, sorted into grades Kindergarten through Second, Third and Fourth, and Fifth and Sixth. Jimmy pulled gingerly into the parking lot and noticed the brick façade coated in a fine blanket of snow. A good snowstorm had a way of making even an ancient edifice look like a refuge.

He took care not to slip on the asphalt, a hazard he wished he could have warned Danica of. If only he could turn back time, volunteer to pick up the groceries on the way home, keep Danica away from town just for that day, Jimmy would do it in a heartbeat.

There was still another fifteen minutes of school, so Jimmy hunkered through the snow and headed straight for the principal's office.

"Mr. Burdick, how can I help you?" The school secretary, Shelby Lowe, greeted Jimmy warmly in all her platinum blond, perfumed glory.

Jimmy detested intrusion into their private lives, but he knew the kids would be out of school now through Christmas break, so he would have to tell these people about Danny. His own terror still fresh, he opted for the short phrase, "There's been an accident."

"Oh my Gosh. Okay. Who was hurt?" Shelby picked up the phone and pressed the principal's button, listening to

Jimmy as she waited for Ronald First, the principal, to pick up.

"It's Danica. She's at the hospital in Rickton and I need to get the kids."

She held up a bejeweled, crimson-tipped index finger. "Jimmy Burdick is here and he needs to get Seth and Lorna Browning. Do you mind coming out here, please?" She nodded as she hung up the receiver.

"Ronald's on his way. How badly was Danica hurt?" Shelby asked more out of curiosity, than true caring. Shelby was fifteen years older than Danica and they'd never been friends. Now Shelby and Toby were a different story— Shelby Lowe and Ashley Browning, Toby's mom, were thick as thieves. Shelby lived in Ashley's trailer park.

Ignoring the question, Jimmy turned to Ronald First.

"The final bell is about to ring, so we'll collect Lorna and Seth as they're on their way out, how does that sound?" Mr. First offered.

"That will be fine. I need to let you know, though, that they won't be back until after Christmas break."

"That's not a big deal, since it's so close, but can I ask why?" Ronald inquired.

"Danica's had an accident," Shelby interrupted rudely.

"What kind of accident? Is she going to be okay?" Ronald asked.

"I don't know," Jimmy admitted grudgingly. "I just need the kids. I need to tell them and take them to her."

"She's at the hospital in Rickton," Shelby repeated as much as she knew, trying to seem well-informed for her boss' benefit.

Jimmy rolled his eyes impatiently. "Danica fell on the ice and she was hit by a car."

Shelby gasped dramatically. Jimmy was pretty sure the first thing she would do when he left was call Toby or his mom. He stared hard at her, willing her to shut up now, even if she felt compelled to blab later.

He continued. "She's having some tests done and we'll know more after."

"I see," Ronald replied. "It sounds like she's lucky to be alive. We'll just go on over and meet the kids, and I'll let you get back to Danica. You will keep us updated, of course?"

"I'll try, Mr. First. She may get shipped out to Spokane. The next few days will be pretty hectic…"

"I understand, of course. I can always call Pop at the end of the week. We usually have coffee on Sundays after church," Ronald said as they continued out of the office.

Shelby Lowe hung on their every word; and as soon as they were out of earshot, she picked up the phone again, her blood-red nails plucking out the number she knew by heart.

The K-2nd classroom was first from the office, so Jimmy and Ronald stopped there first. Mrs. Hansen was reading from something that sounded like Dr. Seuss. Lorna smiled as much at the antics on the illustrated pages as the rhythm of the story. Jimmy's heart nearly burst with love and sorrow. He let Mrs. Hansen finish the story. Then Mr. First cleared his throat.

"Jimmy!" Lorna exclaimed running to him and hugging his legs, glad as always to show off one of her parents to her classmates. Then she noticed the tears in his eyes.

"What's wrong?"

"Lorna, honey, I need you to grab your coat and gather your things as quickly as possible so we can go get Seth. I'll explain everything in the car."

"Is Milo okay?" Lorna was seven, inquisitive, and always incredibly intuitive. Jimmy knew better than to think she'd last until she got to the truck before she started asking questions. She was her mother's girl—that was for sure.

"Milo's good." He replied, knowing that Liz would have everything under control with the baby. "Just hurry, Lorna. I'm going to go get Seth going too, okay?"

"Okay," she shrugged, even though it wasn't.

They stepped across the hall to Seth's classroom. He did immediately as he was asked, sensing correctly that something was terribly wrong. Jimmy was never melancholy when he picked them up. In fact, he usually took them to do something fun after school.

Jimmy, Seth, and Lorna emerged to a white-out. They could scarcely see the truck through the storm. Now the kids knew why they'd had to play in the gym during recess.

They threw their bags in the tool box in the back of Jimmy's truck and hustled into the rig.

Seth and Jimmy took the outer seats. Lorna buckled her seatbelt between them. She'd just barely outgrown her booster seat and Jimmy could tell she was happy to sit up front just like the guys. "Where're we going, Jimmy?"

Jimmy sighed. "No place good, Lorna. Your Momma's hurt," he started, telling them the whole story as they sat there with the engine running, the heater on, their collective breathing turning into trickling vapor on the truck's windows.

The three dissolved into tears, hugging awkwardly across the bench seat of the truck. School was out, but they were blind to it, as the world went on around them while theirs stood still. Then Lorna asked the question that was at the forefront of everybody's mind.

"If Momma dies, Jimmy, will you still be our Dad?"

"I sure hope so, baby girl. I will fight with all I have to make sure, okay?"

Lorna gazed into Jimmy's eyes. He saw in their depths pure trust and a soul innocent of all of the ugliness in the world. As he looked past her to Seth, a boy who knew exactly how awful two parents could be when they fought over two little kids, he said a quick prayer that he would never have to fight that fight.

"Let's go see your mom," he said as his voice cracked once again. He rolled down the windows to clear them of the fog and shifted the truck into gear.

Chapter Seven

As he returned to the hospital, Jimmy found that picking up the kids had been a welcome distraction. Danica was back in the ER, but the hospital's imaging interpretations came remotely from Seattle, so the waiting game was on to see just how injured she was.

Pop took up pacing. Mom and Glenna waited calmly in the chairs outside the exam room. Lorna and Seth walked behind Jimmy, pale and so small.

Mom wondered aloud if it was a mistake to bring them here, at least until they knew more about Danica.

Jimmy heard her softly spoken question. He spoke under his breath in reply as they embraced. "I almost took them to Liz too, so they wouldn't have to see her like this. But they insisted, Mom. They just kept asking, 'What if she dies?' I didn't have the heart to tell them that they might never get a chance to say goodbye."

Mom nodded and hugged each of her grandchildren. The doctor allowed each child a brief time to say 'hello,' accompanied by Jimmy. As a child gripped each hand, Jimmy half hoped that she would awake to their touch. But just as before, Danica was unreachable, still as a wax figure, except the rise and fall of her chest as the respirator breathed for her.

Another half hour passed before results were back and the emergency doctor had a chance to consult specialists in Spokane and Seattle. He gathered them all in a private corner of the ER waiting room.

"I haven't properly introduced myself since I've been so busy with Danica, but I'd like to now. My name is Dr. Mike Moreland and I'm a general practitioner here in Rickton. What many people here don't know about me, though, is that I also spent time before coming here completing a fellowship in neurosurgery.

"While this hardly makes me an expert, I am probably more aware than most G.P.'s of the effects of a traumatic brain injury," Dr. Moreland continued.

"As I said before, Danica is stable, and, as I suspected, she does have a mild to moderate brain injury. It is apparent from her CAT scan that she suffered an insult. How this will affect her function and awareness, I don't know. Every brain injury is different. So far, Danica hasn't shown any signs of consciousness or response to stimuli. She's also not trying to breathe on her own. She is, for all intents and purposes, in a coma and reliant on the respirator.

"Once we answered the question of whether she had a head injury or not, several other experts and I sat down and discussed over the phone her images and her clinical appearance to decide if she should be sent to one of the larger hospitals for surgery or treatment. Our current decision is that we are doing everything we can to help her at this point. Unless her brain starts to swell unexpectedly, Danica can forego surgery for now. We can keep her in Rickton."

"Now wait a second," Pop interrupted. "Am I to believe that she's getting the best care possible if she stays here? A bigger hospital would be so much better equipped."

"I can't disagree with you. But for now, Danica doesn't appear to be getting any worse. The damage is done. We have an orthopedic surgeon who can fix her leg when we are absolutely sure that she's stable, in the next week or so," Dr. Moreland replied.

"And if her brain swells and she gets worse? Wouldn't she be better off somewhere else?" Pop quizzed.

"We can have a *MediCopter* flight here in less than an hour if she shows signs of her condition worsening."

"I want her here." Jimmy said resolutely, his voice barely audible.

"Oh, Jimmy, honey," Marcia soothed. "I know you do. But we need to think of what's best for Danica."

He persisted. "What's best for Danny is to have her kids and me here for her every day. We can't do that if they ship her three or four hours away."

"We could help you, Jimmy. It's not like we wouldn't help with the kids. We could take turns driving and maybe find a place there to stay or rent an RV or something," Pop suggested.

"Dr. Moreland says she'd be just as well taken care of here," Jimmy insisted.

"I know you're all frightened for Danica," Dr. Moreland said. "Let me see if I can make you more confident in my skills as I care for her. I came to Rickton because the State agreed to pay off my student loans if I came to a rural care facility. The hours and stress of neurosurgery made me glad to leave it behind. I have much more time for my young family now. But, I assure you, I have had excellent training. If I sensed that Danica was in any danger, I would be the first to admit that she needed more intense care."

Jimmy would brook no further discussion of transferring Danica. "It's settled then. Do you think Danny is going to be okay, Doc, after she wakes up?"

Dr. Moreland, with his sparkling blue eyes and rumpled sand-colored hair, looked like a boy as he ventured a smile. "I like your optimism, Jimmy. Yes. We need to look forward to Danica waking up. Let's believe that it will happen and we'll handle everything else from there. We'll continue to help her breathe in the meantime and keep a close eye on her neurological symptoms."

Pop shook his head in frustration. "I wish you would reconsider, Jimmy."

Marcia laid a hand on his arm. "Don't, Pop," she murmured quietly. "You know he wants what's best for her too."

Lorna and Seth kept quiet during this discussion. As Dr. Moreland walked away to see that Danica was settled into an intensive care room, Lorna slipped her hand in Jimmy's. "I'm glad you didn't let them send her away, Jimmy."

Jimmy swallowed a lump in his throat the size of a softball. These children really meant the world to him. He just hoped that he wouldn't let them down.

It was nearly two hours later and Jimmy had just come back from calling and checking with Liz about Milo. Milo was sleeping, though it had taken her a good hour to get him to take a bottle. Distress ruled the entire exchange. Milo simply wanted and needed his mom.

Jimmy watched the gentle rise and fall of his wife's chest. So still she was. He wondered where she had gone, where her mind retreated to. He sighed. It was going to be a long night.

Mom and Pop had taken Seth and Lorna to their apartment. Dr. Moreland, after a long day, was preparing to go home for the evening.

Jimmy approached him at the nurse's station. "I want to thank you for taking care of Danica today. I know part of the reason she's still with us was the care you and your staff took with her."

"It's my job, Mr. Burdick. I'm glad she's been strong

enough to hang in there."

"I have one more question. Danny and I have a little boy who's only six months old. She's been nursing him full-time since she had him. Is there any way for her to continue doing it?"

Dr. Moreland's eyes widened in surprise. "I'm sorry. I had no idea that she was still lactating. I guess I should have noticed. I'm sure she's quite uncomfortable by now, though we have no way of knowing how aware she is of it. There are several drugs that will inhibit the production of prolactin. I'll prescribe one immediately."

"Now wait just a sec, Doc," Jimmy said, shifting his weight to his other foot as he discussed a subject familiar, but unchartered regarding the mother of his child. "Is that the only option? For her to stop nursing completely?"

"Mr. Burdick..." Dr. Moreland began.

"Call me Jimmy."

"Jimmy. Until Danica regains consciousness, which could be tomorrow, or could be next week, we'll be giving her TPN, which means total parenteral nutrition. We'll introduce the nutrients she needs to survive directly to her heart through a central venous line. We can give her what *she* needs, but you're suggesting that she feed another person, while she's out."

"Well I was thinking maybe one of those pump thingies." Jimmy flushed as he thought of the few times he'd seen Danny pump. It really was comical how much she'd resembled a glorified dairy cow. They'd laughed themselves silly as they watched the plastic cones stretch and squeeze her poor nipples.

"We could probably figure that out, logistically," Dr. Moreland conceded. "But it would be highly irregular to let a comatose patient continue to lactate."

"Aren't there herbs or vitamins or something you could

give her to increase her milk supply even on, what'd you call it, TPN? I mean, if you can *decrease* the milk, can't you also *increase* it?" Jimmy persisted, much as he'd done earlier in the day.

"Do you honestly think Danica would make this choice if she were able to tell us what to do?" Dr. Moreland asked.

"I just know that she made a promise to herself and Milo to breastfeed him until he was at least a year old. I think if there was any physical way she could keep feeding him, she'd do it," Jimmy said. "Besides, Milo needs his momma. He can't have her right now, but at least he could have a part of her. Something familiar."

Dr. Moreland softened. "I have three kids of my own and the youngest is just three months old. I wonder what I would do for my wife. She's a staunch proponent of breastfeeding herself.

"You know, Jimmy," he continued, "I might be able to arrange it. Let me make a few phone calls. I've never tried such a thing, so I'll need to find out more about the risks. You need to know, also, that if Danica's brain starts to swell and she has to be put on medications to reduce the damage, all bets are off. She'd never be able to take these medicines and continue to breastfeed."

"I appreciate your checking," Jimmy said gratefully.

"In the meantime, I'll have my nurse call the people over in OB and have them bring a pump over. We need to at least relieve some of the discomfort as soon as possible."

"In case she *is* feeling it," Jimmy deduced.

"Let's hope that she is. Any such awareness could only be good," Dr. Moreland replied.

"Thanks, Doc."

"Don't mention it, Jimmy." They shook hands companionably, partners on a mission for Milo and Danica.

Chapter Eight

Danica wafted to and fro on the waves until she panicked as she realized the water was splashing repeatedly over her face. Was there a storm picking up? She couldn't breathe. Something was pressing on her chest.

There was an ache. Not like the pain before, but an undeniable pressure that she yearned to release. Maybe then she could breathe.

Danica tried to rise from the water, but each movement brought further immersion. Now she wished she could grab a hold of the sunshine. When had the water gotten so darn cold?

She tried to swim, but her arms were immobile. Her wedding dress had bound them against her side.

She was going to drown in this miserable lake. She tried to will away the despair. What about her children and Jimmy? What would they do without her?

Then, a familiar tug. A release. And the pressure let off a little and continued to. She relaxed and felt her body float away from shore, no longer carried by the waves and at their mercy. Now she followed a current, a way to somewhere. As her breathing returned to normal and she felt the sunshine once again on her face, Danica waited for the current to take her home again.

Chapter Nine

Jimmy could have gone home for the night; and he would have, but he couldn't tear himself away from the sight of his wife fighting for her life. Every moment, every glance could be the last. At least that's what it felt like. He kissed her goodnight on the forehead and cheek at least ten times, memorizing her velvet skin, the curve of her sable lashes; and then he wound right back up in the blue, vinyl-covered chair in the corner of her room.

Sleep was the furthest thing from his mind, yet somehow it claimed him in the early hours of the morning. He awakened to a low moan from the direction of the bed. He pried his gritty eyes open to see Danica's feet moving. Was she waking up?

Jimmy rushed to her side as one of the monitors let loose with a shrill alarm. A male nurse was right behind him, shoving him out of the way.

"You're going to have to leave, Sir," the broad, young man ordered.

Jimmy backed out of the room as more medical staff swarmed into the ICU. She wasn't waking up. In fact, something was dreadfully wrong. Her eyes were open, but they were rolled back in her head, and her arms and legs were moving, but they were stiff and working in unconscious rhythm. More than one alarm began to blare.

Jimmy made his way numbly to the ICU waiting area just outside imposing double doors. He sat with his head in his hands. What time was it? Why had he fallen asleep? Was Danica dying now? Why did he feel like he had let her down?

He felt a hand on his shoulder. He looked up to see Pop, whose craggy face held a mixture of fear and sympathy. Pop had the kind of leathery complexion that made him look forever forty, even when he'd been younger. But he'd aged overnight, his black shock of hair suddenly infused with much more white than Jimmy had seen before, the lines on his face deepened into puffy wrinkles.

"What's happened, Son?" Pop asked, seeming to sense Jimmy's grief.

"I don't know, Pop. I spent the night in Danny's room, and when I woke up she was moving, but not normally. She set off all kinds of alarms. What if this is it, Pop?" He couldn't keep the terror from his face and he looked skyward because he couldn't stand to see the sorrow in the depths of his father-in-law's eyes.

Pop had been destined for the ICU, but now he sat down beside Jimmy, both resigned to whatever fate had in store for Danica.

It seemed like they sat there for hours, though barely an hour passed. They'd seen Dr. Moreland rush through the big double doors. Now he emerged, his expression unreadable. Jimmy and Pop stood in greeting.

Dr. Moreland cut to the chase. "She's had a seizure, but we've gotten it under control. We'll be doing another CAT scan to see if there's been any change in the amount of hemorrhaging since yesterday. We're still monitoring her intracranial pressure and that remains stable. She's resting now."

"Are you finally going to send her where she needs to be?" Pop demanded.

"Pop," Jimmy's voice contained a warning.

"If her test comes out okay, we'll keep her here. Seizures are relatively common in a patient with traumatic brain injury. Her brain is trying to reset itself and signals get mixed, triggering a seizure. Now that she's had one, we'll give her medication to keep them under control. Jimmy, I checked to make sure the drug we're using is compatible with lactation."

"You what?" Pop demanded.

"Jimmy and I have decided to continue to let Danica produce milk, which we're pumping for her, until she wakes up."

"Of all the hair-brained ideas, Jimmy Burdick. Milo will be just fine, but Danica may well not be. Why can't you just leave this alone? Why are you so centered on you and the kids' needs and not hers?"

Dr. Moreland cleared his throat. "Yes. Well. I'm going to let you two hash this out. Danica is stable again for now and I'll be checking in with her throughout the day. I'll keep you updated."

The double doors opened once again and Danica emerged on a stretcher with five people in scrubs surrounding her with her monitors, respirator, and IV pumps.

Pop stared forlornly after her as they made their way down the hallway to Radiology.

"I don't understand you, Jimmy." He said quietly. "I always thought you loved my daughter more than life itself. It's why I like you."

"I do love her that way, Pop."

"Then why are you willing to put her in danger?"

"First of all, I like Dr. Moreland. He's a smart guy, and I have every faith that he can figure this out. Second, it's what Danny would want."

"Danica would want to live, first of all." Pop insisted.

"Pop, we're only going to discuss this one last time, because ultimately I'm her husband and I'm going to make the choice. Danny is like you. She's opinionated and strong and she's one hell of a parent because if she does nothing else, she makes sure that what she believes is law, whether it's conventional or not."

He continued, as Pop remained mute. "She fought for her kids, for her freedom from her asshole of an ex-husband, and she fought with you when it came to the decision to leave the store and stay home with her baby. Come on. You know your daughter. She's no victim and she's no pushover. She will not let this beat her. Can you have faith in that?"

"I'd like to. What does that have to do with continuing to feed Milo? That's just over the top, Jimmy."

"She could wake up tomorrow or next week. You remember how determined she was to keep nursing him. Toby made her give it up at three months with the other two kids because the babies took too much of attention away from him. Don't you think, knowing Danny, that she would be incredibly disappointed that she couldn't take up feeding her son after she woke up?"

"She may not be in any shape to feed Milo for a while after she wakes up," Pop pointed out.

"We can deal with the breastfeeding issue on a day-by-day basis. If she's in any danger, I'll ask Dr. Moreland to prescribe the medicine that can stop her milk production. Can you just go with me on this, for now?"

"I guess I have to, don't I?"

"Just believe that I have her best interests at heart too, will you?" Jimmy held out his hand. Pop shook it and they took their seats to wait once more.

*M*om and Glenna arrived an hour later with Milo,

Lorna, and Seth in tow.

"Pop tells me that Milo here has some goodies in store for him," Mom bounced him on her hip, as he grinned a warm greeting to his daddy.

Jimmy immediately reached for his baby boy and held him close. "Hey, little man. How's my boy? You seem healthy." He held Milo away as he examined him with a twinkle in his eye. "Yep. You've still got that double chin." He tickled his baby under his chin and Milo let out a delighted giggle.

He turned to the other kids. "How're you two holding up?"

With the resilience of youth, Lorna replied first. "We're okay. Grandma made us pancakes with strawberries and whipped cream for breakfast!"

"Yum." Jimmy's stomach growled and he realized how long it had been since he'd eaten anything.

"There's a plate for you in the oven at your house, Jimmy," Marcia said. "And a few thick slices of maple-cured bacon. You need to go home and get something to eat and some rest."

Jimmy admitted that he was awfully short on both. "Do you want me to take the kids?"

"Are you kidding? The point is to rest. I'm pretty sure you'd get none of that if you took these hooligans home with you," Marcia laughed while Seth and Lorna rolled their eyes. "We've got it covered. Pop is going to take them back to the store. You know how they love playing with the price-taggers? Pop just happens to have some new shipments that need pricing."

"And Milo?" The baby smiled at Jimmy as he heard his daddy say his name.

"We're here to pick up the goods to feed him. He's still not wild about formula, so we'll take what the nurses have pumped and return him to Liz. She's all for being his surrogate mommy for now."

"I suppose she's the next best thing since she and Danny are as close to sisters as any friends'll ever be," Jimmy admitted, though he was reluctant to let his son go now that he had him in his arms.

"How's Danica this morning?" Glenna had not heard about Danica's rough start.

"She just got back to her room. They did another CAT scan and we'll know the results soon. We had a little scare first thing, but everything appears to be under control," said Pop, winking at Jimmy.

"Thank God she's so strong."

"Oh yeah. That's my girl. She'd never let something so insignificant as a run-in with a car get her down," Pop joked.

Seth spoke for the first time that morning. "Speaking of cars, Grandpa. I heard from my friend, Josh…his dad is an ambulance driver…that they're still looking for the car that hit Mom. The driver left before the cops could talk to him."

Pop blanched. He, indeed, did not know everything. Jimmy stopped bouncing Milo too. "What're you saying, Seth? That whoever hit Danny just kept on going?"

"I guess so." Seth gazed regretfully at the two most important men in his life, who were looking increasingly upset. He hung his head and clammed up.

Why did that stupid Josh have to tell him about the car, and why hadn't he kept his mouth shut? He'd kept quiet ever since he found out his Mom was hurt. He should have kept this to himself too. Seth shrugged, tears in his eyes, and walked the opposite direction down the hallway.

Chapter Ten

The two dogs greeted Jimmy outside with the enthusiasm of a fifty person welcoming committee and their excited breath hung on the freezing air. He patted each down thoroughly, needing as much comforting as they did, and noticed that Marcia had taken care of refilling their dishes. He glanced over to see that Laredo happily munched his morning hay as well. The woman truly was a marvel. Danny had often said that her mother had the heart of a saint and the intuition of the good witch—her generosity never, ever waned and she knew just where to bestow it.

Thankful, but emotionally drained, Jimmy entered a house achingly absent of the only people who mattered. Danica had been in a hurry to get to town, so she'd rinsed the kids' cereal bowls and left them beside the sink to stuff in the dishwasher later.

A basket of laundry was waiting by the washer for the previous load to finish. Jimmy was too exhausted to fold the clothes in the dryer, though he knew Danny would be horrified to know that the clothes in the washer had been allowed to sour. Jimmy made a mental note to restart the load after his nap.

The smell of pancakes and bacon seeped from the oven into the air, making Jimmy's stomach issue loud protest as he used the bathroom first and washed up at the sink. Marcia had even brewed a fresh pot of coffee, decaf he assumed, since that's all Danica ever kept in the house while she was nursing.

Jimmy scarfed down breakfast and stripped down to his skivvies, leaving his clothes in the correct section of the laundry sorter. He would not return to his heathen bachelor ways just because Danny wasn't there to remind him to pick up his socks.

A scalding shower cleared away a good portion of the tension he'd felt creeping into his neck. He emerged relaxed and so ready for a rest. The couch beckoned, since he couldn't fathom using the bed without sharing it with Danny.

He was shifting his favorite pillow to the living room when the phone rang, slicing shrilly into the silence. Jimmy jumped and then he felt annoyance as it continued to ring. After the third ring, he realized that the call may be about Danny and he grabbed up the receiver.

"Hello?"

"Hello. May I please speak to James Burdick?"

"Speaking."

"Oh, Mr. Burdick. I hoped to catch you downstairs earlier, but you had already left. This is Amy Loeffler and I'm a billing representative from the Rickton Community Hospital. Is this a bad time?"

A rhetorical question, Jimmy thought, with little good humor. When would be a good time? Without waiting for his answer, Amy What's Her Name pushed forward.

"Mr. Burdick. I'm afraid we have some issues with Danica's insurance. As you know, she might be staying with us for some time and, as a public facility, we are bound by law to treat her; but we do need to keep our doors open..."

"Please get to the point, Ms...." Jimmy pressed.

"Loeffler. Amy Loeffler. Anyway, Mr. Burdick, it seems that the insurance we have on file for Danica Burdick is

State-funded and was designated for child birth and family planning only. Does she have any other insurance that we can use to begin her claim?"

"I assumed that Danny was still covered for all of her healthcare on the State plan, since the kids are covered by the same plan," Jimmy replied, his exhausted brain trying to work its way around the problem being posed to him.

"Sometimes when a woman becomes pregnant, the insurance plan will automatically be converted to a perinatal plan and the other type will be dropped. Perhaps it was just an oversight by the State. I'm sure you'll be able to clear it up with them. In the meantime, we are required to ask private-pay patients for a co-pay that befits the treatment or testing being provided to them."

"And how much of a co-pay are you looking for?" Jimmy finally got the reason for the call. The hospital wanted their money, and they wanted reassurance that they would get it. After all, Danny's care was probably costing thousands of dollars a day.

"I know this is a difficult time and I really hate to bother you when you're dealing with…"

"How much?" Jimmy demanded. He wanted to get this phone call over with so he could just close his eyes and reclaim some of the calm he'd felt right after his shower.

"We would like to ask for one thousand dollars to begin with," He could hear Ms. Loeffler hold her breath.

"I will be at the hospital later this afternoon and I will deliver one thousand dollars to you personally, Amy. Will that be all?"

"When you come in, we'll need to make payment arrangements for the rest…"

"Whatever. Fine. I'll see what I can find out about Danny's insurance in the meantime. Now, if you'll excuse me, I'm going to try and get some rest."

"Oh, of course. Again, I'm sorry to bother you…"

"Goodbye, Ms. Loeffler," Jimmy said as politely as he could manage and replaced the phone in its cradle.

He sighed in resignation. Yes, they needed a bigger house and they had been saving diligently, but Danny's care was more important than any home improvement. He'd go by the bank later, but the first order of business was that nap. He stretched the length of the couch and tried to let his mind go to a better place.

The phone rang again just two hours later. In Jimmy's dream, he was with Danny and she was in a hospital bed, but she was laughing and smiling. She ate an unidentifiable lunch from a lime green plastic tray. Then the alarms started to ring. Suddenly Danny's face turned ashen and her mouth opened in astonishment. Then she turned to sand before Jimmy's eyes. Her body crumbled into a heap of dirt with a blue and white gown lying over the top of it.

Danny! He screamed and sat straight up on the couch. His heart in his throat, he realized that his phone was ringing, thus the sound of the alarms. He ran for it, not knowing how long it had been ringing, and answered it still out of breath.

"Hello?"

"Jimmy? Are you okay? This is Miranda Lobos. You sound winded."

"Oh. Hi Miranda," Jimmy attempted to calm his breathing. "I was sleeping. The phone just startled me, that's all." The image of Danny leaving him crept back into his mind. He shoved the image away and wiped the perspiration off of his face.

Miranda Lobos was Danny's friend and attorney. Hardly contemporaries, given Miranda's thirty year age difference from Danica's, they nonetheless had a closeness born of hard times. Miranda looked out for Danica—after all, Danica was little more than a child when Miranda represented her in the divorce. Danica, in turn, saw to it that Miranda, a long-distance grandmother and baby-lover, had plenty of face-time with all of the kids.

Seth and Lorna loved their 'Aunt Randi' nearly as much as their own grandmother. Milo was quickly becoming a fan as well.

Now, though, Miranda sounded angry. "I'm awfully sorry to hear about Danica's accident, Jimmy. You'll never guess how I heard about it, though."

"I'm sorry, Miranda. There are a ton of people I need to call. I just haven't had a chance…" Jimmy began.

"Jimmy Burdick, I am not getting on your case. You've had enough to worry about without getting on the phone to the couple hundred people who know Danica and you. Nope. I'm not blaming you, but I am spitting mad about the phone call I did receive this morning."

"Don't leave me in suspense," Jimmy begged, as he wiped sleep from his eyes and tried to catch up to Miranda's fury, whatever it was about.

"George Stevens called me at ten and my secretary patched him through to me."

"Stevens? As in Toby Browning's attorney, George Stevens?" Jimmy felt his blood begin to simmer.

"Well, apparently good news travels fast. He heard from his client late yesterday that Danica was in a hit-and-run accident and that she's in a coma and may not live to see tomorrow."

'Damn that Shelby Lowe,' he thought. Out loud he asked warily. "Why do I get the feeling that George wasn't only calling to spread the good news?"

"George would like to file a temporary custody order for Toby so that Seth and Lorna's father can take care of them while Danica is unable."

Exasperated, but unsurprised, Jimmy asked, "When is he planning to haul us back to court? Because you know I won't just agree to this, Miranda."

"I talked him out of asking for an emergency hearing. In every sense of fairness, Toby shouldn't be messing with any of you at all. I think George knows this, but he's honoring his client's wishes. If he files the motion today, I would expect a hearing late next week."

That might be enough time, he thought. Maybe Danny would be awake by then. He was going to call in reinforcements just in case she wasn't.

"I'm not telling the kids about this. They've been traumatized enough as is," Jimmy explained.

"I wouldn't dream of telling them either," Miranda agreed. Jimmy could picture her full, brown curls bobbing as she nodded. Miranda was a gem and he knew she'd fight the good fight for them, as she always had.

"Listen, Miranda. I need to get back to the hospital. Apparently there's an insurance issue too."

"What do you mean? Danica has health insurance, doesn't she?" Miranda said.

"Well, I thought so, but apparently the State plan she was on switched over to cover maternity and post-baby care with Milo and she never got it switched back to full coverage."

"Would you like to have me call her insurance company for you? I might have more influence—a better ability to cut through the B.S, so to speak, because I'm her lawyer," Miranda offered.

"Can you do that?" Jimmy was grateful.

"Just call me later with her insurance card in hand and I'll take care of the rest."

"Actually, I can grab it if you'll wait a second."

Jimmy put the phone down and got the insurance policy information out of the file cabinet. He returned and read out the information Miranda asked for.

He finished with, "You're wonderful, Miranda. Have I told you that lately?"

"You're going to make me blush, Jimmy Burdick. Just doing my job. You give Danica a kiss for me. I'll light a candle for her at noon mass, okay?"

"She's going to pull through this. She has to. For all of us."

Jimmy could hear Miranda get choked up as she heard the uncertainty behind his words and bid him goodbye.

The lonely house creaked around him as he replaced the phone in its cradle. Stress creeped back into his neck as Jimmy sought a glass of orange juice and ate the remaining piece of bacon atop the stove. He drank calmly and contemplated his two phone calls; and then he pictured Danica once again as he had seen her first thing this morning—in the throes of a seizure, eyes rolled back in her head, choking on her respirator.

Fear and desperation like he'd never known overcame him like a crane crashing down from a fifty-story building. It left a crater the size of Texas. For lack of anything better to do to ease his distress, Jimmy chucked his glass across the room where it hit textured sheetrock and shattered into hundreds of tiny pieces.

Slippery   Kimberly Ann Freel

Chapter Eleven

Sibby was too small of a town to have its own police force, so like many of the smaller towns in the county, Sibby contracted with the county Sheriff's department to provide police services. The county seat was in Lewville, but there was a precinct office in Rickton. Jimmy stopped by his bank and then stepped two doors over to the Sheriff's office to see if Detective Pete was working.

Pete Morse, in his off-time, was a pool shark and had whipped Jimmy in many a game at the tavern in Sibby before Danica changed Jimmy's barstool-hopping days forever. He and Pete still met up for a game of pool about twice every six months; and since Milo came along, Jimmy saw Pete even less.

Pete was married too, but his kids were teenagers and they had little time or patience for their parents. Pete's wife, Izzy, was an incredibly lucky bingo player, and she had no beef with Pete going out to the tavern while she played game after game at the Tribal bingo hall. Jimmy imagined that Pete had found another pool partner somewhere so he could keep up his game.

Jimmy took off his black felt cowboy hat and stomped the snow off his boots as he entered the office and approached the clerk. He didn't recognize her.

"Hi. I'm Jimmy Burdick and I'm a friend of Detective Pete Morse's. Is he on duty today?"

With a pure Kentucky accent, unusual in this rural

Washington county, the clerk replied, "Burdick? Ain't that the name o' the gal that got hit yesterday in Sibby?" She popped her gum and batted her frosty blue-lidded eyes at him.

"Yes. My wife Danica was the victim."

"Well. I'm surely sorry about that, sir. Is she doin' okay?"

"You know, Miss…" Jimmy began.

"West. Connie May West." The clerk held out her hand in greeting.

"Connie. I'm really just trying to get a chance to talk to Pete. Is he here today?"

"Oh, sure. Pete's around. I think he's in th' lunch room. If ya'll 'll wait here, I'll get 'im for ya." She flashed a dazzling smile.

Pete appeared in a moment, greeting Jimmy with regret high in his eyes. Pete, of course, knew everything that had happened the day before. He was the second officer on the scene. Lunch today was the first time he had really sat down since the accident. Snow had fallen to the tune of a foot since the day before and it hindered their investigation.

What purely stank about Danica's accident was that it was just an accident until that ignorant soul in the blue sedan chose to drive away instead of owning up to what was clearly a cruel twist of fate. Now the Sheriff's department faced a search for a hit-and-run suspect.

"Hey, Jimmy. How are you?" Pete gestured toward the lunchroom and Jimmy followed him down the hall, his wet boots squeaking on the linoleum floor. Pete poured Jimmy a cup of coffee and Jimmy grimaced as he swallowed down brew stiff enough to chew. That ought to take care of any lingering exhaustion.

"Well, I'm better than Danny is, that's for sure. She's hanging in there so far, though."

"The hospital is keeping us updated on her condition since our charges for the driver of the car will rely on how well she does."

"In other words, if she dies, you have a homicide investigation on your hands," Jimmy put it bluntly.

Pete ran his hand through his white blond hair and shifted his feet restlessly. His normally clear blue eyes were bloodshot. Jimmy felt momentarily bad for torturing his friend, because Pete really was a good buddy. Jimmy clapped Pete on the back good-naturedly, letting him off the hook.

"I just feel awful about this, Jimmy." Then changing the subject, Pete asked, "How's Milo? I bet he's getting big, isn't he?"

"Danny teases me that I just spit him out—that's how much he looks like me. He's just about the happiest baby I've ever seen. He'll smile himself inside out if you'll return it. I'm pretty sure I was never that sweet." Jimmy grinned despite himself.

"I would have to agree with that," Pete teased. "Seriously, though, Jimmy. We are trying to find the car that hit Danica. I'm assuming that's why you're here. We've checked all of the auto body shops to make sure that if anybody brings the car in, they will call us. Trouble is, in the wintertime, so many cars are kept in garages. We might not even spot a car of that description until spring. And what if it's somebody from out of town? We might never know who hit her."

"From what Pop told me, it was Danny who lost her footing as the car approached. It really wasn't like this guy ran her over on purpose," Jimmy offered.

"No, but I just don't understand why he or she would leave," Pete reasoned.

"I got the distinct feeling before I left the hospital that

Pop won't let this one go, so he'll be glad to hear that you're taking the search seriously. That's actually not why I'm here, though," Jimmy admitted.

Pete's curiosity looked piqued. Surely there couldn't be anything more important than the accident. Pete took a sip of his coffee and offered Jimmy an Oreo as he waited for Jimmy to spit out the rest.

Jimmy took the offered cookie and, in man-fashion, stuffed the whole thing in his mouth. Pete waited patiently while he did the same and they both chewed their cookies.

Jimmy began with a question. "What do you know about Toby Browning?"

"Danica's ex?" Pete asked. Jimmy nodded.

"I know that he mostly keeps his nose clean. We've had to haul him in here a few times for petty assaults—fights at the pool hall, that kind of thing; but we mostly kept him until he cooled off and sobered up. I've decided that he's a mean S.O.B., but he tries to avoid us as much as we try to avoid him. Why do you ask?"

"Danny has been in the hospital all of one day and he's already called his lawyer and asked for a custody hearing."

Pete blew out a whistle in surprise. That was pretty low. "Does he hate you that much, that he can't let the kids stay with you while she gets better?"

"Well, yeah. I'm pretty sure he does. I was in one of his pool hall brawls and I got the better of him, but that was before Danny and I were even dating. You're right that he's mean, pure and simple.

"Ever since they were teenagers, Toby's had a hold on Danny. She loved him the way infatuated young girls do. When she married him and found out that he wanted to control how she dressed and talked and whom she spent time with and that crossing him meant bruises, the honeymoon ended. To top that, rumor had it that he was carrying on with a waitress at the pool hall. She stuck it out, though, for the kids, until he rearranged her teeth with a coffee table."

"You've got to be kidding me! How could she have been battered like that without us knowing about it?" Pete was nonplussed.

"She never filed charges. He always claimed to push her or run into her on accident. By this time, Seth was four and Lorna was two. Danny came home from working at The Mercantile to find Seth's left arm in a cast. Seth wouldn't talk and Toby claimed he'd fallen out of bed. It was the last straw. She was packing to leave when he made her pay with major dental work."

"Wow. No wonder you have a serious hate on for the guy," Pete remarked. "Was she able to prove any of this in her custody fights?"

"She had the word of her dentist, and it weighed well in her original custody hearing; but she's lacked proof since then of his being an unfit parent," Jimmy said.

"So where do I come in?" Pete asked, unsure how the police department could help with Jimmy and Danica's latest predicament.

Jimmy sat down on one of the hard plastic chairs and Pete followed suit. "Here's the rub, Pete. I have never been able to figure out what it is that Toby *does*. Danny said he did odd jobs while they were together, even working a little for one of the casinos, but mostly he stuck around the house and helped with the kids while she worked at The Mercantile. They never lacked money, though, because his mom helped them out. They lived in her trailer park, didn't have to pay rent.

"He still lives there now and, other than living in a single-wide trailer, he seems well-heeled, has a nice T-Bird, and an expensive lawyer on speed-dial. Yet he has no job and manages to avoid paying child support because there are no wages to garnish." Jimmy adjusted his collar, his ire up once more.

"I hate to tell you this, Jimmy, but there are many Tobies in this world. His mom obviously never cut the apron strings and he enjoys the good life. Maybe he could tell us where we went wrong."

Jimmy had to chuckle. "You wouldn't be any happier living with your mom and taking hand-outs than I would, Pete."

Pete agreed good-naturedly. "Listen. I've enjoyed chatting with you, Jimmy, but I'm going to have to get back to work. I have a hit-and-run driver to catch."

"Wait, Pete," Jimmy grabbed Pete's sleeve as he rose. "I guess I haven't really gotten to my point, have I? You see, Toby's mom doesn't have a job either. She got the trailer park from some ex-husband years ago and she manages it, but as far as I can tell, that's her only income. Now tell me. How does she afford to drive a brand new Ford pick-up, and Toby a sports car, wear fancy clothes and employ a lawyer who charges two hundred bucks an hour, and who knows what else, on that kind of income?"

"Good question, Jimmy, but how do we know what else she got from her divorce?"

"Rumor has it, and this is purely rumor, that she has a little business going on the side," Jimmy added.

"Drugs?" Pete asked casually.

"Maybe. I came here to ask you if you'd check it out. They're on the outskirts of Rickton, so I think it's within your jurisdiction."

"And what if I don't find anything?" Pete asked.

"All I'm asking is, could you try? I'm just trying to put a dent in all that conceit of Toby's. He's pulled a real dirty trick this time and I'd like to just slow him down a bit, that's all."

"That's not too much to ask, Jimmy. I'll check into it. Who knows? We might just bust up something big," Pete offered.

Jimmy smiled his thanks and shook Pete's hand and returned to the frigid, pristinely white day. He needed to go see Danny.

Chapter Twelve

Mom and Pop found themselves regularly walking to the cafeteria, seeking coffee and an escape from the agony of watching a respirator breathe for their daughter. Glenna had the kids and Liz was with Danica, so both of them decided to take a load off and sit in the deserted dining room for a few minutes.

Everything in the dining area was mauve, from the plastic levelor blinds to the linoleum tiles. Marcia playfully rearranged the silk mauve-colored mums in the mauve vase in the middle of their table. "I think they need more color—how about pink?"

Pop laughed. "You can't be serious. It looks like they took a can of dusty pink paint and just poured it out in here. It's like a scene from a Dr. Seuss movie—everything matches except the people."

"I suppose they were aiming for a relaxing color," Marcia admitted. "But I do feel like I've fallen into a plastic bedpan and I can't get out."

Both of them chuckled. The pair had been together for nearly thirty years and despite the whitening of their hair and the inevitable layer of fifty-year-old paunch around the middle, they still looked and acted like teenagers when the two of them were alone together.

Pop looked into Marcia's sapphire eyes, ringed with worry despite her laughter. "You know, you still look like the girl I met at the drive-in movie all those years ago."

"Oh, right. Back when I still called you Lloyd? Before we felt compelled to buy a 'Mom and Pop' store? I feel centuries older right now," she replied.

"Yeah, I didn't sleep much last night either," he admitted. "Isn't it amazing how wrapped up we can be in our lives, so that we take for granted our own flesh and blood? I never imagined that I'd watch my own child go through the trauma Danica went through."

"It is patently unfair that you had to witness the accident, Pop. I'd be a basket case right now if I'd seen the same thing."

"You know, Milo saw it too. I'm sure he's too young to understand, but he was on my shoulders when she slipped. How much of that do you suppose his subconscious mind might hang on to?"

Marcia reassured her husband. She always did her best to ease his anxiety. "I'm sure his young mind didn't even process it the same way yours did. For all he knows, his mommy did a neat trick. He won't need to know the rest until he's way older."

"Except for now we don't know if she'll make it. It might process differently if his mommy is suddenly gone forever." Pop stared bleakly at his hands, which were clasped as if in prayer.

"She's made it this far, honey." Marcia covered his hands with hers. "If there is one thing I've always loved about you, Pop, it's your unerring faith. Faith in God, faith in us, faith in your daughter—you've had all of these, even when times were dark, when one of us disappointed you. Don't lose faith, because I just couldn't stand that. Your faith could be what's making Danica fight."

A tear slipped unexpectedly from his eye and Pop wiped it away. "Nah. It's not me. She's always been willful, Mom. Do you remember when she was seven and I demanded that she clean her filthy room or I was going to throw everything away?"

"Yep, and she did, only she picked up by packing everything into boxes and bags. She called up her Grandma in Carnation and made arrangements to go live there. The only reason we foiled her plan was because she came to ask us for an umbrella to take with her since she was going where it rained more. She had a well-thought-out plan. It was her will against yours, and she was moving out." Marcia laughed at the memory.

"She wants to live now, because she has so much to live for—Milo, Jimmy, the kids. Her will to live has nothing to do with my faith." Pop said.

"It has everything to do with it, Pop. She is the strong, brave young woman she is, because you raised her to be."

"I seem to recall that you were there too."

"Yes," Marcia agreed. "But I'm pretty sure I gave her the only weakness she ever displayed. I'm the incurable romantic. That's the part that rubbed off when she fell for Toby."

"Toby did plenty of 'rubbing' on his own. You can't blame Danica's weakness for Toby on yourself. He was slick and charming. He was older and he drove a nice car. He took her out on fancy dates. He was mature and capable; and he wanted our daughter, and she wanted him."

"Too bad he ended up being such a putz," Marcia lamented.

"Oh, we always knew he was a putz. Any twenty-year-old who would bed a high school freshman can't be too much of a winner. We just tried to put up with him for the kids' sake once they came along."

Pop rose and walked over to the vending machine. Digging in his pockets for loose change, he purchased a Danish for he and Mom to share.

"That's true. Seth and Lorna are the best thing that man ever did." Marcia stood to get some plates and forks from the counter.

They sat together in silence as they washed their snack down with stale coffee. Liz appeared in the cafeteria doorway, looking wan despite the overworked heater and her wool sweater.

Marcia walked to her and grasped her hand. She led Liz back to the table. Marcia adeptly filled a cup with hot water and put a selection of herbal teas in front of Liz. Her daughter's friend preferred to avoid caffeine.

"Bless you, Mom. I'm freezing today. This should help." Liz shivered and Marcia smiled in reply. Liz' chill had nothing to do with the temperature and everything to do with seeing her best friend lying battered and bruised in a coma as a machine breathed for her. Pop still hadn't gotten used to feeling the same way himself every time he walked into Danica's room.

Liz looked around. "Geez. What did they do here—get a bargain from the hardware store by buying everything from the same dye lot? Was Bob's having a special on mauve that I didn't know about? Because you do know how much I love mauve."

Both Mom and Pop laughed with her, letting some of the tension go that they all felt.

"How'd your night with little man, Milo, go?" Pop asked Liz.

"Well, I'll tell you this, Pop: I won't be having any kids any time soon. He was so sweet when he was sleeping. I swear he looked like an angel and his breath smelled like warmed honey. I just couldn't get enough of watching him. It was then that I envied Danica. But then he would wake up without his momma, and those brown eyes would fill with disappointment, and he'd scream like there was no tomorrow. I'd try to give him formula and he'd spit it out over and over until he finally figured out it was the only thing I had to offer. I'm just exhausted. I don't know how Danica does it."

"Oh, she's got it easy," Marcia laughed. "She just stuffs a boob in his mouth and he's happy."

Liz could only muster a tired smile in reply. "He's six months old now. Can't he have some baby food? We have some really good organic stuff at the store. There are moms that come all of the way from Lewville to get it from us."

"I know Danica was thinking of trying some solid food soon. She's given him rice cereal here and there. I'm sure she wouldn't object if you wanted to try it, Liz." Marcia offered.

"Well I'm going to plan on taking care of him at least the next few nights until Jimmy's ready to take over, so I might try it."

"That's noble of you, Liz, considering how poorly your first night went," Pop said.

"I just know that you and Mom need to help with Seth and Lorna, and Jimmy's probably going to be here as much as possible. Besides, it should be easier now that they're pumping breast milk from Danica for us to give him."

Pop's expression turned grim. He started fidgeting, a sure sign of irritation.

"Is there a problem, Pop?" Marcia asked.

"It's just this whole 'pumping' thing. I'm worried that they're expecting too much from Danica. She has enough of a battle as it is without asking her to keep providing food for her son."

"I've wondered about that too," Marcia admitted. "I'm sure the doctor would cut things off if he thought he was compromising her care."

"I think Jimmy's right. It's what Danica would want," Liz reasoned.

Pop arose from the table, his frustration coloring every agile movement. "Since when does everyone in my daughter's life presume to know what *she* would want? *I* want my grandkids to have their mother. I want my little girl to be okay."

Marcia stood and put a hand on Pop's forearm as if trying to calm him. He jerked it away. "I'm going for a walk," Pop grumbled as he stalked out of the cafeteria.

Chapter Thirteen

The lake dried in a searing summer sun, leaving Danica ashore, only she didn't feel hot. She shivered as if her clothing was still wet. She found that she could walk on the parched lakebed. So she did, but walking was like hovering, her feet so light, her arms like helium balloons. She laughed.

If only the children could see her—she was sure there were children, though it escaped her how many and where they were. She looked down to see her shapeless frock changing colors as vivid as a rainbow, each floating step cycling through colors like the dress was on a fiberoptic wheel. She laughed again. How amazing, she thought, and how random.

At least she was on her feet again and the sun didn't seem quite so bright. Nothing beckoned, but it felt good to be upright, as if activity could bring the blurred landscape back into focus. She was lonely. Where were her loved ones? Why had they left her here?

Confusion and desperate sadness closed her throat and she tried to cry out only she couldn't find the air. Then an invisible force smoothed her hair. It felt like her mother feeling her forehead when she was frought with fever. The touch was cool, soothingly so. She calmed down and continued her hover walk. Maybe if she paced herself, she could walk out of here before nightfall.

But the lakebed seemed endless and the colors on her dress didn't seem so funny, because she soon realized the same pattern played over and over—cracked, muddy, unending landscape and a trudging step—and a shifty muu-muu in blue, green, yellow, orange, red, purple….blue, green, yellow, orange, red, purple….

Jimmy contemplated Danica. Something about her seemed different from the morning. Her color was higher or the respirator was breathing faster, or something. He felt her head, gingerly touching the space where her turban-style bandage met her forehead. No obvious fever, he thought. He asked the nurse if any of her vital signs had changed. Was she trying to wake up?

The nurse gave him a look akin to pity and explained that Danica hadn't shown any progression toward consciousness, but that they would let him know immediately if she did.

Jimmy sat resigned in his corner chair. He dozed.

"Mr. Burdick?" A slight hand tapped his shoulder. "Mr. Burdick? I'm so sorry to wake you…"

Jimmy awoke with a start, taking a moment to register where he was. He looked at the woman before him. Slight and skittish as a barn cat, the woman before him wrung her hands together.

"I'm so sorry to disturb you, really…" The voice gave her away. It was Amy Whats-Her-Name, billing specialist for Rickton Community Hospital.

She held out a limp hand in greeting. "I'm Amy Loeffler. We spoke on the phone earlier. I heard that I missed you on your way in, since I was out to lunch, so I thought I'd find you here."

"I paid the other lady in billing, Ms. Loeffler. One thousand dollars, like we agreed. I wasn't expecting you to track me down," Jimmy replied and shook the offered hand, his voice still gravelly with sleep.

"That was very helpful and I appreciate you being so prompt. Actually I came down to tell you that we're making inroads with the insurance company. Apparently they received some call from a lawyer early this afternoon and they're looking for Danica's paperwork. It seems she may have applied through her medical provider to change her coverage back over after your son was born, but the application was either lost or never processed."

"I was sure Danny told me she'd taken care of that. It's not like her to overlook details like that, especially not when it deals with her health or the kids'," Jimmy said.

"Anyway, I'm still waiting to hear back from them. Until then, I'll hold Danica's billing so that you don't receive bills needlessly." Amy's eyes were lost beneath her pop-bottle glasses, but Jimmy could tell she regarded him kindly. She really had a thankless job tracking down money for a struggling community hospital.

"Thanks for your help." Jimmy said quietly. "I know you'll do your best."

Amy blushed. "I'll be in touch," she said and turned to go. "Pardon me," she said as she stepped around the large-boned, well-dressed Hispanic woman and the two children in the doorway.

Seth regarded his mother seriously, the perpetually happy boy unable and unwilling to smile at his stepfather who looked plenty happy to see him. Lorna bounced over to Jimmy, avoiding the sight of her mother entirely.

"Aunt Randi said we could come see Mommy with her. She promised to explain all of the tubes and wires to us and she said she'd get the nurse to help," Lorna told Jimmy.

Jimmy gave her a squeeze.

"How are you doing, Jimmy?" Miranda asked as she came to his side and patted his shoulder.

Miranda looked over at Danica. Almost unrecognizable, owing to the day-after swelling of her injuries, Miranda could see by the grace of Danica's hands and the ebony hair that peeked from under her bandages that it was indeed her dear friend. Her eyes filled with tears. Poor Danica didn't deserve this. Then she remembered her promise to help the children see their mother and she held the crying in check.

Lorna stood beside Jimmy, her hand in his. She still refused to look in her mother's direction.

Seth remained in the doorway, his stare fixed on Danica, his luminous blue eyes shrouded in intense worry. Seth was the oldest; and before Jimmy came along, he was the man of the house. Miranda had heard Seth vow, when he was too young to know better, that he would always take care of his mommy and his sister. What she saw in his face now was sadness, but also something else—guilt—the weight of the world on a nine-year-old's shoulders.

She spoke quietly. "Seth, honey, come over here with your Aunt Randi."

He did as he was told. He looked into Miranda's huge, black eyes and saw comfort, not blame there. She ruffled his hair, a familiar gesture, and he smoothed it with his own hands, as he usually did.

"Jimmy, can you push the nurse's button, please? I promised the kids we'd talk about all of the things attached to their mom. Everything's not so scary if you know what all of it is for. I want to make sure I'm correct, so I need the nurse's help."

The nurse came and spent twenty minutes Jimmy was sure she could ill-afford, showing Miranda and the children what each wire meant and how they would lead to the monitor at her bedside, and what each tube was for. Jimmy hadn't been privy to most of this himself, so he was grateful for the education. He rested a warm hand on the shoulder of each of the kids, *his* kids.

Seth looked up at him gravely. "Jimmy, can we come home with you tonight? I know Grandma planned to have us over again, but Lorna and I talked it over before we came and we want to be with you, since Mom can't be."

Jimmy momentarily choked on the lump in his throat. He looked at Miranda, whose own tears rendered her silent, and then back at Seth. "I would sure love that, kiddo. I spent too long in that house by myself. It needs you there. It needs all of us and soon your Momma and Milo will be there too."

Seth nodded, still serious, and Jimmy wondered when the jubilant spirit of the boy would return. Would it ever?

Lorna, usually the more contemplative of the two children, smiled triumphantly at her brother and Aunt Randi. "I told you Jimmy would want us more than Grandma and Grandpa," she said.

"Whoa, I don't know about that," Jimmy chuckled softly. "Your Grandma will hate giving you up for the night. Plus, she makes the lightest, fluffiest pancakes in the world. I know, 'cause I had some this morning. You know me. I can barely muster a bowl of cereal."

"That's true," Lorna frowned. Then she brightened again. "But you let us watch TV in the mornings and I'll have all my clothes and my paints and markers and my dolls."

Seth scowled. "You talk too much, Lorna. We know about your stuff already. We're supposed to be quiet for Mom."

"Actually, both the doctor and the nurses have

encouraged us to talk to your Mom," Jimmy explained. "Although I'm sure she would prefer to hear you getting along, she might be able to hear both of you and I'm sure that's music to her ears."

Miranda stood watching the exchange between Jimmy and the kids. She marveled at his ease with them, confirming what she knew from years of practicing family law: Being a good parent had little to do with biology.

"I'm going to go find Marcia and Pop and let them know that the kids are going with you, Jimmy," she said.

Wrapped up in their family cocoon, Jimmy murmured his thanks and continued to converse quietly with the kids. Looking at Danny while the kids bantered, he could swear her expression changed from confusion to peace. She let out an almost inaudible sigh; and her breathing, through the respirator, seemed to resume a more normal pace.

Chapter Fourteen

The only person missing from the Burdick family unit was Milo Burdick. By his frequent enraged outbursts, Liz was pretty sure that he knew he was missing out too. Glenna was minding the store, leaving Liz in charge of Milo once again. It was Saturday and Danica's third day in the hospital.

Giving Milo a bottle was at least easier since they were using the milk he was used to tasting, but he was still acutely aware of the absence of his mother. Liz understood that a baby Milo's age needed floor time so that he could get better at rolling over and sitting up. It was just that every time she put Milo down, he let out a bellow befit of a baby elephant.

So she'd taken to carrying Milo everywhere. He wasn't napping effectively. This meant that she ate and heated bottles with Milo on her hip, and attempted to fold laundry with him lying across her lap in a half-sleep.

She needed to go to The Mercantile sometime and gather Milo's backpack because she knew this was Danica's secret to taking Milo everywhere without physically carrying him. Liz was pretty sure her arms were going to just up and fall off pretty soon. At twenty pounds, Milo was past being a lug and well on his way to being that baby elephant.

She was fixing to call her mom and see if she would stop and pick up the backpack, when the phone rang. She greeted the caller with all of the enthusiasm she could muster under the circumstances.

"Liz? It's me, Steve."

"Oh. Hello Steve. How's The Mercantile in the boss' absence?"

"You know, it's been really busy. I had to call in Nita, the part-time clerk. I think everyone in Sibby is curious about Danica, and this is their way of finding out details."

"Don't give them anything, Steve. Mom and Pop would be furious."

"I would never do that, Liz. You know that. I'm just now getting ready to close, and I wanted to see how you are doing. I know you have Milo. Your mom told me when I went to get a fresh-squeezed juice this morning. How's it going?"

"I'm managing," was all that Liz could reply, contorted as she was with Milo on her right hip and the phone tucked between her chin and shoulder. Milo, curious about the phone, decided to grab it and got a handful of hair instead. His brown eyes glowed with mischief as Liz promptly set down the bottle she was holding, steadied the phone with her left hand, and grimaced at the strands of amber hair Milo held victoriously in the air.

"If you need help, I could send my little sister over to watch him. She's home from college on Christmas break and, from what Mom says, she's plenty bored," Steve offered.

"That's really sweet, but Milo and I are just working on our routine." Liz tweaked Milo's cute little nose for emphasis and he cracked a toothless grin.

"I could come over after work, Liz. I'm sure Milo is happy and healthy. It's you I'm worried about."

Steve's voice dropped intimately, a caress that comforted her and tempted her to bolt at the same time. His offer loomed like an oasis in the desert. Her dearest friend fought for her life in the hospital, and her oldest flame hadn't forgotten how much that would hurt Liz. Her heart told her that she could trust him, but could she truly trust any man? Weren't they all the same, fundamentally?

"You know, I really think I'm okay. Mom will be closing shortly after you do. She's just going to swing by the hospital quickly after work and then she'll be home." Liz squashed Steve's hope for an invitation.

"You can't shut me out forever, Liz. I'm just as worried about Danica as you are. It would do us good to talk about what happened and what might happen to her and her family."

Liz felt a momentary pang of guilt. Of course Steve would need a friend right now too. The three of them had been inseparable for several years when they were adolescents. Just because he was a guy didn't mean that he didn't feel just as wretched and worried as she did.

She could hear his steady breathing in her ear as he waited for her reply.

Foul-smelling, labored breathing in her ear—she flashed back to the struggle, the helplessness, and sheer terror of that fateful night just two years before; and her fear interrupted any sympathy she had for Steve, just as it always had. It was an undercurrent of self-induced psychosis that Liz recognized, but knew she would never surmount on her own. She closed her eyes and swayed, setting Milo down on the floor for a second while she regained her bearings.

Milo voiced his objection and Steve heard him, breaking the eerie silence.

"Liz? Are you okay? Are you there?"

She was breathless as she replied. "I'm here. I'm just a little tired, Steve. Overwhelmed might be a good word for it."

"Please let me help," Steve pleaded.

She forced down the irrational thoughts plaguing her. This was Steve talking, not Tim or Chad or any of the guys from school. "Will you grab a pizza on your way?" She asked in a barely audible voice.

"You bet. I'll run to Rickton and get one. From the sounds of it, Milo's too much work to allow for cooking," Steve observed.

"He's been like this all day. I'm starved. Hey, can you also grab Milo's backpack for me on your way out?"

"Sure. I'll be there in forty-five minutes. Tomorrow's Sunday and we're closed, so maybe I can stay for a while tonight," Steve said and Liz could hear the hope in his voice. She'd opened the door just a crack, and he was ready to jump on through. She was pretty sure she could slam it shut again if she had to.

Glenna held Milo close two hours later. She cradled him in her arms as his exhaustion won out over his fury at being separated from his mother, and he fell blissfully asleep. She wandered back from the master bedroom toward the living room, where his playpen was.

She held a silent finger up to her lips. Steve and Liz nodded their understanding. She placed him gently on his back and covered him with a fuzzy blanket. Glenna blew Milo a kiss as she backed away from the makeshift crib.

Steve, Liz, and Glenna retreated to the kitchen table where they would be within earshot if Milo awoke, but far enough away not to awaken him while they talked.

Steve and Liz had broken out the photo albums from Liz's days as an amateur photographer. Steve and Danica had been, to their dismay, Liz's most popular subjects. Any party, any trip, any occasion that the three celebrated between the ages of twelve and fifteen was nicely recorded and put into albums. That hobby, like many things Liz loved growing up, had been set aside when Glenna's daughter stopped living and started going through the motions instead.

Glenna was surprised to find Steve at the house when she came home from the hospital. Danica's condition was still precarious, unchanged and unpredictable, so Glenna was weary enough. But seeing her daughter's guarded expression and Steve's gallant effort to overcome her reservations made Glenna's heart hurt all the more. It was time that Liz was happy and Steve could give her daughter a good dose of that.

Glenna had no idea how to approach helping her daughter when her own devastation was clear enough. How was it that a young widow could raise a human being with such care and pride and have her turn out so beautifully, only to have every shred of trust and security ripped away by two spoiled, filthy-rich college boys?

Glenna was pretty sure that Liz had never intended for her to know about the rape, but school officials had been informed by one of the men responsible; and they were compelled to notify any student's family in the event of such a crime. Glenna and Liz had never talked about what happened. In a way, Glenna didn't want to know. She simply brought her daughter home and sought to restore every sense of safety and forthrightness Liz had ever felt about the world.

As she watched Liz bent on entertaining Steve, fear and mistrust high in her gray eyes, Glenna knew that she was going to have to do much more to help her girl. It needed to be soon, because Lord knew life was short. She thought of Marcia and Pop and their only child. A child in pain was the worst sort of punishment for a parent, but the loss of a child entirely was unfathomable.

Glenna rubbed the goosebumps from her arms as she realized that, in a way, she'd already lost Liz.

As Steve rose to excuse himself for home, Glenna gave him a pat on the shoulder and a wink. He was a good kid and she hoped he'd continue to be patient while they got Liz back on track. The door clicked shut and Glenna watched Steve shuffle through the snow to his car. When his headlights came on, she shut off the porchlight.

Glenna turned to talk to Liz, to ask her about her day, and to tell her she was proud of her for taking a positive step with Steve. But Liz was already gone. Glenna could tell that Liz had already shut off the day as she walked with her shoulders slumped in defeat and exhaustion toward her room.

Chapter Fifteen

Toby Browning was a divorced father of two, with a penchant for easy women and rowdy bars, shady business dealings and fast cars; but that didn't stop him from going to church on Sunday. If Toby had a bad streak, it was counteracted by the faith that his heavenly Father would forgive him for just about anything.

His mom had taught him to fear the Almighty; and seeing as how he had plenty to fear given the activities of any week prior, he made sure he planted his butt in a pew at the Lewville Alliance Church at nine a.m. every Sunday. As he looked at his gorgeous mom, decked out in a lilac-hued wool suit and a ruffled pink silk blouse, he thanked the Lord for her too. She was the only one in the world who understood him.

He once thought that Danica felt that way about him—that whatever ills he had done, she saw the good in him and loved him for all of his faults and shortcomings. After all, he was a romantic guy, attentive and doting; and he dressed nice and kept himself well-groomed. There was a lot to like about Toby Browning. So what if what his mom said was true—that he had the temper of a rattlesnake and the meanness of a badger? These things only rarely bothered anyone; and besides his mom blamed these traits on his no-good father, who'd run off when Toby was two.

Toby half-listened to the sermon of the day. Pastor was talking about death and the life offered in the Great

Beyond. As the man of God gestured and gesticulated, Toby thought briefly how nice it would be to be revered as the preacher was. Then he turned his attention to his mom, who muttered her own mantra under her breath:

"Lord, I know You're listening to our wonderful pastor and filling us with Your great light while You do it. That's why I'm praying too, because I know You'll hear me.

"Lord, God, please wash away my sins and know that all I do is for the love of You. I'm one of your people, God, I really am, and I know You'll watch over me and my beloved Toby.

"God, I'm just wondering if I can ask for a little better station in life. I mean, I know we've got nice things and a good life and all; but I'm wondering if we could just get a little respect—maybe a more respectable place to live, a lifestyle that people could admire, not covet, You know—because I know You wouldn't like that...."

Toby smiled a little at that. His mom always did that during the sermon. She felt like God might listen to her better because she talked at the same time as the pastor, out of the pastor's hearing range, of course. That's why they always sat toward the back. It was also just like Ashley Browning to pray for prosperity, but not to ask for too much. She didn't want to piss the Lord off, or anything. He, on the other hand, thought her request was totally reasonable.

They all rose to sing the closing hymn. Pastor closed with a wish for the health and safety of his minions as they faced the harsh winter weather and asked them to all please take care traveling in the snow. Toby and his mother exited the quaint white church and she waited on the concrete steps while he brought the car closer. Her lavender suede heels would never hold up to the slushy parking lot.

They drove away with the heater on high, destined

for The Apple Annie Diner for their customary Sunday brunch.

"Good grief, Toby. Weather like this makes me wish we lived way down in the South somewhere," Ashley complained.

"What, so we can get carried off by a tornado or a flood?" Toby replied. His mom had brought up the idea of moving away many times, but Toby simply couldn't imagine living somewhere else. This county was his home, God's country.

"You've got a point there," she agreed. "Listen, Toby. Let's get our breakfast eaten and make our way back home soon. I've got to meet Shelby at the spa at one for a mani/pedi. We've had it planned for weeks."

"You deserve some pampering, Mom," Toby offered, thinking, 'After all, if you're going to keep that fifty-year-old body looking twenty-something, there are a few sacrifices you've got to make.'

"That's sweet, honey." Ashley patted her son on the leg. He was the perfect son, loyal and handsome. He wasn't going to like what she was going to say next, though.

"Honey, I have a chore I need you to do while I'm gone."

Toby rolled his eyes. He had planned to go shoot some pool if his mom was going to the spa.

"Don't go looking all annoyed," Ashley defended. "Lupe came to polish up the trailer on Thursday and she decided to attack the guest room, your old room. She found a whole mess of papers in the bureau and I think they're yours. I didn't recognize them."

"What do you want me to do with them?" Toby groused.

"Well, if they're yours, I want you to make sure that none of them is important before I throw them away. I won't have you cluttering up my house, Toby. I have never let you before and I won't let you now."

Toby glanced over at his bottle-blond, gym-trimmed mother and saw the firm set of her jaw, and he knew he was sunk. He was going to have to waste at least a little pool time going through those papers. They were probably all junk anyway. He hadn't kept stuff like that at his mom's since he and Danica moved two trailers away when Seth was just a baby. Surely nothing would be important enough to keep after all that time.

He pulled into the parking lot of The Apple Annie, and his stomach growled as he thought of his favorite French toast drowning in butter and syrup accompanied by a salty slab of bacon. He loved Sunday—there was nothing like salvation accompanied by indulgence.

"Well I'll be Goddamned." Toby stared in disbelief at the document in front of him. It was two o'clock in the afternoon and he was finishing his paperwork. He'd dug up a treasure in the process.

In all of his thirty years, he had only had one 'real' job. He took a job at a tribal gaming casino when Danica was pregnant with Seth. His mom had convinced him that, as he was about to become a family man, he should at least appear to be able to support that family.

It lasted roughly six months and, through no fault of Toby's, the job came to an end. The casino offered a shuttle service to work from communities around Lewville and Toby decided to take the bus with the rest of the day workers. It left far too early in the morning, six-thirty to be exact, and he could ill-afford the early mornings when his social life required his presence at the Rickton tavern long into the night.

Besides, the casino management wouldn't let him move

past working in maintenance even when, opting for the late bus home, he spent extra time after work with the dealers to learn their job. Dealing seemed more glamorous, and when they refused to promote him, Toby up and quit.

He'd done a few odd jobs since, but mostly his mom kept him busy with her stuff. He didn't consider the casino job a failure so much as a lesson—he didn't like working for somebody else, letting other people call the shots. The benefits had been amazing, though. Thus, the document in his hands.

He shredded everything else from his pile in his mom's office. He walked to his house, cursing the slushy snow, but loving life.

The corrugated metal door banged inward to an olive linoleum-floored entryway. Smelling of the wet dog that had lived there five years before Toby, the trailer was oppressive, dingy, and he wished for the millionth time that they could ditch the trailer park. He and his mom deserved something classier for all of the work that they did. He wondered how soon he could build a house for his mom and Seth and Lorna. When he got the money, he could set them all up in style. His friend Bill was a contractor. Maybe Bill would be at the pool hall.

Toby changed from his church finery to jeans and a flannel shirt. He'd waterproofed his ostrich-skin boots, so he donned those too and a pro-fit Seahawks cap. He felt like shooting a little pool, imbibing a little fire water, and boasting to the masses about his good fortune. Of course, he would have to keep that part a little quiet. He didn't want to look like a complete jerk. He was about to be engaged in another custody battle, after all.

He needed to look and act like the fine, upstanding, father-of-the-year that he was. Toby looked at the faded parchment document once again. This was outstanding.

He stashed it away in his fire safe—something Danica had insisted on owning to hold birth certificates and social security cards and such. He patted it once more for good luck, grabbed a couple of twenties out of the safe before he closed it, and put his wallet in the back pocket of his jeans.

He examined himself in the beveled hall mirror. Ash blond hair feathered and tucked into a baseball cap, vivid blue eyes sparkling with good fortune, and a smile to kill even the starchiest of old ladies—he was ready to go. He wondered when his mom would be home. She was going to love this. But first, he was going out to have a little fun.

The pool hall held its regular motley crew, a Sunday gathering of men who would rather see the lakes shed their thick layer of snow so they could fish. Instead the bitter cold confined them to the indoors. Testosterone hung like a fog over the six emerald green pool tables, the only concession to female company being the two waitresses who kept the libations fresh.

The air was clear, owing to a Washington State law that banned smoking in public places. Instead it was permeated with conversations, punctuated by the thwack of pool balls colliding, and the clink of Budweiser bottles. Toby hung his coat on the back of a red vinyl chair and sauntered over to his usual table. He knew both guys shooting—his friend Otis, who he'd gone clear through school with, and Pete Morse, one of the town cops. Toby steered clear of lawmen whenever he could, but, in rare good cheer, he shouted out dibs on playing the winner of the game at hand and flirted with Cami, a cute little brunette waitress in skin-tight Wrangler jeans and a pink flannel blouse.

Pete sunk the eight ball in record time and put Otis in his seat. Toby tipped his Jack and Coke to the winner and took his cue stick out of its felt-lined case. As he chalked the tip generously, he waited for Pete to break, which he did impressively, sinking two solid balls.

Pete followed with a miss and sat back down at the side table while Toby went after the stripes. He let Toby finish his shot, then another, and then Pete stood as Toby's third shot went wide.

"Pretty sharp shooting—Toby, isn't it?" Pete commented casually, betraying nothing of his earlier conversation with Jimmy Burdick. Pete was off duty, but that didn't ever keep him from still observing the world through the eyes of a cop. Pete sensed that Toby knew he was a police officer; but if Toby was wary of that fact, he hid it well.

"Thanks. I've had a lot of practice. Should've had that last one, though," Toby said.

"I'm a little out of practice," Pete said as his next shot veered to the right of the corner pocket and the cue ball went straight in.

"I guess," Toby chuckled. "Nice scratch."

Toby retrieved the cue ball and lined up his next shot. His body language suggested that this game would be over in no time.

Pete had intentionally missed the last shot with the hope of prolonging the game. He and Toby needed to chat. Pete pressed conversation, hoping that Toby wouldn't make quick work of the rest of the table.

"Yeah, my wife doesn't let me out as much these days since I've been putting in long hours at work," Pete offered. "You play much?"

"Quite a bit. When I'm not working myself," Toby said as he fired off another shot. So far he'd sunk three stripes.

"Oh sure. I understand. What kind of work do you do?" Pete asked as he took a swig of his 7-Up and watched Toby continue to work the table.

"I manage a mobile home park," Toby replied, evasively.

"That so? Huh. I thought those things kind of ran themselves. What, you collect rent once a month, and do repairs, that kind of thing?"

"We got a handyman who comes and keeps up the trailers. Still, you'd be surprised how much there is to do, handling everything else, just makin' sure everything gets done," Toby said, looking impatiently at Pete with an expression that said, 'Back off, nosey cop.'

"Oh, absolutely. My brother has rentals. Pretty thankless job, from what I understand," Pete said agreeably.

"Renting is definitely a pain. My mom is always saying how great it would be to just boot everybody out and turn the park into one great big lawn," Toby laughed.

Pete made a valiant effort when Toby finally missed, to catch up. He sunk two balls and sat back down, chuckling along with Toby at his final statement.

"So your mom lives in the park too?"

"Yep. We've been neighbors for almost as long as we lived in the same house."

"She must be easy to get along with," Pete remarked.

"As long as I do things her way, sure she is. Isn't every female that way?" They both chuckled again as Pete nodded his agreement.

"What's your mom do?" Pete asked casually.

"She spends a lot of time staying beautiful and fending off the aging process. She looks good too." Toby looked Pete in the eye once more. "Now, *Porky*, why don't you stop giving me the third degree and start shooting a decent game of pool?" Toby scowled at Pete. Leave it to a policeman to ruin a casual game of pool.

Pete reddened at the loathing Toby obviously felt for him, but he clammed up nonetheless. Pissed off, he repaid him when Toby finally missed, by then sinking the rest of his balls, and the eightball.

"I knew you had it in you, *Copper*. All you needed to do was stop yammering and start shootin' pool," Toby simmered, his joviality soured. Apparently, he didn't like to lose. "I'm going to see if there's another table where the competition isn't so damn nosey."

"Sounds good to me. Otis here is up for another game, aren't you?"

Otis nodded, licked his lips, and wiped his hands on his jeans before he grabbed his pool stick. 'That Toby is going to get himself in hot water if he doesn't stop shooting his mouth off at the cop,' he thought. Otis'd never talk to Pete Morse that way. The guy didn't forget a thing—like when Otis' little sister carved her name into her ex-boyfriend's driver's-side door—Pete busted her chops good for that one, and he still paid her an occasional 'be good' visit.

"Thanks Otis. Oh, hey, Toby?" Pete shouted after Toby.

Toby turned around, scowling again. "What, Pig?"

"Those are real nice boots. I might have to go into the rental business. Looks like it's lucrative," Pete said icily, flicking a disdainful gaze over Toby's person. Then he fired a lightning quick shot to scatter the balls for his new game.

Chapter Sixteen

It was Monday and Danica still hadn't awakened from her coma, although her vital signs remained stable. Jimmy and the kids fell into the routine of eating meals in the hospital cafeteria and spending all of their waking hours at the hospital.

The exception was Milo. He was spending nights at home now, since Saturday night. He took his Daddy's cue and preferred his crib over a bed without Mommy in it. Marcia cared for him during the day, since Milo hadn't the patience for the long hours of vigil at the hospital.

Even the big kids weren't thrilled about the boredom, but they wouldn't disappoint Jimmy by refusing to follow the routine. Rickton Community Hospital was a small facility, and the employees were like family. They soon came to recognize the Burdick family and offered support and encouragement to all of them.

The admitting clerks took to giving Seth the remote control to the lobby television, and the Radiology crew saw the budding artist in Lorna and repeatedly invited her to spend time in the office drawing with pencils, sharpies, and highlighters. Jimmy remained focused on healing Danica. He spent hours holding her hand and telling her about the news of the world and the state of their family.

Dr. Moreland, recognizing that her condition was neither improved, nor less stable, finally gave permission to the orthopedic surgeon to fix Danica's leg. The fact was that he could decrease some of the pain medications if they aligned and rodded her fracture. It was possible that decreasing the pain medication might increase her awareness enough to make her wake up.

Surgery was scheduled tentatively for Tuesday afternoon. The anesthesiologist, Dr. Hamm, visited extensively with Pop and Jimmy on Monday while the kids kept themselves busy out in the waiting area with their hand-held video games. Pop stood by Danica's bed with his arms crossed.

"So what you're saying is that you don't exactly know how much anesthesia to give her because she's already unconscious," Pop said gruffly, understanding one thing— that this surgery was further endangering his daughter's fragile state.

"That's not exactly true. We mathematically calculate a medication rate based on Danica's weight and age, and we could use that amount. We're just not sure, because she's in a coma, what her level of awareness already is. Most of our anesthesia will be achieved with a spinal block, a temporary deadening of the feeling below the waist. We'll keep the respirator steady, doing what it's already doing, and then we'll just do our best to make sure she's not in any unnecessary pain."

"This won't risk worsening her head injury, right?" Jimmy asked. The most important thing was Danica's brain condition, not her damaged bone.

"No. Dr. Moreland and I are sure that her head injury is actually showing signs of healing on her latest CAT scan. If we keep her oxygen levels unchanged, this shouldn't have any affect at all on her brain processes," Dr. Hamm answered.

"Are we absolutely positive that this hospital is the best place to have this done?" Pop reiterated.

"I have to be honest with you, Mr. Dixon. We had hoped Danica would wake up before we had to fix her leg. So far, she's done very well here and there has been no need to ship her. There are some risks of operating, but the orthopedic surgeon, Dr. Moreland, and I are in agreement that the benefits outweigh the risks."

"We've been over this. She's staying here, Pop. I trust these guys. I really do." Jimmy insisted.

"I cannot do this. I really can't." Pop looked physically ill. "I don't know how you can, Jimmy. I can't give consent to something that is such a huge unknown. It's a big risk. Can't we wait another week or two?"

"Would you like Danica to awake, only to be required to have her leg refractured in order to be fixed, and then to be told that she may never walk normally again, or worse, that she might lose her leg? All of these things are at risk if we wait too long to fix her femur. Her fracture is too serious to have even waited this long," Dr. Hamm persisted.

"Her life is more important than her leg," Pop said simply.

"I have to agree," said Jimmy.

"Her chance of waking up may be increased by the healing of her leg. We have said, less pain, less medication, which may help her regain consciousness. She needs to return to her life also, yes?" Dr. Hamm reasoned.

"Yes. That's important too," Jimmy capitulated.

"Jimmy. You're going to have to do this on your own. I know you love Danica. Promise me that you'll think for a few hours before you sign those consent forms," Pop requested as he waved a hand in dismissal and staggered out of the ICU. Pop's emotional reserves were spent. This decision was going to rest solidly on Jimmy's shoulders. Hopefully, he would make the right choice for Danica, and for the rest of them as well.

Jimmy signed the forms three hours later, then took the kids home to a quiet evening of dinner and movies. They all needed to relax before the big day Tuesday, when Danica would be in surgery for at least four hours. Marcia had prepared a pot of spaghetti for all of them and it waited at home.

Jimmy, Seth, and Lorna kissed Danica goodnight, and Jimmy had a hand on each of their shoulders as he steered them out of her room and into the hall adjoining the ICU. He almost reached to rub his eyes as recognition dawned on him. The man was completely out of context, but the reality of his presence sunk in when Seth said, "Hey, Dad."

Jimmy's blood ran cold. What in the world was Toby Browning doing less than fifty feet from Danica's hospital room?

Toby licked his lips nervously and ducked his head at Jimmy's glare. "Hey kiddos," he responded.

Jimmy kept his temper in check for the kids' sake. Quietly, lethally, he said, "You've got no business here, Toby."

"I knew you guys would be here. I have some good news. I got my lawyer to postpone the hearing indefinitely. I'm just thinking that's the last thing you need right now with Danica being sick and all."

"What hearing?" Asked Seth. Jimmy hadn't given the kids any inkling that their dad was causing trouble again.

"Well, now, Seth, I'm not sure what your dad is talking about." Jimmy fixed Toby with a gaze that brooked no argument. "I'm sure Miranda would have told us if there was something we needed to know about."

"I had a change of heart, Jimmy. That's it." Toby left it at that. Jimmy longed to be alone with the creep to wipe the smugness out of his eyes and the ignorance out of his soul.

Lorna, always torn in alliances, squeezed Jimmy's hand and then went to take her dad's. "Are you here to see Mommy?" She asked with the pure innocence of a child who still believed that love could conquer even the gravest of situations.

"Your daddy's here to give us a message, that's all, Lorna." Jimmy answered for Toby.

"Dad, I think it's time for you to leave," Seth said authoritatively, as if sensing the animosity between the two grown men.

"I really didn't come to cause trouble, Jimmy. Can you tell me how Danica's doing? I did love her once, after all." Toby pretended to be virtuous, but Jimmy felt goading behind the façade.

"It's entirely none of your business how Danica's doing," Jimmy replied.

"Mommy's going to have an operation tomorrow, Daddy. On her leg." Lorna attempted again to smooth things over.

"Oh, really? She must be doing better then." Toby said.

"Dad, Lorna and me will walk you to your car. We're not supposed to visit until next Saturday, but we'll come with you for now, okay?" Seth insisted, leading the way for Toby to leave with him, giving the man no choice but to follow.

Jimmy watched them retreat, cursing himself for being so angry with Toby in front of the kids. Though their biological father deserved every ounce of loathing Jimmy felt for him, he'd always been careful to hide his disdain in front of them, for their sake. This was just over the top coming to see Danica at the hospital.

He did find it interesting that Toby was backing off on the custody suit, though. Knowing Toby, Jimmy would continue to be wary. Like a vulture awaiting the death of an ailing calf, Jimmy knew that Toby would swoop upon them like helpless prey the minute he or Miranda let their guard down.

Chapter Seventeen

There were moments when Danica felt like she teetered on the edge of some giant precipice. It was as if she'd reached the edge of the lakebed and discovered a yawning canyon, and an invitation to jump off the edge and test her frock out as a parachute.

But she sensed the danger in jumping, inherently knowing the choice was irreversible. Something, or someone, held her back, kept her feet under her, so to speak. So she stared into the void instead, admired the luminescence and warmth from afar. She felt unthreatened, but terribly lonely.

She noticed a few moments when the ground came out from under her anyway, but she never fell. She chose not to, and knew that choosing was simply all she had to do.

She sensed love and safety in her lakebed. Not once did she realize that by remaining on solid ground, she selected life over death, or that the afterlife beckoned with an invitation almost too breathtaking to behold and almost too welcoming to resist.

"That's right, Shelby. It's a life insurance policy. On Danica. All the little tramp has to do is die and we'll be two hundred and fifty thousand dollars richer." Ashley

Browning dipped her spinach leaf lightly into her dressing and nibbled it delicately, savoring the Goddess dressing as if its name could infuse her with its qualities.

"Where in the world did that come from?" Shelby asked, incredulous.

"The tribal casinos got a one-time deal to buy permanent life insurance policies for its members and employees with government subsidy. Toby got the papers while he was working there and decided to put his policy offering in Danica's name—his reasoning was clear: He and the kids could be rich if she died. If he died, he could've cared less whether she got rich. Toby's listed as the beneficiary and since it's a permanent policy, it's good forever."

"Why didn't he just knock her off before she could take away the kids?" Shelby asked curiously.

"Well, Toby has never been one to stay on top of paperwork. He simply forgot about the policy. Otherwise I'm sure Danica Burdick would have had an 'accident' sooner."

Shelby's ice blue eyes lit with amused malice. "So I hear she's just barely clinging to life. Whatever can you do to make sure she doesn't hang on too awfully hard?" She bit into her fried chicken wrap.

"I guess they're doing surgery today to fix her leg, or so Lorna told Toby. With any luck, knowing the fine Rickton Community Hospital, they'll kill her before we have to consider helping her out at all," Ashley laughed and took a drink of her sugar-free cowboy lemonade.

Shelby laughed at this too. Befriending and unerringly agreeing with Ashley had gotten Shelby Lowe a place to live, frequent visits to the spa, and even more frequent lunches to Godbey's, the best, freshest food there was to eat in Rickton. It paid to be close to the Brownings. As far as Ashley was concerned, Shelby was one of them.

"Did you water our little friends today?" Ashley was a businesswoman foremost and Shelby, though she was her best friend, was also an employee of sorts.

"Of course. I watered them before work. You should have seen me trudging around in the snow between trailers seven and fifteen. God, I hate the wintertime. I felt like a cat trying to make its way across a puddle. I make my steps as long as possible and choose where my feet go so I don't get cold and soaked."

Ashley laughed at this. She would have felt the same way trying to get around in the trailer park in Shelby's work shoes.

"What's amazing is that as far as those guys are concerned, it's the tropics, even in the dead of winter," Shelby commented.

"Well I should hope so, with what I pay for electricity for your trailer and the other four. As far as the PUD knows, though, I just have wasteful tenants with terrible insulation," Ashley said.

"This tenant would be feeling better about it if hot flashes weren't attacking me with a vengeance. I have to put my make-up on in the car or it all melts away!" Shelby lamented.

"You know, I haven't really had any trouble with those. My massage therapist told me to take black cohosh and have a daily non-fat soy latte and it's working like a charm." Ashley said, offering the best advice she knew, as she usually tried to do.

Poor Shelby really did look a lot older than she herself did. No wonder her body responded in kind. If Shelby would exercise her fat rear end with Ashley five days a week instead of just once and skip the fried chicken wraps and opt for salads, she might be able to kick some of her metabolic issues. But then, even with work, few women of fifty could match Ashley's youthful good looks. She patted Shelby's hand sympathetically. At least Shelby was a loyal friend, even if she needed a little help in the looks department.

Ashley noticed out of the corner of her eye an obviously faux redhead approaching them from another table. The woman wore a lime polyester pencil skirt with some sort of lime and orange blouse and a brown leather bomber jacket with black above-the-knee vinyl boots. Ashley noted her garish parrot green eyeshadow as she teetered toward them in apparent recognition. "Well, hi Shelby. How are ya'll doin' today? I haven't met your gorgeous little friend here." She had a face like Bob Hope and, just as friendly, the woman shoved out her hand. "Connie May West."

Ashley grasped her hand limply. Shelby made the introductions. "This is my best friend, Ashley Browning. Ashley, this is Connie May. She's the clerk at the Sheriff's department here in Rickton."

Ashley raised her eyebrows at this. Why was Shelby friendly with the clerk for the local police? She smelled trouble.

"Shelby and me met when I brought my little 'uns to school about a month ago. She was real nice showin' us around 'n all. I don't know too many people 'round here since I jus' moved out from Kentucky, but Shelby, she was real sweet," Connie May gushed.

"Just doing my job." Shelby smiled sweetly in return.

"Oh, it was so much more, but I won't go interruptin' ya'll any more. I gotta git back t' work." She gestured to the bags on each arm. "I picked up burgers fer th' guys. Wouldn't want it to git cold! It was nice meetin' ya, Miss Ashley."

"My pleasure," Ashley replied smoothly. She fixed Shelby with a glare as the fashion disaster tapped away from them in her high-heeled boots, balancing her burdens carefully on each arm. Ashley meanly hoped that Connie May would fall flat on her ass when she hit the icy sidewalk. What a perfectly awful woman.

"Are we making new friends, Shelby?" Ashley asked acidly.

"Ashley, really, I was just being friendly, doing my job, like I always do. You know how women like that are. They'll cling to whoever gives them the time of day."

"Yeah, well don't let her get too clingy. You can't afford to screw with the delicate little balance you've got going working for me, and for the school. Your other job might have to disappear."

"You just get the extra money, Ashley, and it sounds like neither one of us will have to worry about other jobs. The lap of luxury, right? Two girlfriends and not a care in the world. That'll be us, girl, you'll see." Shelby smoothed Ashley's ruffled feathers as only she knew how. Whatever she did, she couldn't afford to jeopardize her relationship with the Brownings.

Chapter Eighteen

At the hospital, the entire Danica-support team gathered in the main waiting room. Miranda, Pop, and Marcia convened in the corner, holding their vigil with the comfort of prayer. Liz and Glenna borrowed Maria from Bob's Hardware for the day to run Wren's while they waited out Danica's surgery. The two of them, Jimmy, Seth, and Lorna took turns holding and entertaining Milo, who eventually tired of the excitement and fell asleep in Jimmy's arms.

They were two hours into Danica's surgery when one of the nurse's aides from the ICU came to give them the news that she was doing well. There were a few blood pressure drops at the start of surgery, but both had leveled off almost immediately. The surgeon had inserted the rod into her upper leg bone and the bulk of the work was done.

Her family received the news with a collective sigh. They resumed their positions and began quiet conversations. One of the other waiting room occupants, a portly man, about as tall as he was wide and bedecked in a tartan plaid overcoat, approached Pop. His white hair ringed the sides and back of his head and he carried a matching mackinaw hat in his hands.

"Hi Pop. It's been a long time," the man said in greeting. His smile was brilliant white like his hair and his eyes like merry little slits in doughy pastry.

"Lou! You're right it's been a while. Good to see you.

What are you doing here?" Pop pumped the other man's hand, genuinely surprised to see his old acquaintance.

"Oh, I had to come in for a few tests today," Lou replied.

"Nothing serious, I hope." Pop said conversationally.

"Just routine. No worries." Lou slid his hands into the pockets of his trousers and regarded Pop, who remained seated. "How about you? What are you doing here?"

"My daughter, Danica, was in an accident. She's having surgery on her leg today."

"I'm sorry to hear that she's been hurt. She'll be okay, then?" Lou inquired.

"It's sounds as though the surgery is going well and they're ahead of schedule. She's been in a coma for about a week, though, so we won't know for a while how that will work out." Pop shifted, uncomfortable with sharing too much with a man he barely knew.

"Pop, listen. I've been thinking about that spat we had at the Sibby Gun Club. I know it's been ages ago, but I want you to know that I was in the wrong there. I really was…" Lou's face turned crimson and he reached to loosen his collar.

Pop was alarmed. For all intents, Lou looked about ready to have a coronary and Pop couldn't figure out what in the world they'd even talked about. By now Jimmy and Marcia, who had been avoiding his conversation, not wanting to bother with introductions, were both hovering, listening to their words. He gestured to the chair across from him.

"Have a seat, Lou. Please. Those tests don't have anything to do with your heart, do they?"

"The tests? Oh, no. Really. They're nothing." Lou sat, breathing as if he'd run a mile.

"Not to be rude, but our family has had a lot of

stress lately. I truly can't remember what you and I talked about the last time I saw you. What's it been, six months? Longer?" Pop probed gently, afraid to cause Lou another fit.

"We were discussing zoning." Lou coughed and took a deep breath. "You thought the downtown Sibby area should remain entirely as it is—commercial and residential—and that the historic homes lining the main street should remain private homes. I have other ideas. I live in Rickton and I've seen the benefit of requiring businesses to operate out of the houses on Main Street when it is entirely zoned commercially. The economic stimulation there was tremendous once there were more businesses for patrons to see."

"Ah, yes. I remember now. As I recall, you'd given a bid on a few of those homes in Sibby. You're a developer, aren't you?"

"Actually, I'm a venture capitalist. I even discussed investing in your business, suggesting that you expand into a department store, using the next floor of your building."

Pop stared hard at Lou. "I had really forgotten about that. I dismissed your idea and then moved on. Expansion is just not for me. What you surely don't know about me is that I'm one who likes a debate, especially with a fellow rifleman. It's forgotten, Lou. No need to fret over the disagreement."

Lou reddened again, this time with embarrassment. "I took it a little too seriously, then, Pop? It is my business, after all." His eyes sought the lobby door. "I think I just saw a lab person walk by the window there. I'm going to go see if my results are ready to take with me. You'll excuse me?"

As excitable as a grasshopper in a jar, Lou suddenly popped up and made a beeline for the door. "It's been nice catching up with you, Pop. Give your daughter my regards. I hope she gets well quickly."

"Good luck with your tests, Lou. Thanks for the good wishes."

Pop stared after Lou as the lobby door swung closed behind him.

It was Marcia who spoke. "What an odd little man!"

"Was that Santa Claus, Jimmy?" asked Lorna. Minus the mustache and beard, the man was the closest she'd ever seen to St. Nick himself. It was getting close to the holiday after all.

Jimmy chuckled. "Nope. Not Santa Claus. Tell me, Pop. Did he manage to buy either one of those homes on Main in Sibby?"

"You know, I'm not sure. Louis Jacobs is just another man I met at the club with an interest in guns. I never took his posturing about economic development seriously. This is Sibby we're talking about."

"He certainly seemed serious enough about it," said Marcia. "You never told me you got an offer for a partnership in the business."

"You're my partner, Mom. Obviously it wasn't important enough to even warrant a mention," Pop soothed his wife. "Just chalk it up to locker room talk—a pissing match, so to speak, about whose ideas could take Sibby the furthest."

"Good Lord, let's hope that man doesn't get anywhere near a locker room anytime soon. He's liable to collapse tying his tennis shoes," quipped Glenna, who had taken in the whole conversation with intense interest. Lou Jacobs had paid her a visit or two over the last year also, and unlike Pop, Glenna took him seriously.

Liz went outside to get some air once the good news

about Danica was announced. It hadn't snowed for two days, but the air remained bitterly cold and the skies the gray of tarnished silver, as if the storm lay in wait for another round.

She sought her cell phone, punching the numbers with increasingly numb fingers. Steve would want news on Danica. Liz still held Steve at arms' length, but mutual history forced her to keep in touch with him. As she waited for him to pick up, she thought of Steve's chestnut curls and his square jaw that always looked like his shave was at least a day old. She thought of his green eyes, flecked with gold, that always seemed to warm a shade when he spotted Liz. Sometimes it was almost as if he loved her. She wondered if that could be true…

"The Mercantile." His voice shook her from her reverie.

"Steve. Hi. It's Liz."

"Well, hey there, Liz. How's Danica?"

"She's holding her own. They're closing up her incision. Things have been looking good."

He let out an audible sigh of relief.

"How are you holding up?" Steve asked.

"Oh I'm fine. Just helping with Milo and hanging out with Danica's family."

"You sound cold," Steve sounded amused, a gentle warming of his voice that curled her toes.

"I am cold. I ran outside to use the phone and get some air," she admitted.

"I wish I was there to warm you up." The comment brought about an unexpectant flush and made her want to turn tail and run.

"Steve. Um. I've gotta go. I just wanted to tell you how Danica was doing."

"When are you going to tell me what happened to you, Liz?" Steve asked almost inaudibly.

"I don't know what you're talking about." She evaded. This particular conversation was off-limits, even with Liz's mom.

"Someone hurt you. You weren't like this before you left. Listen, I haven't tried to talk to you about this in person because you won't let me within five feet of you to hold a conversation."

Liz listened, debated hanging up, but decided to let Steve continue.

Taking her silence as acceptance, Steve said, "I knew when you took off to college that I had no shot in hell of making you happy because I was a small-town boy. You were off to bigger and better things. Any childhood crush I had on you would be lost on a woman who was going to become a doctor and save the world one body at a time.

"That was okay. I tried to move on. I dated a few girls, but no one measured up to you, Liz—brilliant, confident, good at everything you tried to master; and you loved to laugh, and put Danica and I in stitches too.

"So all of a sudden you came back, degree in hand, and, from what I understood, acceptance to Vanderbilt, one of the best med schools in the country; and you decided to hang out in Sibby and help your mom with the store instead.

"That I could have chalked up as homesickness, a desire to work for a while and save up your money, or something. But here's what's got me worried sick about you Liz, enough to take a retail job, when you know what I love most is being out in the open air: I haven't seen you laugh like you used to at all, not once. Oh sure, you joke around a little, but those silver eyes of yours don't ever look happy. They look haunted.

"I've known you forever, Liz. When are you going to tell me what in the world happened to my audacious girl?"

Steve finished.

Her voice was a whisper, her tears freezing on her lashes, "I can't."

"Liz? It's just a voice you're talking to. I don't have to touch you, and you know I can take anything you have to tell me."

She let out a shaky sob. "I'm cold. I have to go inside now." She flipped her phone closed and took in another tremulous breath.

Out of the corner of her eye she saw a man emerging from his car—medium height, medium build, an average-looking guy—and she saw Chad. She fled back into the hospital as if being pursued, knowing that she couldn't ever really hide, because she saw Tim or Chad everywhere, heard them in every male voice, and feared them with almost every waking thought.

Chapter Nineteen

George Stevens took off his reading glasses and rubbed his eyes, sighing deeply. His meeting with Toby Browning hadn't gone exactly as he'd predicted. The man changed his mind daily about what he could do to make his ex-wife Danica miserable. He wanted to drop the current custody bid, and George, for the life of him couldn't figure out why. This was probably the best shot they'd had of gaining full custody, since Danica hadn't improved; and Seth and Lorna were left in the care of their stepfather.

George had a private eye do some serious dirty digging on Jimmy Burdick when he and Danica first became an item. The man was squeaky clean, as good as a man gets. They couldn't prove him an unfit step-parent, but he and Toby could certainly argue that, lacking a biological connection, Jimmy had no rights to the Browning kids.

This one-eighty Toby was doing was a mystery to George. It wasn't like he enjoyed doing Toby's dirty work, but the Brownings paid well, and Ashley Browning, well, she catered to a few of his other needs. George's wife had all of the sex appeal of a standard poodle; but she suited his social needs well and paid no mind to his tendency to work too much. Ashley looked past George's bad toupee and jowls and shored him up until he felt like a modern-day Valentino. Oh, the things she could do to him.

George, flushed and sweaty with thoughts of Ashley Browning high on his mind, rose shakily and poured himself a scotch from his office mini-bar.

Perhaps it was best not to bother the Burdicks at this point. After all, he'd made enemy enough of Pop Dixon when he'd taken on Toby's case in the first place. He had been one of Pop's first friends in the area when they tied in a decoy shootout at the gun club. George and his wife had twin girls one year younger than Danica. Marcia and the wife had gotten along famously, and they'd had dinner parties and their girls had run around together for a while.

The whole friendship, more than fifteen years-worth, ran aground when George was *persuaded* by Ashley Browning into taking Toby's divorce and custody case. The most recent attacks on Danica and her family had been completely Toby's ideas. Lord knew Pop had enough to hate George for, but George's remorse could never restore a friendship he missed dearly. It was his largest human failing—that he couldn't shake himself of his need for Ashley Browning.

It was lunchtime, so George downed the last swallow of his scotch, put on his wool overcoat, and walked to his blue Lincoln, planning to tiptoe it on over to the Diner on Easy Street. Fluffy snowflakes began to drift from a silver sky. He scowled. George abhorred this winter weather. Just like a morning meeting with Toby Browning, it brought nothing but trouble.

Rico's Diner felt like a tropical oasis compared to the weather outside. Shouts from the waitresses to Rico, who presided over the grill, resounded over the top of clanking cups and forks scraping up the last scraps of grease-laden morsels.

Candy, a petite brunette in a lemon-yellow pinafore, recognized George when he walked in the door. She winked and gestured with her coffee pot to his regular table.

"Are you having the usual, George?"

George rubbed his ample tummy, vowing to do at least a few minutes on the rowing machine when he got home, then he replied, "Yep, B.L.T. on rye, but you better make it fat-free mayo this time, Candy."

"Sure thing. Can I get you something to drink?"

"I'll have a Coke."

The waitress watched George reach into his breast coat pocket and finger his shiny silver flask. Candy smiled sadly and walked over to the counter to dispense him a Coke, leaving about an inch of headroom so George could add his poison.

Pete Morse watched with interest from the bar counter as George Stevens dumped a measure of whiskey from his flask into his glass. He had no idea old George was a boozer. George held himself well, even in the courtroom, where Pete had gone to testify on occasion. Aside from his jowls and his constantly red face, Pete would have had no idea that George drank regularly. Pete did know, however, that George was Toby Browning's attorney of record.

Pete had heard from his lawyer buddy that George also went to eat almost daily at Rico's. Thus, lunch had turned into an odd sort of stakeout. Lemonade in hand, Pete made his way to George's table.

"You're George Stevens, right?" Pete held out his hand in greeting.

George shook it firmly, though he looked hesitant as he looked Pete's uniform over. "I'm George Stevens."

"Detective Pete Morse. I've seen you in court a few times. You are quite an eloquent barrister, compared to most of the lawyers that hit these parts, anyway."

"Well, I appreciate the complement. I enjoy that part of my job myself." George gestured to the seat across from him. Evidently, the praise warranted a simple gesture of politeness. "Won't you join me?"

"As long as you're not expecting anybody, sure," Pete replied.

Their meals arrived and Pete spent a moment staring longingly at George's B.L.T. before digging into his own green salad with ranch. "That sure looks good."

"It *is* good, Pete. I have it nearly every day. Can't resist Rico's greasy bacon, tart tomatoes, and crispy lettuce," George took a big bite for emphasis.

"Yeah, well, I had to loosen my uniform belt a notch this morning, so I'm in for a skinny lunch. My wife gets on my case when my paunch exceeds its usual limits."

George laughed at this. "My wife likes to smother me with as much gravy and salt as she can get her hands on. Mine must want me to die of a coronary. In fact, I'm sure that would suit her just fine."

Pete laughed along with his lunch companion. He then ventured into the subject that had propelled him across the room in the first place. "Say, didn't I see you down at the station one time with Toby Browning? We'd brought him in to sleep off a bad night at the Pool Hall."

"I make it a policy not to discuss my clients, Pete. It might have been me, or maybe not," George admitted.

"Do you know Toby?" Pete pressed on.

"I do know Mr. Browning. Yes." George said.

"I have a sister who wants to rent a mobile toward the outskirts, because she's got horses south of town to take care of. The Brownings' place is nearby. Do you know if they have any vacancies in their trailer park?" Pete actually had no idea where his only sister was, but George didn't need to know that.

"Well I'm quite sure I don't know what their renting situation is, but I haven't run up any agreements recently.

They could very well have an opening," George said warily.

"You mean to tell me, out of the twenty mobiles that they have out there, that you haven't had any turnover of tenants recently? They must have some pretty faithful renters." Pete commented, munching on a spinach leaf and staring George in the eyes.

George's eyes evaded, looking up and to the left. A lie, Pete noted, as George replied, "I wouldn't know about that. Ashley takes care of most of that business herself." Pete saw the deepening of George's ruddy complexion when he mentioned Toby's mother.

"That's okay, George. I'll try to get ahold of Toby directly to ask about the rental. I can't remember what Toby said he did for a living when we booked him. Do you know where he works?"

George chewed faster. He seemed suddenly anxious to be through with his lunch. He took a deep pull on his glass of whiskey and soda. "I don't know if Toby is working right now."

"Huh. I thought with all of your fancy legal fees, what with being at his beck and call and all, that for sure you'd know how it was he was paying you. You know, in case he didn't pay his bill or something," Pete suggested innocently.

George reddened even more and stammered. "Ashley takes care of the bills. I've never had to deal with Toby about money." He finished his sentence, and Pete noticed smugly that George realized he'd already said too much. He wondered if it was Ashley Browning that George was afraid of.

George stuffed the last of his sandwich in his mouth and indelicately downed the last of his Coke. Throwing a twenty on the table, he said in parting, "Nice talking with you, Pete, but I'm in sort of a hurry. Lunch is on me today."

"That's very kind of you, George. Thanks. It'd be great to visit with you again sometime. I'll buy then, okay? By the way, your shoes don't really suit walking all of the way back to your office, do they? You might want to step next door to the shoe store and see if they have any waterproof shoe covers."

"I'm driving, Pete. My shoes should be just fine." George stared longingly at the door.

Pete's reply was subtle, but it was enough to make George sink back to his chair with resignation. Pete said, "I know you are not going to get in that car in front of me when I just saw you put a shot of booze into your Coke fifteen minutes ago."

"What do you want from me, Detective Morse? It's snowing. Surely you don't expect me to walk?"

Pete stood and patted George Stevens on the shoulder. "I can do better than that for my new lunch buddy. It would be my pleasure to give you a ride. Besides, we'll get a chance to talk some more."

George followed Officer Pete Morse dutifully to his car, where Pete offered him the front seat, thank God. Curse Toby Browning, he thought, as Pete's barrage of questions continued. What kind of trouble was his client in now?

Toby was on a fact-finding mission. He'd learned from the kids that Danica survived her surgery, a blow to his plan to have Rickton Community Hospital take care of his ex-wife problem for him. Lorna, bless her little heart, had also told him all about the machine that was breathing for her mommy. Apparently she was just as stable as could be as long as that machine kept breathing just when it was supposed to.

He could fix that. All he needed to do was to find out how to disrupt the breathing machine. He had a way with females, so he was pretty sure he could charm the information out of some saucy little nurse. The biggest part of his problem was that he was sure Jimmy Burdick would never let him get within a mile of Danica's hospital room again.

He was going to have to enlist the help of the kids. He hated to do it, because it would mean they'd be close by when their helpless mother died. But he couldn't take a chance that she'd do it on her own. There was too much money at stake. She could stay alive like that for years, a vegetable. She really was better off dead. Toby was just taking the decision out of God's hands. It was a good thing God forgave the faithful.

Tomorrow was Saturday—time for his unsupervised twelve hours with the kids. Seth would be suspicious—a chip off the old block, so smart and all. But the heart of a child is so open, he figured he could soft-soap the two of them into believing he needed to see their mother for old times' sake, to try and coax her back to life, for all of them.

It would be simple, really. Toby sat in the hospital cafeteria during the busy Friday lunch hour, watching the staff come and go out of a hideously pink room. It was time to strike up a conversation.

Chapter Twenty

Milo awakened that Saturday morning with a gut-wrenching cry of despair. As Jimmy picked him up, he curled into his daddy's chest, and tears flowed freely down his chubby cheeks. Jimmy, try as he might, couldn't stem his son's sadness, because he knew in his heart that what his baby needed was Danica. Sometimes Jimmy wished he could cry like that too. He scooped the poor little guy into his arms; and with Milo still sup-supping into his shoulder, pulled a bottle filled with breast milk from the fridge and shook the bottle while the pan warmed.

It seemed like so much trouble when all that his wife had to do was whip out a breast, latch him on, and let him go to town. She'd been in the hospital for two and a half weeks now, with no significant change in her condition. Dr. Moreland warned that, though her head injury had stabilized, the fact that she hadn't awaken from her coma led to deep concerns that she might not wake up at all. If she stayed in her coma longer than a month, they would have to make painful decisions about whether to continue to feed her through a tube and to continue with the respirator. They would have to decide if the life she was living was all she would ever be able to do, and if that was the life they wanted for their beloved wife, mom, and daughter.

The prospect of any such decisions simply sent Jimmy's heart into his toes. He could maintain the household, get ready for the holidays, continue to work while Marcia helped with the kids, and continue with life as normal; but he couldn't face the prospect of losing Danica forever. There had to be some way to bring her around.

Christmas was just three days away and Jimmy, who'd never been too good at conversing with God, had been praying in his incoherent fashion for a Christmas miracle.

Danica's family and friends had already decided that the day would be centered around Rickton Community Hospital and Danica, in particular. Mom had bought six turkeys, five bags of breadcrumbs, ten bags of potatoes, a case of green beans, and twenty pumpkin and apple pies. With the help of many friends' ovens and stovetops, she was preparing a feast that would feed the entire hospital staff for both the day and night shifts on Christmas. She figured it was the best she could do for the people who had cared so wonderfully for her daughter.

They couldn't bring a live tree into the ICU, so Jimmy borrowed a lovely ceramic tree from Glenna so they could do their traditional morning gift exchange at the foot of Danica's bed.

Danica loved Christmas and embraced every moment of it, from the gingerbread houses to the green and red hand towels in the bathroom. She even had a Santa toilet seat cover that graced the kids' toilet every Christmas. She lit up on Christmas like the most brightly decorated house in town, especially when she got to see the kids open their gifts from 'Santa.' Jimmy had never met anyone who loved Christmas as much as his wife. That's why he knew they were due for a miracle on that, of all days.

Shared custody with Toby meant that every other year, Toby had Seth and Lorna on Christmas morning; but that never stopped Danica from celebrating Christmas Eve in the same manner as Christmas day.

Jimmy frowned as he remembered that Toby was coming to get the kids today at nine. Toby had them today and on Christmas Eve this year. Jimmy would have to get them up and packed pretty soon.

He fed Milo his bottle, finally calming the baby, even as Milo's eyes remained filled to the brim with tears. Jimmy melted into his son's chocolate orbs, such a mirror of his own. This year was to be even sweeter with the addition of Milo. It was their precious boy's first Christmas. Jimmy knew that Danica would rather die than miss out on that event.

He thought again of the very real possibility that Danica could die. Another fifteen days and they would know if this Christmas would be the last. What would become of their family? Jimmy felt his own eyes fill with tears as he rocked Milo in Danica's cushy glider rocker and sent another disjointed prayer toward the heavens.

Toby was right on-time, for once. He met Jimmy, Seth, and Lorna at the gate where he normally parked. Snow had fallen heavily the night before, but Jimmy had taken the snowblower to the driveway and sidewalk, so the kids would be safe trudging out to Toby's sports car in their snow boots.

Jimmy carried Lorna's pillow and bag of stuffed 'buddies', wondering for the hundredth time why her father couldn't just get duplicates of some of Lorna's favorite things so she didn't have to pack them back and forth so often. According to Seth, their shared room at Toby's was pretty bare-bones; but he always kept the kids entertained by renting videos and taking them out for ice cream, an outing in the park in the summer and hot chocolate and sledding behind the trailer park in the winter.

Toby was the 'fun' daddy, the entertaining one, as

opposed to Jimmy's pragmatic, steady type of fathering. This never bothered Jimmy because he knew they respected him and adored him all the more for his guiding presence in their daily lives. Besides, Danica wouldn't want it any other way. She'd much rather see Seth and Lorna spoiled with love and patience, than with sweets and cheap entertainment.

"Hiya, Jimmy." Toby was unusually cordial. Mostly he would take the kids silently and leave, but today he seemed to want to strike up conversation.

"Toby." Jimmy answered and urged the kids toward the door of the car. Milo was asleep in his crib and he would need to check on him soon. He had no desire to converse with Toby.

"I'll have the kids back at nine tonight, just like usual," Toby offered.

"Sounds fine," Jimmy replied and turned to leave as Toby put the kids' stuff in his trunk.

"Hey, Jimmy? Are you going to see Danica today?"

Jimmy turned in complete annoyance toward his nemesis. "I can't see how that's any of your business, but yes, I am. I see her every day."

"That's got to get old, what with her doing the same thing all the time," Toby said, his ignorance bared for all to see.

"She's my wife. I love her and I can't wait to see her open her eyes again. I want to be there when that happens. Not that you would understand that." Jimmy stared hard at Toby.

"What time do you think you'll be going?" Toby pressed.

Jimmy marveled at Toby's audacity. He kept himself from balking or losing his temper in front of the kids, a move Jimmy knew Toby would take advantage of. Toby could restart his custody bid any day and Jimmy didn't want to see that happen. He replied icily. "I've got a few things to take care of, but I imagine I'll be there by this afternoon."

"That takes dedication, man. Really. I thought no one could ever love Danica like I did, but Jimmy you really do take the cake." Toby was complementing Jimmy. Now Jimmy was absolutely sure that the man was up to something, though for the life of him, he couldn't figure what.

"I'll see you this evening, kiddos, Toby. I've got to go check on the baby." With that, Jimmy turned on his heels and the conversation was over.

Toby sniggered, in a rare good mood, returned to the warmth of his car and eased away into the snowy landscape with his children under his tutelage for at least the day. God-willing, maybe it would be forever. They would have the best nannies money could buy; and as far as he was concerned, the handsomest, most fun dad in the world.

No more child support (not that he paid it anyway), no more Danica, no more sharing. He turned up his Toby Keith CD, winked at himself in the rearview mirror, and yelled, "Hey kids, wanna sing along?"

Chapter Twenty-one

Danica's lake had turned to a bed of clouds and she alternated floating on her cloudy bed and wandering aimlessly on the shore. Time had lost all meaning, but she was feeling restless, nonetheless. She was lonely, but unsure who or what it was she longed for. The light that beckoned her stood firmly at her back; and she had lately refused to even look at it, choosing instead the safety of her cushiony sky.

Suddenly, she spotted a break in the heavens above and a streak of emerald and indigo burst through like a comet. It was headed straight for her! She got to her feet quickly and tried to run, but it was as if a huge weight hung around her calves, keeping her from running or taking flight. She couldn't go fast enough! The lakebed turned to quagmire, and the beautiful, awful vein of darkness swung around to face her. It swept her forehead first. She opened her mouth to scream and tendrils of dead air flew into her nose and mouth. No sound emerged, no way she could cry for help. Danica felt her throat constrict as her cloud-world turned black and she was sucked into the void.

Alarms sounded from room one of the ICU. Her respirator had ceased and the patient was arresting. The nurse's aide flew to the phone.

"Code Blue, ICU One STAT. Code Blue, ICU One STAT."

The milieu descended. The aide's first thought as she rushed into Danica's room was, 'Oh no, the children.'

Lorna and Seth pressed against the far wall of the room, their eyes wide in horror. Their father, whom the aide had only seen just this morning, stood in front of them and tried to shield them from the view of their mother, who lay dying in front of their eyes.

"I'm sorry. You'll all need to leave the room now." She said as calmly as she could while other staff pushed a crash cart into the room and the male day nurse began to apply chest compressions. She went immediately to the drug drawer to get the epinephrine and atropine and other supplies she knew the doctor would need for running the code. The respiratory therapist checked the respirator and found it not functioning. He immediately disconnected it and attached a bag to the tube down Danica's throat, applying much needed oxygen to her system.

Dr. Moreland appeared in operating-room scrubs, fresh from assisting with a c-section. Thank God that he was in-house for this crisis. He'd grown to respect and admire Jimmy and Pop and their cohesive little family. This patient needed to live to return to the people who loved her so much.

He shoved past Danica's two older children and a man he didn't know. That was strange. Where was Jimmy? He arrived at Danica's bedside to find his staff doing just what they were trained to do. They were breathing for the patient and applying chest compressions. So her heart had already stopped.

"Get the crash cart charged. I'm going to shock her. Nurse, give her one milliliter of epi, please, through the central line."

The nurse complied. "The cart is charged, Doctor."

Dr. Moreland held his breath and said, "Clear."

Seth could see his mother's torso rise off the bed as an electric shock went through her body.

"What did you do to her, Dad?" Seth turned to Toby, his blue eyes filled with rage and fear. He knew instinctively that his father had something to do with his mother's condition. Toby had been standing by the machine that breathed for her. He had been murmuring softly to Danica and holding her upper arm. Seth hadn't seen him touch the machine, but then Toby's body was between Seth and the buttons.

"I did nothing, Son. I swear."

"Daddy, did you hurt Mommy?" Lorna chimed in, tears streaming down her face.

"I was just talking to her. Maybe I just frightened her, you know since she hasn't heard my voice in a few weeks or something," Toby hedged, trying to lead the children away from the viewing window to Danica's room. 'Mission accomplished,' he thought, while feeling slightly sick about what he'd just done. Now he just had to appease Seth.

"You pushed something, didn't you?" Seth said, wrenching his arm out of Toby's grasp. "I knew it was a mistake to let you see her."

"I was just whispering kind words to her, Seth. You saw me."

"I know you did this. Just leave me alone. If Mom dies, I'll never forgive you." With that, Seth ran out of the ICU.

"Don't go after him, Daddy. Stay here with me and hold my hand." Lorna insisted, focusing still intently on what was happening in Danica's room.

"We should go, baby. They're going to take care of your mommy, Lorna, honey. You don't need to watch this," Toby tried to coax Lorna away.

"I'm not leaving," Lorna insisted as she wiped away tears and, instead of crying, focused all of her energy on her mother. She just had to be all right, for Milo. Lorna's baby brother needed his mommy. Lorna couldn't be mommy to all of them.

Just at that moment, Jimmy walked in. "Oh no. What's happened? What are *you* doing here?" Jimmy looked at Toby with all the disdain he deserved.

Lorna said in monotone, as if she were a galaxy away, "Mommy's not going to die, Jimmy."

"She's *what*?" Jimmy focused finally on what was happening in Danica's room. "Danny?"

"I can feel her here. She wouldn't leave us." Lorna said, still in her fugue.

Jimmy's fear and confusion turned to fury, all directed at Toby, a man who had no business being here. His words were lethal. "You better not have anything to do with this, Toby Browning, or so help me, Danica will not be the only one who needs saving."

"Hey man, I just brought the kids to visit," Toby said weakly.

All three held their breath as Dr. Moreland stepped back from the bed. "Okay. We have sinus-rhythm. Keep breathing for her until we can get this respirator restarted and reset."

"Doctor, she's trying to take breaths on her own, between squeezes," the respiratory therapist said, amazed that the patient should be doing this.

"Hold off for a few breaths. See if she continues," Dr. Moreland said, almost afraid to breathe himself as he waited for Danica's chest to rise.

All six of the people working on Danica paused to watch the rise and fall of their patient's chest. Then she did it again, and again, picking up in rhythm and depth. Danica was breathing on her own.

Dr. Moreland refused to hope that this would continue, ordering the tube to stay down Danica's throat for now, planning to track her progress over the next few hours personally. He turned to see Jimmy, Lorna, and the unfamiliar man through the window. He'd better talk to them and reassure them. After all, what they'd all seen was some kind of miracle. He struggled to think how he could explain it, when he wasn't even sure how it had happened himself.

"Hi Jimmy. She's okay for now," he said immediately.

"That's good. Why isn't she on the respirator?" Jimmy knew enough from the past two weeks to know that something had changed.

"She arrested, Jimmy. We're not sure why, but we think the respirator may have malfunctioned. Her heart stopped, but we were there in time to restart it."

'Blasted alarms,' Toby thought. He should have known to silence or disconnect those first.

"So she's okay now?" Jimmy asked, confused.

"She's better than before. For some inexplicable reason, when we restarted Danica's heart, she started breathing on her own again too. If she continues, and I don't want to get your hopes up, she won't need the respirator at all. All she'll need is a feeding tube until she wakes up," Dr. Moreland explained.

"You say *when* she wakes up. Does this mean she's made progress toward coming back to us, Doc?" Jimmy asked, biting his lip as he waited for the answer he wanted to hear.

"Suffice it to say that I thought we might have lost your wife today, Jimmy. She proved me wrong, in a miraculous way. I'd like to think her chance of waking up has improved greatly based on this latest feat."

"I told you she wouldn't leave us, Jimmy," said Lorna as

she tugged his hand reassuringly.

"Thanks, Doc." Jimmy said and kissed his daughter's head.

"Anytime. I'm going to stay here for a few hours and track the breathing until I'm sure it's okay to discontinue the respirator. Why don't you and the kids and this gentleman go have a coffee in the cafeteria until you can visit Danica properly?"

"This gentleman is leaving," said Jimmy flatly. "This is Danica's *ex*-husband, Toby Browning."

Toby nodded and waved unenthusiastically at the doctor. Dr. Moreland nodded in acknowledgment.

"Hey, Doc. One more favor?" Jimmy inquired. "Is there any way you can check to see if the respirator was tampered with?" He looked at Toby pointedly, who looked about ready to turn tail and run.

"I can look into that," Dr. Moreland replied, catching Jimmy's drift.

"I need to go find Seth. He and Lorna and I need to go Christmas shopping. Last minute stuff, you know." Toby touched Lorna on the shoulder and pointed toward the exit.

"Not so fast, Toby," Jimmy said. "I think you and I need to go find Seth together."

Pete Morse wasn't on duty, but he did what he could to help Jimmy try to incriminate Toby. According to Jimmy, the oldest kid was pretty sure that his dad might have done something to mess with Danica's breathing machine.

The machine had been shut off during Danica's arrest, making the settings impossible to retrieve. The best they could do, since she didn't need the machine anymore, was to dust it for prints. The hospital volunteered to give Pete some time with the respirator in one of the spare patient rooms.

Word had it that Toby had charmed one of the nurses the day before in the cafeteria into telling him more about how the machine worked. Based on circumstantial evidence alone, Pete thought they almost had enough to arrest Toby.

When it came down to dusting for prints, however, Pete was disappointed to find hundreds of smudged, unrecoverable prints covering the machine. Apparently the staff needed to wipe it down a little more often. Finding Toby's print would be like finding the proverbial needle in the haystack.

The case boiled down to Toby's word against the kid's and Jimmy's gut. They'd never get charges to stick in such a case. Jimmy was forced to drop it, but Pete made a vow. That guy was every sort of bad, and if he'd stoop to killing a helpless woman in her hospital bed, in front of her children, then he needed to be taken out.

Pete was going to nail Toby Browning if it took his last breath to do it.

Chapter Twenty-two

Liz sat by Danica's bedside and held her hand, feeling somewhat appeased by the stillness, the quietness of Danica's breathing. It was so much more peaceful than the sounds of the respirator, which had reverberated throughout the room. Danica looked almost normal and aside from the low-toned beep of her heart monitor, Liz could almost believe that her friend simply slept heavily.

She needed to get back to the store to help her mom with the Christmas Eve crowd. There were sure to be oodles of people shopping for last minute natural gifts and ingredients for their families. Liz had been in charge of the gift inventory this year and she'd made some brilliant choices. She enjoyed picking out vivid soy candles she'd discovered from a local artisan, a selection of gourmet teas and hand-painted teapots, and wooden, American-made toys. These and other items made this their busiest Christmas season yet at Wren's, an ironic twist to the same winter that landed her best friend near death.

Liz had helped her mother bake bread and cinnamon rolls that morning. She was tired because they began at three a.m., but the women knew it would be necessary to their increasingly loyal customers when they fed their families for the holidays. They conversed while they worked.

"I've noticed Steve calling on you more than usual

these days," Glenna began subtly.

"I talk to him almost more often than I talk to you, Mom." Liz exclaimed, as she greased the baking pans in preparation for the cinnamon rolls.

"And are you okay with that?" Glenna asked.

"Steve's harmless, Mom. We've been friends forever."

"I don't think it's friendship he's after, Liz, honey," Glenna said wryly.

"I don't have anything else to give him." Liz stopped what she was doing and looked her mother in her weary eyes. The heartbreak and confusion there nearly took Glenna's breath away. What could she say? She'd failed her daughter fundamentally and she knew that, by not getting her help sooner; but what could she do now to make it better?

"You made me agree never to talk about it, Liz." She said quietly, handing her daughter a measuring cup for flour.

Liz took the cup and began carefully measuring out flour for the dough. "I *can't* talk about it, Mom. I just want to put it behind me. Pretend to live a normal life. I'm just having a hard time doing that when it comes down to trusting someone besides you."

"You've already given up every dream I know you had for yourself. I think you need to talk about it. Ignoring what happened just doesn't seem to be working for you. Now you have a chance with a super guy, and I can tell he truly cares about you. I can see in your eyes that you care about him too, regardless of what you say about friendship." Glenna pressed, trying to say the right thing to her daughter, for once. She kneaded the bread dough thoughtfully, expertly, kept a grimace of pain at bay, and waited for Liz's reply.

"I'll think about it, Mom. Okay? I just need some time."

"You've had time, honey. I think it's time to face what happened before it strips you of absolutely everything. Life is short. Just look at what's happened to Danica. You just let me know what I need to do to help."

Liz put dough covered hands around her mother's neck and gave her a messy hug. "Oh, Mommy, you always do what you need to do. Don't look so sad. You love making bread. This will work out too, just like the lumps in your dough. I promise."

Liz sighed now. It was a promise made out of sleep deprivation and low blood-sugar, but she knew Glenna would consider it binding, nonetheless. Besides, she wanted to feel better for her own sake, too. It was time to tell her story. Danica had always been her confidante. But Liz had refused to share this, even with her oldest friend.

"I've been doing a lot of reading, Danica. It's a mixed bag on whether you'll be able to hear me and remember what I tell you. I guess that makes you the ideal person to talk to. So here goes:

"Do you remember how hard we cried when I had to leave for college?" Danica's breathing remained steady as her friend continued. "It felt like I was leaving for war and that I'd never see you again. I knew the next time I'd be back was Thanksgiving, and it felt like a century away. Those first years were awesome, though, and you called me uppity when I came home because I was learning all these big words and hanging out with all of these rich college kids. But, teasing or not, you were my rock, Danica. I never met another girl there that could be my friend like you could.

"I was almost finished with my Biology degree and it was nearly Christmas break of my senior year. I met a few guys in my Microbiology lab that knew about a party on

Slippery

Saturday at the U. I rarely did that, you know, partying, but it sounded like fun; and both of the guys, Chad and Tim, were already accepted to medical schools too. They seemed like good guys. Chad was built like a linebacker, broad and tall; and he had these eyes like ice, the pupil and the outer rim of his iris were the only color in them." Liz shuddered as she remembered just how cold those eyes could be.

"He had a killer smile, though, and jet black hair, like yours. He was going to medical school in California, so he could be closer to home. I liked him, but it was his friend Tim that I was really intrigued with. Tim was tall too, but lanky, and he had this deep voice, like a radio ad announcer. His eyes were hazel, like a really complicated piece of amber, and he had wavy, dark blond hair that made me want to run my fingers through it. He was extremely bright and he'd been accepted at several medical schools back East and he hadn't made a choice yet.

"I never dated either one of these guys because they never asked, but the three of us had met at the library a few times and studied for tests together. They were gentleman. I thought so, anyway. I had a scholarship, so I lived in the dorms, but both of them came from wealthy families, well-connected with the University. They had an apartment a mile from campus. I took the bus there to meet them before we all went over to the U District to the party, which was at a frat house.

"I'd never seen a house like that, Danica. The front was all windows, lit like the heavens; and it was obvious that a party was already in full swing by the time we got there. Tim drove his Audi and we circled the block and parked down the street a ways from the house. We went inside, letting ourselves in because the hosts were otherwise indisposed. You'd have been amazed. Every piece of furniture was removed from the place. There were folding chairs here and there, but no real furniture. They'd taken every built-in cabinet and taped it shut with duct tape. Several of the larger windows were taped across also with masking tape as if they needed to be reinforced.

"The beer and wine coolers flowed like the Amazon and I took part too, since I was old enough. It was fun and I was the center of attention with the guys and their pals from the U. Tim kept complimenting me on my smarts and tugging at my curls affectionately as he teased me about blowing the curve in most of our advanced classes. Chad just hung back and smiled."

Liz paused and took a deep breath. Danica's expression never changed. This was the hard part and she had never, ever put this event in her life into words. She half-sobbed, half-hiccupped and shored herself up to tell the rest of the story.

"I think they assumed that I would never remember the night. As a matter of fact, I'm pretty sure that they banked on that. And I was pleasantly buzzed, floating through the fun, laughing with everyone. But I wasn't drunk. Tim tucked a finger under my chin and asked me if I would like to go upstairs with him. I figured the upstairs was like the downstairs—no furniture, no beds—what could be the harm? I thought it was weird that Chad followed us, like a puppy tailing his master. Tim didn't say anything.

"There were people necking, and doing unmentionable things to each other in each of the first two rooms we came to. I got a little uncomfortable, realizing that Tim meant to have time alone with me; and I had no idea of his intentions. We weren't even dating, so what could he possibly expect?

"Tim and I ducked into the third room and Chad was right behind us. Before I knew what was happening, the two of them had hauled me into the adjacent bathroom and they started touching and ripping clothes, their mouths, their hands everywhere." Liz's eyes filled with tears and she sobbed again. "I fought, Danica. I did. I scratched and tried to kick. I even fell out of their grasp long enough to bang my head on the edge of the sink and put a big goose egg on my forehead. But Chad was huge and he held me like a vice while Tim, the guy I'd been so attracted to, raped me then and there. I kind of disappeared inside of myself then; and I don't really remember completely the rest, but I do know that Chad took a turn at me. But that wasn't the end. There was more, but it's really jumbled and unclear. At some point, I passed out completely.

"It was clear in the morning, though, that they had left me there. I didn't even know exactly where I was in the U District, so I gathered my clothes and my beat up body and wandered around until I could find a bus stop. I rode the first bus all the way downtown, and then I remembered which number bus would take me back up the hill to my dorm.

"I must have looked like Hell. My lower lip was cut from biting it. My clothes were ragged. I had circles of black makeup under my eyes and my hair was matted with blood and tears. All I knew was that I needed to get home and get clean, get rid of the stench and the shame of those two horrible men.

"I got home, got a shower. Luckily I had my own room, so I didn't have a roommate to explain things to. Then I went to bed and I slept and slept for what seemed like days. I didn't even want to eat. Just sleep and forget.

"I woke up in terror on Monday morning when I had a dream that I was pregnant. I had forgotten about that. I knew enough from your pregnancies with Seth and Lorna, that these things weren't always planned; and I knew that Chad and Tim had certainly not had time to use anything when they were going at me. I went back downtown to the Family Planning Clinic and got a day-after pill. I didn't tell them the sex wasn't consensual. I didn't want to make a big deal out of things, to tell the story, so I pretended it didn't happen. And I didn't get pregnant, so that was easy to do.

"Except for that I slept all the way through that Christmas Break. You probably remember that I wouldn't come see you and the kids and Mom and Pop. I know you thought that was odd, but you had your hands full with Toby, so you didn't press me. And my grades fell when I got back to school. My mom might never have found out what happened, except that Tim grew a conscience and confessed to a professor about what he and Chad had done. After much coercion, he even told the Provost who their victim was.

"The boys were crucified at the University, their future educations obliterated, but they were not charged criminally. I was allowed to leave school after Spring Break with enough credits to get my degree, since I'd done summer courses. They waived my religious studies requirement and they let me go home. It was well-known that I was accepted to Vanderbilt and that I had a very bright future, but I didn't want it. My spirit was crushed, Danica. It still is. Every bit of ambition and intelligence I had was shoved into the pit of my existence."

Liz sat quietly then. Her story was out. There wasn't much else she needed to say. It was funny though. She felt spent, but stronger, more shored up somehow by saying the words out loud. Danica's expression never changed. Liz giggled a nervous giggle.

"I'm just real brave, aren't I? Telling you, of all people, my troubles—a lot of help you'll be!"

Liz held her breath when it looked almost as if Danica blinked. She watched her intently for at least five more minutes. Then Liz chalked the movement up to illusion, created by the wobble of her own head or eyes.

Liz looked up from Danica's face to see Jimmy darkening her ICU doorway.

"Hi Jimmy."

"How's our girl today?" Jimmy asked, giving Liz a lazy, exhausted smile. He didn't look like he'd slept much.

"She's a miracle. It's so nice to hear her breathing on her own."

"Yep. The sweet sound of silence. Well, almost." Jimmy admitted.

"I could do without the sound of the monitors too," Liz said. She rose to put her coat on.

"I didn't mean to chase you off," Jimmy said.

"Oh no, you didn't, Jimmy. It's Christmas Eve. I need to go help Mom with the store."

"That's helpful of you. You are a good girl, after all, aren't you? So what'd you ask Santa for this year, Liz?" Jimmy asked conversationally.

Liz looked very serious, her gray eyes like steel washers. "Santa can't help me with this, Jimmy. But here's what I want: I want courage. I want to be unafraid. I want to grow to trust people. And I want Danica to wake up."

Jimmy nodded, melting Liz's reserve with his liquid coffee gaze. "I hope you get everything you wish for," he said. Then he sat down in the chair where she'd bared her soul to Danica and grasped his wife's hand, brushing a kiss across the back of it.

Liz knew she was on her way to getting her Christmas wishes, because hope permeated this room. The words, the ugly, awful story she'd just imperatively uttered—they disappeared like vapor in the desert the minute those two loving hands entwined.

Liz needed to call Steve.

Chapter Twenty-three

Pop watched the Sheriff's deputy exit his cruiser and make his way gingerly to the sidewalk in front of The Mercantile, which Pop had cleared with the snowblower earlier. It was nearly time to close on this Christmas Eve; and dusk was closing in, letting the shop windows shine like beacons to the motorists passing on the highway.

"Those dangling blue lights sure make this shop look inviting, Mr. Dixon," the deputy commented, taking off his mackinaw hat.

"Oh yeah, Steve here took care of the decorating this year. Did a good job, didn't he?" Pop watched Steve duck his head modestly. "Mom usually does it, but we haven't had much time to think about the niceties of the holiday since our girl is in the hospital."

Pete held out his hand. "Pete Morse. I'm from the Sheriff's office in Rickton."

"Pop Dixon. You're the fellow Jimmy called after that weasel Toby went after my daughter at the hospital."

"Jimmy and I met playing pool. He's one of the good guys. I'm happy to help him out however I can."

"Me too. To what do I owe the pleasure of your visit, Officer Morse?"

"Call me Pete. I wanted to let you know that we've located a vehicle that may match the description of the car that hit Danica. Before we go check it out, I wanted to see if you'd like to come along. You got a good look at the car, didn't you?"

"I witnessed the whole blasted accident, unfortunately. We're getting close to closing time here. I would like to go, but what good will it be looking at the rig in the dark?" Pop asked.

"There are streetlights where we're going. The car was spotted in Lewville, on a city cul-de-sac, and the owner has no idea we're checking it out. We didn't want to stir up trouble, if it's the wrong car."

Pop reached for his wool jacket. "Let's go then. Steve, Marcia is in the back. Have her help you close up, will you?"

"Sure thing, Pop," Steve replied. "Hey, Pete? Can I ask whose car you're looking at? Do you know who the driver is?"

"Well now, here's what's ironic about this trip, and I expect you all to keep this under wraps. This blue sedan belongs to a man named Victor Billings."

"I've never heard the name. What's so ironic about him?" Pop asked, confused.

"I'm surprised you've never heard of him," Pete replied. "He's Ashley Browning's ex-husband."

"Well, crap, Vic. I have no idea why the sheriff would keep sending a cruiser by your place. It's not like I have anything to do with you nowadays," Ashley sat at her vanity, admiring her sweet reflection. She tucked the phone into her shoulder and sprayed the atomizer into the air over her head, taking a dab off the applicator and applying it to each of her wrists. Scent should be subtle, but intriguing too. She wrinkled her nose in distaste as her ex-husband continued to rant. She really didn't have time for this. She had a party to go to.

"Victor, honey, I stopped giving a flying frog leg about

your business when we split more than fifteen years ago," she placated Victor Billings.

She loathed even the sight of him nowadays, since he'd let himself go. When they met, he was cute—his floppy dishwater blond bangs charming before they'd become an unsightly combover. His dancing blue eyes and adventurous attitude in the bedroom had far made up for his loosening mid-section. She should have expected him to get fat and ridiculous, after all, he had been entirely too old for her in the first place. She had just wanted stability, a daddy for Toby; and Victor's business dealings, though shady, were lucrative.

They'd only been married for five years—long enough for Ashley to get ownership of this trailer park and a quarter of Vic's assets. She'd even let him keep his name, going back to her maiden name, Browning.

"Well, now, Vic. There's no reason to get offensive," Ashley fumed as her ex-husband started to insult Toby, something he'd done entirely too much during and after their short marriage. "I'm positive that Toby would never implicate you. He hasn't been in any trouble. I told him to keep his nose clean after the last time he got in a fight at the pool hall. And he has. Really. He's such a good boy."

She listened briefly to Victor, who chipped away at her calm demeanor. "Yes, I know he's not a boy anymore, but he does lots of work for me now, Vic. He's been a great help to his mother. He loves and supports me, something you would know nothing about. Now, if you're done harassing me, I would sure like to slap this phone back down on its cradle. It's a holiday. I've got somewhere to be."

Two last insults and Ashley did hang up, without saying goodbye. Land's sake, she couldn't fathom why Victor would connect trouble with the law to her or Toby. They were much too good at what they did, above suspicion, really. She shrugged, unwilling to let Vic's trouble continue to get her ire up.

Victor Billings was perspiring as he calmly replaced the receiver. Why did his housekeeper insist on turning up the blasted heat so high? You'd think a woman in her fifties would have enough hormonal issues to keep her fingers off the thermostat.

Of course his sweat had nothing to do with the repeated passing of the police cruiser through his isolated cul-de-sac. It was baffling since he'd most recently been doing business on the up and up. He'd grown tired of the criminal element in drug dealing. Time and wise investments had given him the freedom to rise above shady business dealings. His most recent deals benefitted the community and local businesses as well as they padded his pocket.

That didn't mean he had always been quite so philanthropic. In fact, he needed to brush up on the basics of statutes of limitation and such. His lawyer, George Stevens, was only a phone call away, should any of these police cruisers decide to stop. For now, he played it cool, kept the thick, brocade curtains drawn, and comforted himself with a gin and tonic.

When the doorbell rang, Victor jumped so violently that his feet nearly left his socks. He dumped the remainder of his drink in the kitchen sink and made his way to the door just as the doorbell erupted a second time.

It was an officer in uniform and a strapping older man in *Dickies* coveralls and a wool cap.

"Can I help you?" Victor wiped the beads of perspiration from his chin and upper lip with the back of his hand.

"Are you Victor Billings?" The officer spoke first.

"I am."

"I'm Officer Pete Morse and this is Pop Dixon. Sorry to bother you on a holiday, but we're here to ask you a few questions."

Of course they were. Wasn't that how the conversation always started? Then you said a few casual lies or half-truths, and you were on your way to the pokey anyway.

Out loud, Victor said, "Well sure. The weather sure stinks, so I'd rather let you in, if that's okay." After all, he had nothing to hide here—all they'd see was modest, comfortable bachelor furniture and cathedral ceilings.

"That's real friendly of you, Mr. Billings," the officer commented. The other man remained silent. Suddenly, Victor placed the man's name.

"Say, aren't you the guy who owns The Mercantile in Sibby?" Victor inquired.

"I am," was Pop's simple reply.

"I thought so. I've had some business dealings with a man who owns some Sibby real estate. He's mighty familiar with your little town. I've helped him with a few investments. That's my business," Victor stated, knowing full well that the rumor mill might place his business in a few other, less desirable places.

"That so?" Pop replied. "Sibby's a small town, almost not large enough to be of any interest to investors. Who's your associate? Maybe I've talked to him."

"Lou Jacobs."

"Right. Yes. I saw him just the other day. I didn't realize he'd had any success buying up those old properties. Guess I'll have to ask him about that the next time I see him," Pop said casually.

"We have another connection too, Mr. Dixon," Victor continued as Pete looked on with interest.

"What's that?" Pop's curiosity was piqued. He'd really expected little but stonewalling from anyone involved with Toby Browning. Victor Billings was defying the neat little stereotype Pop had assigned to him. After all, Victor had been married to Ashley for a time.

"Well, your daughter used to be married to my former step-son. Small world, isn't it?" Victor remained amiable, though he sought his handkerchief in his back pocket to keep the sweat on his brow from dripping into his eyes.

"Actually, Mr. Dixon's daughter is the reason we're here." Pete interjected.

"Really?" Now Victor was flummoxed. He didn't even know the girl.

"Danica was hit by a car three weeks ago," Pop offered.

"The car's description matches the sedan you have parked out front, Mr. Billings," Pete Morse added.

Victor let out an audible sigh of relief. "Is that why I've seen so many police cruisers yesterday and today?" He asked.

"Would there be any other reason?" Pete asked.

'Typical cop. Looking for trouble,' Vic thought, his genial smile never wavering.

"Nope. I can put your minds at ease though, gentlemen. I bought that car just two weeks ago in Ellensburg, at an auction. It couldn't have been your vehicle."

"Do you have a Bill of Sale?" Pete asked. He needed reasonable evidence to let the obviously damaged blue sedan off the hook.

"As a matter of fact, I do," Victor said. He walked a bit unsteadily to his sofa table and pulled out a crisp sheet of paper.

Pete looked the paper over. "Looks like we've got ample reason to leave you alone, Mr. Billings. I apologize for taking time out of your Christmas Eve. You don't happen to know where the car originated, do you?"

"Actually, it did come from this county. The clerk at the auction commented on that when he took my cash. I remember him saying that the car was getting to return to where it came from." Victor was helpful now that it looked like he was truly out of the woods, so to speak.

"I'm going to need a copy of this Bill of Sale so that I can track the original owner down, question him too." Pete said.

Vic nodded agreeably. "Sure. You can take that with you and bring it back once you've made a copy. It was a real bargain. I'm going to fix the car up a little in the spring and try to resell it. But I'm not planning to do anything major with it until then, if you need to do anything with it."

"Thanks, Mr. Billings. I wish all car owners were so cooperative," Pete commented. "If it hadn't been for the driver of that car leaving the accident scene in the first place, we wouldn't be here at all."

Pete and Pop tipped their hats and bid Victor Billings goodbye. Victor let his shoulders relax as soon as they were out the door. That was easy. Perhaps his past never would catch up to him. He was sure trying to keep his nose clean now, unlike his no-good ex-wife and her loser son.

Victor poured himself another gin and tonic, this time adding a slice of lime. Everything was going to be just fine. He held his crystal tumbler up in the air, toasting the holiday and his own good fortune.

Chapter Twenty-four

Marcia was deeply concerned about Seth. It was Christmas Eve. Usually on this evening, Seth and Lorna were restless as houseflies, flitting from house to church to bed with unmatched exuberance. Their enthusiasm for the holiday had not dimmed with their increasing ages, but it was clear as Seth's haunted eyes examined his gingerbread house creation that his heart was simply not in it this year.

Marcia left Lorna to finish trimming her eaves with red licorice strings and went over to her grandson whose own house lacked any adornment, save the frosting outlining the doors and windows. He fingered gum drops absently.

"Can I have one of those?" Marcia said gently, disrupting Seth's reverie. His eyes twinkled briefly as he put a gumdrop in his grandma's mouth; and she turned her eyes skyward, feigning ecstasy. But he did not smile.

"Yum." Marcia ruffled his hair. "Want me to help put some of those on? We've got to start getting ready for church in an hour or so, after Milo wakes up from his nap."

"Do we have to go tonight, Grandma?" Seth's expression pleaded.

"Why, Seth Browning, I don't believe it," Marcia exclaimed. "You love going to church on Christmas Eve and watching the nativity play. Your sister is even going to be a shepherd this year."

"Yeah, Seth," Lorna scolded. "Just because you're not in the play doesn't mean you get to skip going to church tonight."

"Shut up, squirt," Seth said. Even his fight lacked luster.

"Lorna, why don't you go see if Pop is back from his errand yet? He may have your costume ready downstairs. It looks like your gingerbread house has just about all of the candy decoration it can hold." Marcia was eager to talk to Seth alone, without his sister egging him on.

"Okay. But when can I eat it?" Lorna reluctantly left her perch at the kitchen table and made her way toward the staircase.

"Well you can't eat it now, that's for sure. Now scoot." Marcia replied and laughed as Lorna literally scooted away.

"Good thing you sent her downstairs, Grandma. I was pretty sure there wouldn't be any candy left for my gingerbread house," Seth commented.

"It's not like you were using any of it, Seth. Honey, you need to talk to me. I'm worried about you. This is your favorite time of year, but you don't seem to be enjoying yourself at all."

"How can I have fun when Mom is lying in a hospital bed, barely even breathing on her own?" Seth cut to the chase. "This is Mom's favorite time of year too, and she might not even live through it. How can you and Pop and Lorna pretend like everything is normal?"

"Your mom would be incredibly disappointed in me if I were to spoil Christmas with worrying and grieving. This is a miraculous time of year, Seth; and, even if something were to happen to myself or Pop, your mom would still make sure that you, Lorna, and Milo had a happy holiday. That's what moms do."

"What do sons do, Grandma? Because that's what I'm trying to figure out," Seth said frankly.

"What do you mean?" Marcia, above all, knew that the answer to that question would reveal what was bothering Seth.

"Well, I'm a son, and all I've done is make Pop and Jimmy upset about who might've hit Mom with their car. Then I let my dad almost kill her." Seth reddened, fighting off tears, as it dawned on Marcia just how deeply upset her grandson was. He wasn't feeling sad about his mother's accident and hospitalization. He was feeling guilty, and responsible. She enveloped him in a hug as a sob escaped her throat.

"Oh, baby. Okay," she soothed, smoothing down Seth's silky black hair and trying to will away the hurt as they became a soggy, sobbing mass right there on the kitchen floor.

She held him like that for a time, thanking the Lord that Lorna and Pop were busy elsewhere, and that Milo continued to take his nap. When Seth's heaving sobs subsided, she held him at arm's length to see if he felt any better. He still looked miserable.

"Seth, honey, you need to understand something. I know that before Jimmy came along, you considered yourself the man of the house. You looked out for your mom and Lorna, didn't you?"

Seth nodded solemnly.

"You know, your mom getting hurt, that was out of your control. It's okay to be sad about that. Look at Pop and me—we're a mess about it and we're all grown up. When your mom gets better, she'll be glad to know that you cared that much, but she would never, ever want you to think you were somehow responsible."

"But Dad, he hurt her..." Seth began.

"And I told myself a long time ago that I would never say something hateful about your father in front of you, because, well, he is your father; and I wanted you to respect him as you would any other adult. But, God help me, I believe Toby Browning is as dirty and low-down as the devil himself if he did what we all suspect he did." Marcia took a deep breath and continued.

"You are not to blame for what he did either. Toby is the only guilty party here, and he will have to answer to the Almighty for his sins. It was out of your control, Seth."

"Jimmy said the same thing," Seth admitted. "But I still feel like I should have kept him away or done something to keep him from hurting Mom."

"I don't think any of us believed that Toby would stoop so low. Heavens, even I didn't know he hated Danica that much. How could he when she gave him you and Lorna?" Marcia worried her lower lip, at a loss for an explanation.

"Can we go see Mom after we go to church?" Seth asked, wiping at his eyes with his shirtsleeves.

"Of course we can. I'm sure Steve, Glenna, and Liz will want to see her also. They're coming with us."

"Oh, no," Seth whined. "I like Steve and all; but if I have to watch him and Liz make googly eyes at each other for two whole hours, I'm gonna be sick."

Marcia let out a surprised giggle. "I hadn't noticed the googly eyes," she remarked.

"Yeah well, it's pretty hard to ignore. Steve's a good guy, though, so if Liz likes him, I guess that would be okay."

Marcia gave Seth another squeeze, making a mental note to ask Glenna about Liz and Steve later that evening. Was Steve finally getting through Liz's reserve?

"Let's go wake up your brother. If Milo sleeps any longer, there won't be any of us getting to sleep before Santa Claus hits the neighborhood."

Steve and Liz held hands all the way through the service and nativity play. Glenna and Marcia smiled knowingly at each other. The change in Liz was palpable and Glenna sent up more than a few prayers of thanks. Glenna didn't know what had brought about the change, but she was grateful nonetheless. She relaxed and enjoyed the ushering in of Christ's birthday, courtesy of Lorna and her Sunday school classmates.

Seth clapped the loudest for Lorna when she finished. A more animated shepherd never existed. Though Lorna had coveted the role of Mary this year, Marcia suspected that the director would see fit to give it to her next year. Never mind that she was only seven years old—the girl was born for drama. But then, they had always known that.

They all filed out of the church at midnight—Mom and Pop, Glenna, Liz, Steve, Jimmy, and the kids. Milo rubbed his tired eyes as he was strapped into his car seat.

"Just one more stop, Buddy," Jimmy soothed and kissed his baby's head. He called to the others, "I'll see you all at the hospital. The staff knows we're coming and they made an exception to the normal visiting hour rules so we could all be there on Christmas with Danny. But we gotta be real quiet, okay guys?"

"Let's do it," replied Pop. "I'll lead the caravan, if that's okay with you, Jimmy."

"Of course," Jimmy said and they proceeded in their three vehicles to Rickton Community Hospital, just a fifteen minute drive from the Sibby Alliance Church. The roads were blessedly clear and the night shone with stars, the magic penetrated only by the Christmas tunes that Seth had cranked up on the radio.

"I hate that your mom is missing this," Jimmy commented to Seth, who sat beside him in the passenger seat of the diesel.

"She's with us in spirit, Dad," said Lorna from the backseat. "Grandma said so."

"Well, your grandma's a wise woman. I think she's

probably right." They continued in silence until they all pulled into the deserted parking lot of the hospital.

Danica looked beautiful, as if she was only sleeping peacefully. The nurses had bathed her the best they could and dressed her in a soft pink gown. Her raven hair was brushed carefully over each of her shoulders. There were white twinkle lights around the room's doorframe and a wreath on the door, lending the area the sharp scent of pine—the smell of Christmas.

Jimmy went into the room first and, as he'd gotten accustomed to doing, picked up his wife's warm hand and kissed the back of it. "Merry Christmas, Danny," he whispered, a catch in his voice.

The kids were next. They leaned carefully across Danica's chest and gave her soft hugs. Milo let out a low whine. He recognized his Mommy, but he was nowhere close to understanding why she wouldn't open her eyes and reach out to him.

Mom and Pop looked at each other helplessly, then joined hands and went together to their daughter's side. Pop was choked up, so Marcia spoke for the both of them. "It's Christmas, Danica, honey. You don't want to miss this. Everybody is here and we love you and we need you. Won't you try to come back to us?"

They watched intently for a blink, for a pause in Danica's steady breathing—some sign that she heard them. Nothing happened.

Liz and Steve continued to hold hands. Steve's voice was heavy with emotion as he said, "Danica, you've gotta wake up and see this. She's holding my hand. Our Liz is finally here with us, all the way. It's going to be like when we were kids again. We'll be inseparable. All we need is for you to wake up and join us."

Still nothing. They had all hoped and prayed for a Christmas miracle, but it was not to be.

Pop was not giving up, though. "People, I want to thank you all for being here with Mom and me and our lovely daughter. I know none of you would have missed it. Danica's not waking up yet, but that doesn't mean she won't. If there's anything God has taught us, it's that miracles are not to be predicted or expected. I just think Danica would be grateful as heck that you are all here. Will everybody please join hands? Jimmy and Mom, you take Danica's hands. I would be much obliged if you would all pray with me."

Jimmy laid Milo on his Mommy's chest and he lay there quietly, as if he understood just what he needed to do. Pop led them all in prayer as they stood vigil over Danica's bed for nearly twenty minutes. Milo fell asleep there, and Seth and Lorna began to sway on their exhausted feet.

"I need to get the kids home to their beds," said Jimmy quietly.

"We all need to get home to our beds," Pop agreed, punctuating his statement with a yawn.

"We'll see you in the morning," said Marcia, giving Danica's hand one last squeeze. It may have been a figment of her imagination, but it was almost as if Danica squeezed back. As Jimmy pulled his sleepy baby from his mother's chest, Marcia hoped desperately that she had.

Chapter Twenty-five

"For Christ's sake, Toby. It's Christmas Day. It's not like I can do anything at all in the courts for you today." George Stevens was exasperated. Why had he ever given Ashley Browning his home phone number, whether she had him by the nuts or not? Toby was going to send George's stress levels well above heart attack level, especially if his wife found out that he was pulled from her perfect little family Christmas party by business on Christmas Day.

"It's just that Mom and I were at church and praying, and suddenly she had this epiphany. It was as if God put the thoughts in her head himself," Toby exclaimed.

"Oh, do tell. I'm on the edge of my seat," George replied sarcastically.

Toby continued with exuberance, not catching George's wry wit. "We want to sue to get Danica taken off of all life support."

"She's already off her respirator," George replied. And if Pete Morse was to be believed, Toby might have had a lot to do with that. 'It may be time to distance myself from the Brownings,' he thought to himself.

"But they're still feeding her. My mom read about this case in *People* magazine where a woman was kept alive for decades, just by the feeding tube alone. The husband ended up suing to have it discontinued so that she could finally die in peace. Hasn't Danica suffered enough? Shouldn't she be allowed to die with dignity, George?"

"But, Toby, you're no longer married to Danica. Why would any judge in his right mind believe that you have her best interests at heart?" George sat with his head in his hands, talking into the phone quietly as he hoped that his wife wouldn't notice him gone just yet.

"Because I do, George. She's the mother of my kids. Lorna and Seth wouldn't want her to suffer either. I bet they'd be thankful to me in the long run for freeing her from life lived as a vegetable in a hospital bed."

"I highly doubt that your kids would be thankful to you for ending their mother's life," George said.

There was silence for a moment.

"So will you take Jimmy to court or not?" Toby pressed. "You are my lawyer, after all, and I'm not going to drop this."

George thought of all the times he'd filed custody motions on Toby's behalf, and at Ashley's irresistible pleas, and he'd felt sick doing so. Danica was a good mom and Pop's whole family was above reproach. They didn't deserve the grief he'd already inflicted upon them in the name of Toby Browning. Still, there was Ashley to consider. He dug deeper.

"Is this about custody, Toby? Again? I mean, do you want Danica to die because you want the kids to yourself, for good?" George asked, wanting to understand this latest assault.

"It's not that I want Danica to die," Toby lied. "It's just that I don't want her to suffer. If it's up to that wimpy, bleeding heart, Jimmy, he'll let her go on like this forever."

"He is her husband," George defended, knowing he'd do the same for his wife, out of respect and responsibility. Love or no love, it was his obligation.

Toby's voice became a whine. "I love her, George. I really still do. Why else would I want to make her so miserable for marrying Jimmy Burdick in the first place? Don't I have any say in what happens to her?"

Toby had a point, George thought. He might be able to argue this from the standpoint of the interest of the children. He needed to end this conversation and get back to his wife's party before she hung him up to dry for doing business on Christmas day.

"Okay, Toby. I'll see what I can do, but you're going to have to give me a few days to prepare the motion. That means you leave me alone for the rest of the holiday, you hear me?"

"Oh sure, George. Hey, I'm sorry to bug you on Christmas. Thanks a lot." Toby hung up the phone, as excited as he was the day he found out he was going to have a son. He would get his hands on that money and his children, Danica and Jimmy Burdick be damned.

It was three days after Christmas when Miranda Lobos made another heartbreaking call to the Burdick household. Jimmy answered the phone breathlessly, and Miranda could hear Milo in the midst of a giggling fit.

"You sound wonderful, Jimmy. It's been ages since I've heard laughter from any of you," Miranda remarked.

"Lorna and I were just entertaining the baby. He likes looking at silly faces, especially if they're upside down. Seth is operating the video camera. This is just a kick!" Jimmy laughed into the phone, enjoying the moments of lighthearted freedom that laughter allowed. They all needed it so badly.

"Oh, wait, maybe I should put Milo down before all of the blood rushes to his head." Milo giggled again as Jimmy swooped him to the floor.

"Well, crap, I just want to hang up the phone now," Miranda lamented. "Why don't you just call me back when you all are down in the dumps again?"

Jimmy chuckled again. "Geez, Randi, you make it sound like we're a pretty glum bunch a good part of the time."

"Well I can't exactly expect 'happy, happy,' with Danica hurt like she is," Miranda remarked.

"No, that's true." Jimmy's breathing evened out. Suddenly he realized that Miranda might be calling with bad news, thus her reluctance to end their fun.

"What's going on, Randi?" He asked, alarmed now.

"Why don't you call me back?" Miranda suggested.

"Nope. Spill it, Miranda." Jimmy demanded.

"George has filed a new motion with the courts. I've already called Pop, and I'll be representing him and Mom too."

"Custody again? I thought he was going to drop that," Jimmy asked in frustration. "And why would Mom and Pop need to be involved?"

"Oh, Jimmy. I wish it were that simple. That I could handle. This is so much worse. Are you sitting down?"

Jimmy remained standing. "I am not going to sit down if Toby is bringing another fight at me. Go ahead, Randi. Out with it."

"Toby is suing to have Danica's feeding tube removed, so that she can be allowed to die without any life-saving measures."

"He can't do that. That's ridiculous. He's not even married to Danny anymore. He has no business getting involved in any kind of decision like that," Jimmy argued, suddenly angry beyond all reason.

"I'm afraid he's going to get away with it," Miranda remained calm.

"And why is that? Because he has an expensive-assed lawyer and he can buy off a judge?" Jimmy could not conceal his fury.

"No, Jimmy. He's filing on behalf of his children. Toby is arguing that it is in their best interest not to prolong Danica's suffering."

"That's absolutely untrue. Neither of them would ever agree to this."

"They won't get a voice in this, Jimmy. No judge would allow children to be dragged into such a case. Toby, as their only healthy parent, would be acting as their representative."

"Damn him. We've got to fight this, Randi, with everything we've got." Jimmy could almost hardly stand to breathe as panic gripped him. They were just a few weeks from making such decisions themselves should Danica not wake up. Jimmy couldn't handle Danica's death at Toby's orders, Toby's control. It would leave him more bereft than if she had died on the road before she reached the hospital.

"I'll do the best I can, Jimmy, but you need for Danica to wake up. Seriously. Pull out all the stops, because if she doesn't, there are some extraordinarily painful days awaiting all of you," Miranda predicted.

Jimmy hung up the phone. Seth and Lorna were watching him. Even Milo had grown solemn, his chocolate gaze seemed to realize the depths of Jimmy's dread.

Seth took Jimmy's hand. "What's Dad done now, Jimmy?"

Jimmy couldn't speak; fear and grief rendered him mute. He simply gathered his precious children on his lap and held on for dear life.

Chapter Twenty-six

Pete Morse washed down a tuna-salad sandwich with an unsweetened glass of iced tea. The lunchroom was empty, save Connie May West, who'd just sat down with split pea soup in a Tupperware bowl. He smiled and waved to be friendly. She smiled back, her lips a melon-colored ring around slightly yellowing teeth with a gap between them.

She took his friendliness as an invitation. Connie May picked up her bowl and teetered over to him on ruby high-heels that looked like they came straight out of the *Wizard of Oz*. Her red-white-and blue polyester caftan was cinched neatly at the waist by a broad black vinyl belt. Her titian hair was amazingly defiant of gravity, thanks to the bouffant Connie May had teased it into.

"Well, hi there, Pete," Connie May drawled. "Looks like yer wife packed you a fine lunch."

"Oh, she doesn't pack my lunch. She's liberated, you know. She packs her own lunch and leaves me some of the tuna salad so I can make my own sandwich."

"Where's she work, Pete? She must be real busy if she doesn't take th' time to pack her hubby's lunch! 'Specially since yer out all day protectin' the likes of th' entire county." Connie May exclaimed.

"My wife does odd jobs—several days a week she's a clerk at a boutique in Lewville. She does a few days a month at Bob's Hardware in Sibby, and she's a licensed massage therapist, so she works in appointments at our home in between all of that. Plus, she plays a mean game of bingo."

"Whew. She is busy, ain't she? Do ya'll have kids?" Connie May took delicate sips of her soup straight from the side of the bowl. She defied convention, but still managed to look lady-like.

"We do. Joanna is eighteen and due to graduate in the spring. Will is sixteen and it seems like I haven't seen him since he got his driver's license. They're pretty busy with friends and school. It's a good thing their mom taught them how to make their own sandwiches too!" Pete munched his Cheetos thoughtfully. He suddenly missed his family. They were all home today, five days after Christmas, enjoying the last of Christmas vacation.

"Yer s' young, I never woulda expected you to have teenagers. Shoot, I'm older 'n you and my little'uns are still in grade school."

"We got married when we were eighteen—Joanna was unexpected—but she's been a joy from the minute she arrived, the easiest kid in the world to raise. It's a good thing, too, because Izzy—that's my wife—and I weren't nearly prepared to be parents at that age. I think the way you're doing it must be much easier," Pete admitted.

"Well, it sher would be, except my ex is a louse and I'm doin' it all by my little self." Connie May put on a pouty face for emphasis.

"We could track him down and give him an old-fashioned lesson in beating a deadbeat dad," Pete joked.

"Oh, Pete, yer much too sweet t' do somethin' that dirty. Besides, he's too far away. I wouldn't want t' put anyone through findin' him in my hometown. What a dump." For a moment, Connie May's lifetime of disappointment shone through her carefully arranged, sunny façade.

"I have another bad guy to go after right now, anyway,"

Pete shared.

Connie's blue eyes shone. She loved knowing what kind of work the good guys were doing. "Do tell, Pete Morse."

"I heard from Jimmy Burdick yesterday that his wife's ex, Toby Browning, is suing to have her life support removed," Pete said.

"Well, that don't make any sense. What would he want with killin' off his ex-wife?" Connie May asked.

"That's exactly what I need to find out, Connie May. Why would an ex-husband give a thought to his ex-wife's welfare? For some reason, Toby Browning wants Danica Burdick dead. I need to find out why."

"Shouldn't the lawyers be goin' after that answer?" Connie May deduced.

"I'm sure Jimmy's lawyer is exploring that. However, I have other reasons for wanting to tail Toby Browning. It seems his *associates* have been less than forthcoming about what it is that Toby does for a living to pay for all of these lawsuits he's filing. There's some kind of shady business with the Brownings."

"Ya know, Detective Pete, I have a new girlfriend who's real tight with Ashley Browning. Th' snob gave me th' cold shoulder at the eatery th' other day when I was gettin' burgers. I'd be happy t' get t' know Shelby better, and find out what they might be up to." Connie May offered.

It dawned on Pete that this might be exactly the break they needed. "Would you do that for us, Connie May? It might be dangerous, getting into the investigative part of police work."

"Shoot, if it meant I might get to do more than manage th' phones and th' messages, I'd do jes' about anythin'. I wanna see some real action, Pete."

Pete laughed. Connie May West was a force to be reckoned with, all in a fashion-challenged, deceptively sweet package. He nodded in agreement.

Connie May slurped up the last of her soup and clicked her heels over to the sink to rinse out her bowl. "Ya'll 'll excuse me now. I got me a phone call t' make!" She exclaimed, her excitement palpable. "See ya, Pete Morse."

"Thanks, Connie May. You're the best," shouted Pete as she clattered on out the door.

Shelby watered their little 'friends', fanning herself as she repeated the daily ritual. Shelby couldn't wait for winter to get over, so that this blasted heat wouldn't be so hard to handle. It was like having extremely cold air-conditioning in the summer and then going out into one hundred degree heat. The difference in temperature made the extreme all that more intolerable.

She needed to scoot or she wasn't going to make her afternoon coffee with Connie May West. Apparently business was slow at the Rickton Sheriff's precinct and they were letting Connie May leave early. Shelby was still out for Christmas break, so she was happy to have something to do outside the house. She swore she never left her sweatpants and terrycloth slippers if she didn't have something to dress for. Ashley had taken her out to shopping and lunch the day after Christmas, but she hadn't had any reason to go out since then.

She knew Ashley would be sore at her for going out with Connie May at all, but Shelby really wanted to make other friends too. Connie May was fresh and sweet. She had a different perspective in life, as if being from outside the County made her somehow more worldly than Ashley and all of her cronies. Besides, nobody truly *liked* Ashley Browning. They all simply sucked up to her, Shelby included, though she would never, ever let Ashley know that.

Shelby wanted a real girlfriend; and if she met with Connie May away from the trailer park, Ashley would never even know. She could never bring Connie May over to her house anyway, because of the hulking pot bushes that made the southern half of her trailer look like a bona fide terrarium.

She dressed in wool gabardine pants and a cashmere sweater—there were some pleasures a single woman must indulge in and good clothes were some of them. Ashley would never have hung out with her if she dressed in public like she did in the confines of her home.

Shelby knew that Connie May would appreciate her taste in clothes as well. Though Connie May could use a few points on style, she always dressed to the hilt also.

Her phone rang. The caller ID said it was Victor. She let the machine pick it up.

"Shelby, darling, it's Vic. It's been a while since you've called. Don't go letting Ashley harass you about seeing me. We're both single people and you make good company. It's understandable that she would be jealous, but you must know that I would treat you far better than Ashley ever could. Besides, I have a fancy new car for us to go about town in. I'd love to pick you up for dinner. Just name the time and place. Call me." Click.

Shelby reached for the phone and then pulled her hand back. She didn't know when her coffee date would end with Connie May, and she knew Ashley's panties would really get in a bunch if she got together with both Connie May and Victor, in one day, even.

Heavens, her social calendar was taking on a life of its own. She'd call Victor tomorrow. She needed another reason to get dressed up anyway.

Shelby smiled at her reflection in the hall mirror. Even without make-up, her face shone, thanks to last week's facial. She had good bone structure and thick, bottle-blond tresses. Her eyes were cool and sparkly. She was a little tall, and a little thick around the middle, but Victor Billings found her attractive, nonetheless. Maybe it was time she moved from the Ashley Fan Club and started doing a little for Shelby.

Shelby threw on her matching wool peacoat and suede boots, grabbed her make-up bag so she could apply it in the frigid car, and headed out the door.

Connie May was nervous, but then she'd done plenty of meeting up after work with girlfriends before, in Kentucky. That's all this was. Shelby would never know that it was an inquisition.

There was a hip little bistro two blocks off main in Rickton. Connie May sat and admired the dyed concrete countertops and floors and brick walls decorated with artistic graffiti. You would never find a joint like this in the deep South. This was a culture and décor unique to the Pacific Northwest and she loved it.

Shelby came in the door, dressed to the nines, in pants and a coat that must have cost her a fortune.

"Lord, girl, you look like you came straight outta a Spiegel's catalog!" Connie May exclaimed.

Shelby joined Connie May at the bistro bar and replied frankly, "This is how you dress, honey, when you have a good job and no kids. I'm constantly amazed at how well put together you are with two little kids to get ready every morning."

"Well I dint do much with 'em today, jest shoved 'em with their jammies in th' car 'n took off t' daycare. I should be there now, instead of out playin' with a girlfriend," Connie May admitted.

"How are Halley and Hugh, anyway?" Shelby asked.

"Well, right now they're boreder than a penguin 'n the desert. I can't wait 'til school starts again."

"They've got such great teachers too in the fifth and third grades. You're lucky to have them in the Sibby school and not in Rickton." Shelby did love her school and had great loyalty to Mr. First, despite Ashley's insinuation that her job was expendable.

"I know that. When we landed here, I could see that Sibby was a good l'il town, not like the backward, no-good hole that I grew up in and where I met the kids' daddy. Besides this's far 'nough away that he'll ne'er find us neither."

"Is that a concern? Would your ex-husband come after you guys?" Shelby asked the question with as much thrill as worry.

"Oh, no. Least, I don't think so. He'd have t' leave his beer and his poker-playin' buddies long 'nough t' even look. I don't see that happenin'."

She changed the subject. "Whatta ya want for coffee, Shelby? My treat. They gotta coffee menu longer th'n my mom's telephone cord!"

"How about just a plain mocha?" Shelby suggested.

"Heck, honey, there ain't nothin' plain 'bout somethin' with chocolate in it." To the barrista, she said, "Two grande mochas hot 'n skinny 'n no goin' easy on the whipped cream."

"Sounds great," Shelby said, relaxing and realizing that an outing with Connie May would never prove to be dull. She mirrored Connie May's enthusiastic smile as something shifted inside of her—not apprehension, but the feeling that she was doing something good just for the sake of happiness. This woman in front of her was about to become a very good friend.

As if reading her thoughts, Connie May's face suddenly

became serious. "Shelby, I hope this don't spook you, but I jes' got the weirdest feeling. You and me, we're about to become th' best o' friends."

As they received their mugs, Shelby held hers high. "Let's drink to that, Connie May."

Connie May gave an answering "here, here" and, as their mugs clinked together, felt the tiniest frisson of fear slide down her spine.

Chapter Twenty-seven

Danica remained in a void, the space around her colorless and odorless, like being in a vacuum. She could see her loved ones around her and hear them talk to her. Liz appeared in all of her frizzy-haired glory, beautiful and melancholy. Danica's instinct was to wrap her arms around her best friend. She reached to do so and found that she only reached through her. Liz was a hologram.

The same happened with Jimmy. Jimmy appeared anguished and distraught, so Danica gave all of her power to comfort him. This time she tried to touch him with her mind instead of her arms. Jimmy dissolved before her eyes and faded into the void.

Similar things happened with Mom and Pop and with Lorna and Seth. She sensed them at different times, felt and heard their thoughts and words. But she was unable to reach back to any of them.

Stymied by this, Danica grew frustrated and wished again for her lakebed, for the glorious luminescence of the light that had guided her, given her hope, and a sense of choice.

Now she could choose nothing. She could only sit in her void and watch her family and friends suffer and grieve, powerless to comfort them.

Greater frustration came from an innate sense that someone was missing from her rotating circle of friends and loved ones. Someone with extraordinary importance evaded her and she couldn't draw his or her identity out. Danica had an inkling that should that one person appear into her holographic vision, she would be able to grasp him or her and be sucked back out of her personal Hell.

Anything would be better than this. She longed for color. She longed for light. But most of all she despaired to embrace the one person that could make it alright.

Miranda walked up behind Jimmy as he stood at the foot of Danica's hospital bed. He said nothing and just stared intently at his wife's gentle to-and-fro breathing. Miranda touched his shoulder.

"Jimmy. What are you doing? It's almost time to leave for the hearing," she said gently.

"I'm willing her eyes to open, Miranda. Then there wouldn't have to be a hearing," Jimmy replied, his hope of watching Danica open her eyes never wavering.

Miranda sighed deeply. How many times had she wished for such a miracle herself? She'd managed to get the hearing put off for ten days, but now the holidays were over, and the judge wanted to hear this issue today.

Jimmy broke his gaze away from Danica's face and looked frankly at Miranda. "I dreamed that I could do it, Randi. If I stared long and hard enough or if I held her hand, that I would turn the key that could bring her back to us."

Miranda's eyes were the color of midnight, mirrors of her war-hardened soul. She'd seen enough of family law to know that Jimmy's troubles were far from being solved by a stare or the holding of a hand. She was also Catholic, and she'd asked for and seen plenty of miracles.

"Wouldn't that be wonderful, Jimmy? Keep trying. Really. But right now, we need to get to court so you can get more tries."

Turning back to Danica and lifting her cool hand, Jimmy said, "Okay, baby. I'm going to fight for you, so you need to do the same for me. You and I have always presented a united front to Toby. I need you to do your part now and help me ward him off again. He can't win, Danny. You understand that. You wake up. Wake up and I'll be back to see your gorgeous eyes in no time." Jimmy squeezed Danica's hand, kissed it gently, and followed Miranda out of the Rickton Community Hospital.

Dr. Moreland had always been in scrubs when Jimmy saw him at the hospital. Jimmy was taken aback to find the good doctor in a suit and tie. He looked suddenly more slender, more vulnerable. Jimmy realized he needed to order up more of Mom's mashed potatoes for the Doc, a man who had become his hero. Miranda had asked for help from the doctor and a few of the hospital staff. All sat behind Jimmy, Mom, and Pop on the defendants' side of the courtroom.

Toby, Ashley, and George Stevens sat on the opposite side, plaintiffs in a case that could ultimately decimate Danica's family. Jimmy noticed Pete Morse slip into the back of the courtroom quietly as the judge came in. Pete sat at the back on Toby's side.

The clerk called the case to order and George presented his and Toby's argument, on behalf of the children, to have Danica taken off any measures that would prolong her life. Miranda argued back that Danica's accident was a fairly recent event and that she hadn't been given an appropriate amount of time to heal and recover, that removing her feeding tube would amount to starving her to death when she was still very much alive.

George brought in a parade of experts who testified that Danica's condition had very little chance of improving; and that, if kept on the feeding tube, she could live for years as a 'vegetable.' They cited several cases where families used every resource to sustain the life of an individual who would never wake up. Every expert weighed in on the psychological impact the financial stress and waiting could have on the family, particularly the children.

Miranda had to admit that George and his witnesses made a powerful argument, but now it was her turn. The judge turned to her. "Ms. Lobos?"

"Your Honor, I have just two witnesses to call in response. You've seen the affidavits of three of Danica Burdick's nursing staff. I have asked them to be here today, should you have any questions about their statements. In the interest of time, I'm going to call first Danica's doctor, Dr. Michael Moreland."

Dr. Moreland was sworn in. He sat nervously on the stand, definitely out of his comfort zone.

"Dr. Moreland, can you please tell me first your qualifications and your staff position at Rickton Community Hospital," Miranda began.

She highlighted his impressive credentials and experience. Dr. Moreland was a star witness, intelligent and confident, but not boastful. She guided him through testimony about Danica's condition and other similar cases he might have overseen during his fellowship. She asked him about the uncertainty that surrounded neurological injuries. After all, no one really knew what was going on inside the injured brain as it healed. Miranda hoped that the uncertainty would lead the court away from giving up on Danica. She asked another question.

"Dr. Moreland, in your opinion, do you think, given

time, that Danica will awake from her coma?"

"That's the thing, Ms. Lobos. We don't know. There is no way of knowing. She's breathing on her own and her vital signs are stable. I expect her to physically be able to wake up any time."

He continued. "Of course, it is widely known that a coma that lasts past one month becomes statistically less likely to be short-term. She is approaching the one month mark; but since she's weaned herself off of her respirator, I give her better odds than most at recovering even beyond that month time period."

Miranda paused, wanting to dramatize the final question. "Dr. Moreland, again in your opinion, do you think removing Danica Burdick's feeding tube would be the equivalent of starving an innocent, helpless person to death?"

"Objection, your Honor," George Stevens rose from his chair. "Ms. Lobos is trying to inflame the court into believing that my client wishes Danica Burdick ill-will. On the contrary, as we have proven, we simply wish to look out for the interests of the children."

"Overruled," the judge replied. "You may answer the question, Doctor."

"Danica is helpless in her hospital bed. The only link she has to life right now is that feeding tube, and, yes, we would be starving her to death if we removed the tube or her IV fluids."

"Thank you, Doctor," Miranda invited Dr. Moreland to step down.

"Next, your Honor, I would like to call Detective Pete Morse to the stand."

Pete was sworn in. His testimony was a gamble for Miranda because most of what he would be saying was hearsay, but she needed to cast doubt in Toby's direction.

She summoned courage, stood all of her five feet five inches tall, and began her line of questioning.

"Detective Morse, you were called in by Jimmy Burdick to the Rickton Community Hospital on the night of December 21st. Can you tell me what that call was about?"

"Jimmy Burdick told me that Danica's respirator had malfunctioned while Toby Browning was in her room with the kids. He suspected that Toby had tampered with it, so he called me to check it out."

"Objection, your Honor," George stood quickly, his neck reddening. Surely Miranda didn't think she could get away with implicating his client in a court of law for a crime he hadn't been charged with. "This line of questioning is completely irrelevant to the case at hand. Ms. Lobos is attempting to sully my client's good name." Somewhere in the back of the courtroom, someone coughed a laugh.

"Your Honor, I am not asking the Court to believe Mr. Browning's guilt for the incident on the 21st. I'm simply trying to cast doubt on his motive for removing life support," Miranda argued.

The gristled, old judge glared at both attorneys. "I'll allow the line of questioning for now, Ms. Lobos, but keep to the point, please."

"Of course, your Honor," Miranda turned her attention back to the detective, knowing she'd won a small victory.

"Detective Morse, why in the world would Jimmy suspect Toby had anything to do with the respirator mishap?"

"There were several things: According to Seth Browning, his father was next to the respirator when it failed and his mother arrested. Also, a nurse from the ICU remembered Mr. Browning being in the cafeteria the day before and asking about how the machine worked. Finally, there's the fact that Toby Browning hates his ex-wife…"

"Objection, your Honor," George jumped out of his chair once again.

"Sustained. Detective Morse, please stick to the facts," the judge warned.

"Let's move on to the next question, Detective," Miranda suggested. "That sounds like some pretty convincing evidence that Mr. Browning may have turned off the respirator. Why wasn't he ever charged with a crime for this, Detective?"

"What I've mentioned is purely circumstantial evidence. I wanted something concrete, so I tried to get fingerprints off the respirator itself. There were too many other sets of prints and I couldn't find anything clean. I was forced to drop the case."

Miranda glanced at Toby Browning. If looks could kill, she would be writhing around on the hardwood, she decided. "No further questions, your Honor."

"Mr. Stevens, would you like to cross-examine?" The judge inquired.

"Yes, your honor." George rose and adjusted his collar. "Detective Morse, isn't it true that you have a grudge against my client?"

"I wouldn't say that, no." Pete replied honestly. "I'm just doing my job, as I've been doing for nearly twenty years now. I've learned to spot somebody dirty, and I'm pretty sure Toby Browning is guilty of everything Jimmy Burdick and I suspect him of."

"Objection, your Honor. Hearsay," George bellowed.

"Sustained. Detective Morse, this is your last warning. You also know, as a veteran law enforcement officer, that you cannot make assumptions or conjectures under oath." The judge chastised Pete.

"Yes, your Honor," Pete looked mollified.

"Any further questions, Mr. Stevens?" The judge asked.

"Just one, your Honor. Detective Morse, Toby Browning was married to Danica Burdick and had two children with her. There is a lot of shared history, perhaps even love, still there. He'd be responsible for the death of the mother of his children. Can you tell me, if Mr. Browning has it in for her, as you say he does, what his motivation could possibly be?" George waited. He had Pete over a barrel, because he had been unable to answer such a question himself.

Pete paused, thinking the question over. George Stevens had him, but he wouldn't go down easily. "Custody, maybe? He's fought for custody of the children several times since the divorce."

"But he never tried to harm Mrs. Burdick before over the custody issue," George argued. "What could possibly motivate him to hurt her while she lies helpless in a hospital bed?"

"You know, I haven't figured that out yet," Pete replied honestly. He shifted his uniform-clad body and stared hard at Toby Browning, his blue eyes like lasers boring through the plaintiff. Toby simply looked away. "I'm going to find out the answer to that question, though, Mr. Stevens, if I have to work umpteen hours of unpaid overtime to do it." Toby's gaze snapped back up to Pete, who gave him a malicious smile in return.

George watched the game of wills with detached amusement. He'd proven his case. Toby would probably win. Why, then, did he feel like such a horse's ass for taking it on in the first place?

"Your Honor, the Plaintiff rests." He sighed and sat down.

"Ms. Lobos?" The judge asked.

"Defense rests also, your Honor."

"I'll need to take a short recess to review the affidavits at hand in my chambers. I will return shortly with my decision," the judge said as he swished his robes through a wood-paneled door. Miranda just stood and watched him go, her hands on Jimmy and Pop's shoulders. Now she prayed.

Chapter Twenty-eight

Glenna Stone wiped her hands on her apron, the pain in her shoulders almost unbearable now that her baking was almost finished. She had an appointment with her doctor later that afternoon to go over some tests. Glenna hated to admit she needed medication, but unbeknownst to Liz and everyone else, the burden of keeping the store going was proving to be entirely too painful.

The phone rang. She walked listlessly to the front of the store to answer it. "Wren's Market," she intoned.

"Glenna, it's Lou Jacobs. We need to meet." The voice at the end of the line was confident and welcome to Glenna's exhausted ears.

"You're right, Lou. We've put this off long enough. When can we have lunch?"

"I've arranged for George and Victor to meet me tomorrow at the Bistro two blocks off Main in Rickton. Can you make it?"

"Does George Stevens really have to be involved?" Glenna asked. "He's been a key player in a case affecting some very good friends of mine. I can't say he's my favorite person right now."

"He's our lawyer—mine and Victor's—Glenna, and darn good at what he does. Can I ask what he's done to upset you?" Lou asked.

"Well, thanks to her doctor, my dearest friends' daughter, Danica, is being spared some time—two weeks to be exact. But after that, thanks to George and his scum of a client, Danica will be systematically starved to death if she doesn't awake from her coma."

"That's terrible," Lou exclaimed. "It's, of course, none of my affair what kind of cases George is taking on. I am sorry to hear, though, that Pop Dixon's daughter isn't fairing so well. It would be tragic if she died."

Glenna was taken aback. She didn't know Lou was close enough to Mom and Pop to be aware of Danica's plight. "I didn't mention who I was talking about, Lou. How did you know I was referring to Pop's daughter?"

"I, um, er…Well, I assumed such, since I saw you at the hospital with Pop the day that Danica had surgery… Besides, Danica is not a common name."

"Oh, right. I forgot about that," Glenna was relieved. She didn't want Pop to know about her dealings with Louis Jacobs, at least not yet. She was reminded, once again, what a small town they all lived in.

"Anyway, back to our meeting, Glenna. Can you be at the Bistro tomorrow at one o'clock?"

"Oh, um sure. I'll have to call over to Bob's and see if his clerk, Maria, can cover my lunch hour. Liz, my daughter, is out of town." 'Which made the meeting all that much more fortuitous,' thought Glenna.

"Why don't you confirm with me in the morning? I'll be in the office then," Lou suggested.

"I'll do that, Lou. Thanks." Glenna replaced the phone in the charger. Liz was going to be devastated to know that Glenna intended to sell the store. Wren's Market had been their brain child, a miraculous salvation to a tiny general store that had seen better days. But Liz was gone, off to college, shortly after the conversion to natural foods, and Glenna suspected that her daughter would be on to much bigger and better things very soon, thanks to Steve. The market had outgrown its usefulness to Glenna and her family. The legacy of the tiny Sibby grocery store would end with Glenna Stone.

Steve and Liz were taking a tour of her old stomping grounds. He, too, loved the brick Victorians that lined narrow, one-way streets. She showed him from the car her favorite three-mile run. As her face filled with longing, Steve became conscious that Liz loved Seattle and missed it, as much as she feared returning to the place where her trauma lingered.

Steve still didn't have the whole story from Liz. He knew that she'd had a change of heart about him, and he was hugely grateful for that. He also knew that she was struggling with issues well beyond anything he had the faculties to cope with, but he coaxed, cajoled, and comforted her as best he could.

When Pop asked Steve to make the hairy winter trip across the Cascade Mountains for a buying show from a premier Northwest sporting goods company, Steve wanted to take Liz. For one thing, he needed a navigator as he negotiated the tricky city streets. For another, he wanted the company of a real person and not just a DJ or an audio book narrator. Liz was definitely his favorite choice of companion.

As it turned out, Steve realized that this visit was therapeutic for Liz. As he examined Liz, her wild curly hair framing her face against the rain-spattered window, he asked a question. He held his breath as he waited for the answer. "So are you going to tell me what happened here, Liz?"

Tears popped instantly into her silver eyes. In a tiny voice, she replied. "It didn't happen here."

"You were somewhere besides Seattle?"

"No. I was in Seattle, but it wasn't here. I love it here," Liz replied.

"Do you want to go there?" Steve pried gently.

"Do you think it would help?" Liz asked, her face a picture of vulnerable beauty and terrific fear.

"I'm not sure, Liz, honey, because you haven't told me, but it's worth a try."

So Liz gave Steve directions to the frat house in the U district, the one that she had last travelled to at night in the back of the car, yet she still knew exactly where it was and what it looked like. The house looked placid in the late afternoon, surrounded by the landscape of a drizzly Seattle winter. There were twinkle lights left in each of the front picture windows from Christmas. Occupants had apparently returned after the holidays, as evidenced by luminated desk lights in the upstairs windows.

"How in the world could that be? It looks so ordinary," Liz said, her voice a mixture of wonder and fury.

"Will you tell me what happened here, Liz?" Steve asked, pleading, for the first time truly convinced that they needed to get to the bottom of this before it pillaged their fragile bond forever.

Her stony gaze met his. He knew she would see trust there in the depths of his autumn-colored stare, not blame.

"I can't... Oh, my God, Steve. I have to. I have to tell you. But you have to promise me that you will not judge me."

"Whatever happened to you, Liz. It doesn't define you. I have loved you forever, since we were awkward teenagers learning how to kiss. I want to do more of that, by the way," Steve deadpanned. "But I want you to feel better. To do that, you have to tell someone."

"I did. Tell someone, I mean. I told Danica. I know that sounds stupid, I mean, because how is that going to help me? She's in a coma. But it did help me feel better. That's why I'm here with you. No, I need to tell you for *you*, Steve. So you know what you're up against and why I'm definitely damaged goods."

Steve waited and Liz only paused half a heartbeat before she spilled everything right there in front of that filthy, rotten house. Steve kept his expression neutral until she mentioned that Chad and Tim hadn't been prosecuted. Then he felt like he could strangle them both single-handedly. She finished her story spent, but appearing at the same time fortified, as if a weight had been lifted.

Steve hugged her. "Thank you for telling me." He swept her hair away from her face. "You know it wasn't your fault what happened, right?"

"I do know that. Logically, anyway. But the experience has still capitalized every thought I've had for the last three years."

"What can I do to make it easier, Liz?" Steve was genuinely concerned.

"You've already done everything you can, Steve, by listening. The rest is up to me. I would take dinner, though," she teased, lightening the mood.

Steve laughed, started the car, and flipped on the headlights to ward off the impending night. He still hated driving in the city during the day. Night was all that more daunting. "You name the place, darling. I'll try to aim the rocket here in the correct direction."

"I know this great Thai place that we can go to. It's not far. But we're only going there if you'll let me drive," Liz goaded Steve. She knew how he preferred country roads to the fast pace of city traffic.

"I thought you'd never ask."

They both chuckled and traded places as Liz hopped in the driver's seat and left the frat house behind for good.

Slippery   Kimberly Ann Freel

Chapter Twenty-nine

Victor Billings whistled off-key as he exited his blue sedan and headed for the outer door of the Bistro. He was feeling quite randy following his date with Shelby the night before. She was all woman—graceful curves, musky sweet fragrance, and every nail, hair, and piece of clothing neatly in place. She reminded him of Ashley, which normally would have sent him running the opposite direction. Ashley was a serpent, every kind of wily-mean a woman could muster.

Shelby, though, was well-groomed like Ashley, but she was genuinely sweet. Shelby was an opportunist, as were most older unmarried women he'd met. And there were probably reasons she had stayed single through middle age, but Victor assumed that insecurity topped the list. That could evolve, he decided, and he wanted to see more of Shelby Lowe.

Besides, it felt covert and thrilling to be dating the woman closest to his nemesis, Ashley. Victor sighed and tried to shove aside his thoughts of the two women as he prepared mentally for his business meeting. He was present at this meeting solely as an investor. Lou Jacobs had some brilliant ideas in mind for the town of Sibby. It was a unique and potentially profitable idea, and Victor intended to lend as much capital as he could to the project.

Glenna Stone was the only business owner, with the exception of Mom and Pop Dixon, who still maintained ownership on Main Street in Sibby. She would never know until after their transaction that Lou, Victor, and a few other investors, already owned everything else. It had taken them nearly a year. Bob Rickton had held out until after Thanksgiving, when it became clear that the Christmas season would fall into the toilet along with the rest of the economy.

Wren's Market was surprisingly solvent and Victor suspected that he and Lou would have a hefty price to pay to add that and The Mercantile to their holdings, but they had the investors. Now all they needed was to motivate the remaining business owners to sell.

Victor, George, and Lou greeted each other like the cronies they were, all handshakes, smiles, and pats on the back. Glenna walked into the Bistro five minutes later, her head covered in a cap of turquoise worsted wool. The brightness of her hat emphasized the wan set of her features. Victor realized with a start that the woman looked ill. Would that help or hinder their transaction, he wondered.

"Gentlemen." Glenna greeted them confidently, but warily.

They placed their lunch orders and made small talk. Lou impressed them with tales of a week-long trip he'd taken to Florida during Christmas. George tried to make nice with Glenna, ignoring his own role in the decisions surrounding Danica Burdick. She maintained civility with George, but only barely.

They munched on salads and rolls. Glenna wiped her mouth primly with her napkin and started in on the business at hand.

"Lou, I know you've been offering to buy Wren's Market for the better part of a year, now. Truth be told, I've been hanging on to it for my daughter, as my father did for me. She's been helping me with the business and we are making quite a go of it.

"I've had news, though, that I might not physically be able to continue what we're doing at the store. I also sense that my daughter's destiny does not lie in Sibby, ultimately. Opportunities like yours don't arise everyday and I've no desire, if I decide to sell the store later, to see it sit on the market for a year or two while I wait for an interested buyer."

The three men murmured their agreement, waiting for Glenna to continue.

"I have one further question, though. I'm aware that you've purchased all of the other properties on Main Street, with the exception of The Mercantile. Bob told me as much when I asked him point-blank about it. Obviously you have a master plan for the town, and I can imagine that The Mercantile would be important to finishing your project. Have you approached Pop yet?"

Lou fidgeted, uncomfortable under Glenna's frank examination. He knew that she and Pop were friends. The fact was, he was terrified about approaching Pop, for many reasons, the first of which was the exchange they'd had at the gun club. Pop would fight tooth and nail to keep his store, this Lou knew instinctively.

Lou decided to take a gamble, and lie. "Nothing in my plans would possibly involve The Mercantile, Glenna. Pop's made very clear his desire to keep things as they are in Sibby. I have nothing but respect for Pop and my plans are simply to build my dreams around him. His business is thriving, much as yours has, so I've decided I should just let it be."

Glenna looked at Victor and George, whose heads bobbed in agreement. She appeared satisfied that the selling of her own business would never amount to betrayal of

Mom and Pop. Glenna brightened agreeably. "All right, then, I've had my attorney, Miranda Lobos, prepare a Bill of Sale. I've made three copies, so you can all examine my asking price and my terms. I suspect this will be fair and amiable for all of us."

Lou was surprised and delighted that Glenna was so well-prepared for their meeting. Victor cleared his throat loudly when he read the price of the store, but Lou saw nothing ill-informed about the amount. Glenna simply knew what her business and the building were worth. He was relieved that she wanted to sell at all.

George examined the document and verified its fairness from a legal standpoint. By the time dessert and coffee came around, Glenna realized with a flip of her full stomach, that she had just sold Wren's. And she hadn't consulted Liz. She shook off her trepidation and jumped up from the table with a sudden need to fill her lungs with the fresh winter air.

Her body creaked in protest as she rose, and she realized it was all for the best. She had unleashed a burden. Liz would understand, especially when Glenna explained what the doctor said. She knew that conversation would be even harder. Putting her merino wool wrap over her shoulders, Glenna exited with as much grace and dignity as her ravaged body could muster. She prepared to do battle at the store with some of tomorrow's cookie dough and looked forward to the day when she would no longer have to.

Lou left the bistro in Rickton in his truck and took the short drive up the highway to Sibby. It was a breathtaking winter day, the snow reflecting diamonds toward the azure heavens. This day was getting better by the minute. He could almost forget that the funding for his little project wasn't exactly limitless and that he still had a holdout that he hardly dared to approach again.

Pop presented a challenge in every way. First, Lou admired the man—Pop's way of disregarding conformity and paving his own way, his obvious dedication to his family, and then, there was his aim. There wasn't a rifleman in the county that could hold a candle to Pop Dixon.

Just the thought of the man behind a rifle aimed at him was enough to give Lou the shakes. But Pop had no reason to suspect Lou of the things he was guilty of. It looked as though he would get away with all of it.

Lou forced calm to flow through his arms to his fingers gripping the steering wheel. He made every effort to lighten his thoughts. What would he call his little town, once he'd had it incorporated? After all, he would have no opposition to changing the town's name. Who would dare when Lou owned every last business in Sibby?

He couldn't call it Louville, since Lewville was so geographically close. What about Jacobstown? That had a colonial sound to it, which would be fitting. Or he could use another name entirely, not tied to his own, like Grand Butte or, heaven forbid, Victory, after Vic Billings. He chortled a little at the last. Vic was so small-time, a crook, really; but he believed in Lou's project, so that put money firmly in Lou's corner. Lou genuinely didn't care where that money came from.

Lou pulled up to Bob's Hardware. He puckered his mouth distastefully and tsk-ed under his breath at Bob's garish sign. Whether he was a Rickton or not, Bob should have had better sense than to spend the kind of money he did on that sign, especially when Lou was going to have it taken down and destroyed the minute all of the Sibby holdings were his. Oh, he might offer to resell it to Bob. Bob Rickton, after all, was vain first; and anything with his name on it was sure to be valuable to him. That meant more capital for Lou.

Lou was making quiet changes to the store. If anybody noticed the shift in inventory to trinkets and souvenirs from hardware, nobody commented. In fact, passers-through found the new items appealing, and that was the idea. People were going to want to stop in Lou's new town and he was going to give them fun memorabilia to take with them.

Wren's would remain a natural food destination, after all that fit well with today's green consumers; but he was going to attach a small café by expanding into the empty lot next door. He might even offer for Glenna to still make their bread and baked goods, though he suspected she would leave town once she had her money.

This project was Lou's lifeblood, his obsession, and all was going as planned. If only he hadn't complicated things by hitting Danica Burdick with his blue Olds sedan. He'd hated to part with that car, but it had been necessary. He hoped that his visible blanch went unrecognized by George when Victor pulled up to the restaurant in the very same car. The underside of the bumper was even still dented.

He was also disturbed by the news that the young woman might die after all. Lou didn't fault George for taking the case against the Burdick family, but it made Lou's position against Pop all that more precarious when he approached him about buying the store. Lou was sure not to gain any points with Pop Dixon by having George Stevens as his attorney of record.

What a complicated mess. Lou did wish good things for the Dixon family, though. In fact, coffees in hand from Maria's fresh pot near the Bob's Hardware register, he decided to pay them a visit to show his good will.

Lou found Pop at the counter, examining a catalog and frowning at something. He looked up when the door chime

Slippery   Kimberly Ann Freel

rang. "Lou! It's nice to see you on this fine day. Come on in." Pop's greeting was just the start Lou was looking for.

"Hello, Pop. You're right. Sibby is positively gleaming on this sunny day. I brought some fresh coffee from across the way for you and Marcia." Lou offered his compostable coffee cups.

"That's mighty charitable. I didn't know Wren's served coffee. Is it organic?"

"No, no. I meant it came from Bob's," Lou explained.

"Bob's Hardware?" Pop tasted the brew. "Hey, it's pretty good. I'd have figured it to contain a measure of hydraulic fluid if it came from Bob's."

Lou laughed nervously. "Oh, well, Maria is apparently experimenting with offering free gourmet coffee to customers."

"I'll bet Bob loves that." Pop commented wryly.

"You know, Bob isn't as involved in the day to day as he used to be." Lou was vague.

"Oh, yeah. I had a run-in with Victor Billings the other day. You know him, right?" Pop asked. Lou nodded reluctantly. "He said you were making some real estate purchases in Sibby. Guess you're getting to know the other business owners better too, huh? Well, it's nice to welcome you as a merchant, Lou. Any idea what you're going to do as far as opening shops?"

Mom heard the two men conversing and joined them at the counter. Lou gestured to the other cup of coffee and she accepted it graciously.

"Well, I'm still researching the best way to attract customers to Sibby, since we are a bit off the beaten track."

"That's never been a problem for Mom and me, or for Glenna since she specialized. You just have to think of a niche that hasn't been filled in the county," Pop offered.

Lou smiled, as if the idea hadn't occurred to him. "I'm

sure I'll think of something." He changed the subject. "Say, I'm surprised to see both of you here. Isn't your daughter in the hospital still?"

"We're headed over there for a meeting with the doctor as soon as we close. I'm afraid to say she hasn't gotten any better, Lou, since the last time we talked. I'm still praying, though."

"I'm sure that helps," Lou said. "When you're not so preoccupied, I'd like to talk to you some more about business in Sibby, maybe get some pointers or offer you more ideas for expansion, or maybe you'd like to partner up with me on some of my ideas…"

Pop cut Lou off. "Now, Lou. You know how I feel about changing The Mercantile. We talked about that before."

Lou felt chastised and he stammered. "But you ought to listen to what I have to say…"

"It's been said, Lou." Pop interrupted once more, an edge to his voice. "If you'll excuse us, Mom and I have other things to think about right now. The business is just fine; and it will suit you better if you leave it alone, though, again, I do welcome you to do with your own establishments what you will."

Lou reddened again, like he had at the hospital, though Mom wasn't sure if it was from anger or excitement. Without a reply, he blustered toward the door as they both stared after him. Just before he exited, as the door chime signaled his departure, he had one last comment for them both.

Under his breath, almost too low for them to hear, he uttered these words: "You're going to be real sorry folks." And the door popped shut in his wake.

Chapter Thirty

Toby's children weren't speaking to him. He'd gone to The Mercantile to pick them up for his weekend, only to have Seth and Lorna refuse to go with him. Toby's first reaction was to rail at Mom and Pop for poisoning his kids' minds against him, but then Seth piped up and defended them, saying that he'd heard about the lawsuit at school, not from them or Jimmy.

Damn Danica Burdick and her mouthy family. Those were *his* kids, and how was he ever going to explain to them that he was looking out for them when they wouldn't even talk to him? He figured they would get over it eventually, but he didn't want them to blame him, ultimately, for their mother's demise. If they didn't forgive him, who would be their dad, after all? Not Jimmy Burdick. The courts would see to that.

Damn that Pete Morse, too. Ever since he'd made the threat in the courtroom, Pete was having Toby tailed constantly. Apparently the Sheriff Posey was giving Pete enough of his own head to put police resources to work trying to catch Toby at something. Well, Toby wasn't that stupid, or that easily caught. He was careful about whom he did business with, and there was no way that Pete could outfox him, no matter how much he followed Toby around.

The other person who needed to be taken to task was Shelby Lowe. Toby wasn't quite ready to damn her yet, because poor Shelby was just a bit slow on the uptake. She didn't know that by associating with that ugly bitch from the Sheriff's office that she was risking blowing the lid off the whole operation. Toby would set her straight. In fact, he was going to see her right now.

When Toby walked in to Shelby's office at the school, she looked like she'd swallowed a whole pickled habañero. Her body stiffened and her face turned red. In a choked-up little voice, she paged her boss on her intercom, "Sir, I need to step out to the lady's room. I'll be right back."

With that, she grabbed Toby by the arm and marched him outside the front door of the school. Amused by her discomfort, Toby let her do so.

"What, on God's Green Earth, are you thinking marching into my place of work like that, Toby Browning?" Shelby hissed, keeping her voice low.

Toby smiled arrogantly. "I just knew I'd get your attention."

"You'll get my attention, alright, and your momma's when I tell her to spank your skinny butt. And don't think she won't either, just because you're all grown up," Shelby threatened.

"My mom is the one who sent me."

Shelby was speechless. Toby continued.

"You don't think my mom is stupid enough to let you go and cavort around town with the likes of Vic Billings or Connie May West without finding out, do you?"

Shelby squirmed. Ashley was following her, or having her followed. Either way, Shelby couldn't refute what Toby was saying.

"Listen to me, Shelby, and listen good. Either one of those people could annihilate our little project out at the trailer park. You've been useful to us; and my mom, Lord help her, really likes you. But neither one of us will put up with you associating with the cops or Mom's ex-husband.

Is that clear?"

Shelby's expression remained unchanged, the threat rolling off her back as she stared Toby down defiantly. "Since when do you or Ashley control me, Toby Browning?"

"Since it could be really conveniently arranged for you to just go away. It's not like you have anybody looking out for you or anything. Except for maybe those two new friends you just made, but then they could have any number of accidents too."

Shelby's instinct was to slap Toby in that smug, weasely face of his, but the clear threat he presented was enough to make her behave, for now. She didn't want Connie May or Vic to suffer the repercussions of her daring. Instead, she demurred. "I have to go back to work, Toby."

"And what am I going to tell Mom?"

"I'll stay away from Vic and Connie May. Your secrets are safe. I wasn't going to be dumb enough to invite them over or anything anyway. Besides, Connie May is just wily enough that she may have been an asset. I was going to ask Ashley to let her in anyway. It's your loss." She bit at her cuticles, working that angle a little more. "Just think how valuable it would be to have an ally in law enforcement, Toby."

He stared hard at Shelby to see if she was serious. "Crap, girl, you've really let that woman get to you. She works for the cops, get it? People like that have one loyalty, period, and that's to catch the bad guys. What do you think you and me are?"

"Well, we're not Bonnie and Clyde, that's for sure. Cut the tough act, Toby. You're just a thug wannabe. Just go run back to your Momma and tell her that she can cut out the insecurity act. I love Ashley and she knows that," Shelby attempted to put Toby back in his place.

Slippery

"You behave, Shelby Lowe, or I'll come visit you at school again, and I won't go quietly."

"Just go, already," Shelby pleaded and made her way shakily back into the school.

Connie May West had taken a few shopping trips with Shelby and, taking style points from a woman who was obviously the master, she'd toned down her wardrobe just a notch. Pete Morse teased her that she looked like she was going to a funeral because she'd substituted a little more black, brown, and houndstooth for her chartreuse and royal purple get-ups.

Pete knew, though, that Connie May had forged a real friendship with this associate of Toby Browning's and that it was killing Connie May to know that she would have to betray her new friend. The usually gregarious clerk was forlorn and moody, and only Pete knew exactly why. Connie May was not cut out for deception. She was as sweet and honest as the day was long and it ate at her to be otherwise.

Connie May still hadn't shaken her sense of dread about messing with the Brownings either. It was the second week back at school, on a Tuesday, when she discovered just why. She went to pick up her 'li'l 'uns', as she called them, at school and who should be chatting them up, but Toby Browning himself.

She knew him only by the mug shot that Pete Morse had posted at the station, so she was taken aback to see that he was so tall, with a wiry muscular build that made him appear as threatening as he obviously meant to be. He smiled maliciously at Connie May.

"Halley and Hugh and me were just catchin' up," Toby said, putting a hand on each child's shoulder. Halley, who was nine, looked at her mother uncertainly, knowing she was going to catch heck for talking to a stranger. Hugh, her eleven-year-old, just looked at Toby with admiration. He wasn't a stranger. He was a parent and that made him okay in Hugh's book.

"Mr. Browning, here is Seth and Lorna Browning's dad. He's offered to take us boys hunting together sometime. Since Dad's not around, I thought you'd think that was okay..." Hugh stopped when he saw that his mother had gone white as a sheet. "Um, Mr. Browning, I need to go get my bag."

"Halley, why'nt you go do th' same?" Connie May suggested. She watched the two kids go back into the school—her whole world in two scrawny, stringy-haired bodies, enveloped in oversized winter coats, so they would fit into them more than one year—and she turned back to Toby in mother-bear mode.

"Just what is it you want, *Mr. Browning*?" She drawled. "It sure as heck ain't makin' friends with my li'l 'uns."

"You better stay away from Shelby Lowe, Connie May." Toby cut to the chase.

"Or else?" Connie May asked testily.

"Let's just say I know where your children play, Connie May. I would hate for anything to happen to them."

Connie May's breath left her in a whoosh, sending vapor flying into the January air. She saw Halley and Hugh coming back out of the building, so she rushed back over to them, anxious to get them to daycare before Toby could reach his car and see which direction they were heading. Unwilling to let her children see her panic, she teased them. "Come on, li'l chickens. I don' wanna have t' pluck any feathers! Momma Hen is in one big fat hurry t' git back t' work!"

Halley and Hugh laughed as she chased them through the six inches of snow on the playground back to the car in her high-heeled boots.

They were breathless when they sat in the back seat. Their mom leaned over, in all seriousness, and said, "Hey, urchins, do Mama a favor and stay th' heck away from Toby Browning. He's a bad egg, chickens, take my word fer it."

The two nodded in acquiescence as Connie May feared that staying away would never be enough. Friend or no friend, Shelby Lowe meant trouble and now it was affecting her kids. She'd tell Pete that afternoon that she was out. He'd have to solve this one on his own.

Shelby Lowe sat at her desk after school, managing the office while Mr. First saw all the children onto the bus or into their parents' cars. She was filing her acrylic nails down to nothing, thinking about Toby and his threats. She cursed quietly when the edge of a nail lifted. She was going to have to go get that one filled sooner than later or it was a goner.

She heard a gasp at her colorful word and looked up to see Seth Browning examining her with profound interest.

"Did you actually say a curse word at school, Ms. Lowe?" He asked, his sapphire eyes round with mischief.

Shelby laughed despite herself. "Don't tell Mr. First. He'll make me stay after for detention."

"Oh, come on. Grown-ups get to curse all of the time, and no one makes them write 'I will not say the D-word' two hundred times on a blackboard instead of going to recess. It's what my mom would call an 'injustice'." Seth said knowingly.

"I will try to refrain. There are definitely better ways to express oneself," Shelby offered.

"Yeah, but sometimes a good D-word makes you feel a whole lot better." Seth stated. "Like when all of the grown-ups around you are fighting over you and trying to make decisions without asking what you want. Then it feels good to shout out a D-word or two."

Shelby looked at Seth thoughtfully. This was a child wise beyond his years. Looking at his eyes, she saw Toby Browning, but that was where the similarity ended. His shock of black hair, his winning smile, and the completely fresh view of the world—these were all his mother's traits. Shelby didn't know Danica well, but she had seen them together enough to know.

Besides, Toby Browning was as cunning and slick as a wolverine and just as dangerous. This child didn't have a mean bone in his body.

"How's your mom doing, Seth?"

"She's still sleeping awfully hard. Pop keeps talking to God and asking if he'll bring her around. I hope it works, because Lorna and me are pretty sure it would kill Jimmy and Milo if Mom died."

"What about you, Seth? Has anyone talked to you about it? How would you feel if that happened?" Shelby had worked with kids this age long enough to know that often they lacked the vocabulary and the opportunity to express exactly how they felt. She'd always tried to treat the kids with respect, knowing that they had their own feelings about most things.

Seth wrinkled up his face. He looked worried and sad. "I can't believe she might actually die. It's not fair. Milo needs her."

"You need her." Shelby said matter-of-factly.

"Yeah. And Lorna too. I think everyone forgets that, though, 'cause we're older, so we're supposed to just accept whatever happens and be good and go to school and do our homework and all that. Even Dad, he just went off and tried to do what was best for us by suing to have Mom die. He didn't even ask us how we felt.

"That's why I like you, Ms. Lowe. You always think to ask how we feel." Seth's eyes shined with what looked like genuine admiration.

Shelby was touched. Her infatuation with her job grew. Here is where she made a difference, not in a stuffy trailer filled with marijuana plants. Her admiration for the Brownings fell another few notches. It wasn't like Toby or Ashley would ever give her the credit this nine-year-old was giving. She patted Seth's head. "You can stop by and tell me how you're feeling anytime, Seth. For now, you need to find your sister and look out for Miranda. Your grandma called earlier to tell us that she would be picking you up from school."

"Huh. I wonder what Jimmy and Grandma and Grandpa are up to today. I figured you would know where they were, since they haven't shown. It all makes sense now, though. Aunt Randi is never on time. She says it has something to do with not enough toot in her refried beans."

Shelby laughed out loud. 'Out of the mouths of babes,' she thought. "I know one thing for sure, Seth. If they didn't come to scoop you and Lorna up themselves, they must be up to something pretty important, because I can't think of anything that would be more fun than having you around."

Chapter Thirty-one

Dr. Michael Moreland knew he had just two options to save Danica Burdick's life and he was about to meet with her husband and her parents to go over them. Normally, they would be given plenty of time to explore treatment options and test out theories on traumatic brain injury. They would be allowed to *practice* medicine. The courts this time, though, were putting a rush on the deal. Dr. Moreland was challenged with a timeline in a case that had no clear, easy solutions.

Jimmy Burdick, and Mom and Pop Dixon looked like hell. None appeared to have slept since the court hearing two days prior. Dr. Moreland, too, felt like he had grains of sand in his eyes, the result of poring over medical journals two nights in a row instead of sleeping. The four of them sat down like warriors plotting a battle.

"I've come up with a couple of ideas to try and help Danica," he began.

"Let's have them." It was Pop, ready for any solution that could save his girl.

"The first option is to basically lie and say that Danica needs to be transferred for care at a bigger institution, that we question her stability here, and that she needs care from more experienced doctors. The benefit would be that they could try more experimental treatments, and Miranda may be able to argue that you need more time to make sure that they work.

"The two disadvantages of this option are: One, that Miranda may not be able to get the court to agree to another hearing, regardless of whether Danica is transferred; and then we will have wasted time doing so. Two, Toby may use a worsening of her condition as an excuse to get to pull the plug, so to speak, sooner," Dr. Moreland explained.

"Plus, you'd have to lie, which I cannot ask you to do," Pop insisted. "You have ethical standards to uphold, Doctor, and I have believed you when you said Danica can get the best care here. Please do not lie and compromise your values to protect our daughter."

"I'm prepared to do so, Sir."

Pop merely teared up and shook his head, grateful, but shattered that it would have to come to this.

"You mentioned that there's a second option," Mom said hopefully.

"Yes. I've done a lot of Internet and medical book research over the last two days, and I think I've found a drug that might increase Danica's level of awareness enough to bring her around. It's experimental as a treatment for brain swelling, though it's had other medical applications. We can use the drug here at Rickton Community, if I create a protocol for it."

"Let's try it." Jimmy said automatically. "I think that's much better than the alternative. I'll sign off right now if you want me to, Doctor."

"Now, wait a second, Jimmy. You have been adamant about continuing Danica's lactation. I've read up on this, and there is no way that she can continue to breastfeed with this drug on board. Milo will have to be weaned," Dr. Moreland advised.

Jimmy started to respond.

"No." It was Pop. "I won't even hear of it, Jimmy

Burdick. You will choose Danica's life over her son's well-being this time."

"Pop…" Marcia warned.

"It's okay, Pop," Jimmy cajoled. "I have no objection to weaning Milo if it means we can save Danica. I've always said we could stop any time if it looked like it would threaten her getting better. This is that time. I agree one hundred percent with using the drug."

The four of them looked at one another, unsure what to do next. There were no arguments, just a collective need to try for another miracle.

"One more question, Doc."

"What's that, Jimmy?"

"Can I bring my son in one more time to nurse with his Mommy?" Jimmy choked up on the last words. His heart broke that Milo might never get a chance to share that closeness with his mother again.

"I think that's a fine idea, Jimmy." Dr. Moreland agreed, as Mom and Pop nodded too, crumbling at Jimmy's anguish.

"I'll call Glenna and have her bring Milo over right away. The other kids will be fine with Miranda for the rest of the evening." Mom offered, touching away a tear from Jimmy's cheek.

Jimmy nodded and left the room to go to his wife, to talk to her a little more, and will this hurt away.

He was at her bedside, telling her the story of how he fell in love with her, when Marcia returned with Milo. Always stoic nowadays, Milo looked back and forth between his dad and his mom with wondering eyes. He was seven months old already, and sitting up real good, so Jimmy put him on the bed next to his mother, positioning himself next to the baby in case he tried to fall off. Milo did what came naturally and laid his head on Danica's chest. She breathed as if she was sighing.

Marcia absorbed the poignancy of her daughter and grandson lying together and prayed silently that it would not be the last time. Then she gave Milo and Jimmy their privacy with Danica, leaving her digital camera on the tray table.

"Danny, Milo is here," Jimmy said. "I know you and I decided together a long time ago that we were going to give Milo the best nutrition in the world for the first year of his life, and that you were going to nurse him that whole time, and even longer if you decided to.

"I've been honoring that decision, Danny, the best I know how," Jimmy choked up. "Because I knew you'd be furious with me if I didn't think of our little boy first. You'd lay down your life for any one of your kids. That's the way you are. If you could, you would choose Milo."

Milo lay watching his daddy, looking every bit like he knew what Jimmy was saying. He began to whimper softly. "I know, Buddy. It's not fair, is it? To have your Mommy sick like this."

Jimmy rubbed his baby's back and Milo settled back down with his head on Danica's chest. By impulse, Milo began to root around for Danica's breast.

"So, Danny, I hate to tell you this, but this is going to be the last time you get to feed your little buddy. It's down to crunch time, and Dr. Moreland thinks that he might be able to get you better with some experimental medication. We have to try to bring you back to us.

"I've got a camera and I'm going to record this for you, so you can hold this moment in your memory when you get better. That's the best I can do, Danny."

Jimmy looked over at the ICU nurse who'd entered the room quietly to help Jimmy position Danica so she could feed her son. Her face wet with tears, she approached the bed wordlessly. Jimmy took the lead.

"If you could help me roll her on her side, Milo always nursed best and longest with her in bed. We might have to take the top of her gown off first."

They unbuttoned Danica's gown and positioned her on her left side, stuffing pillows behind her to prop her up. Jimmy laid Milo gently on his right side where he instinctively rolled into his mother and latched on.

Jimmy watched the miracle of a mother nursing her infant like he had the very first time she'd held their son in her arms, when he was fresh out of her womb. Out of the corner of his eye, he saw the nurse reach for the camera. He turned to take it from her.

When Jimmy turned back to mother and son, he witnessed the second miracle, for Danica had taken arms that were limp and lifeless a moment before and wrapped them firmly around her nursing son. He could barely see their bodies through his tears, as Jimmy took pictures that would capture this moment for the rest of their lives.

The nurse recognized that the patient moving her limbs was a significant neurological change. She left the room long enough to summon Dr. Moreland who was waiting outside at the nurse's station. Dr. Moreland, Mom, and Pop rushed the doorway and gave a collective gasp. Danica's eyes still weren't open, but she cradled her little boy exactly as she had so many times before her accident.

Danica's void suddenly filled with light and she began walking down a lane lined with hundred-year-old oaks. At the end of the lane, less than fifty yards away, was the person she had been looking for: Milo. Where had he been all this time? He sat playing with a brown-spotted puppy. He looked up and smiled at her, a toothless grin that shone like the sun, his eyes the color and clarity of real maple syrup.

She reached out and grabbed him, hoping against hope that he wasn't a hologram too. He reached back and they shared an embrace as old as time. Milo. She held him to her breast, knowing that she would never let go, and, with the light behind her, Danica started once again to walk along the path that she knew would take her home.

Slippery   Kimberly Ann Freel

Chapter Thirty-two

Pete Morse and George Stevens had a standing lunch date at Rico's Diner once a week. Their agreement to meet there was unspoken. Pete just showed up and sat at the counter every Wednesday, and George sat at his table and ordered something greasy. Pete ordered a salad and sat and joined George. The only thing that had changed was that George was leaving his flask at the office nowadays. No sense getting Detective Pete's ire up.

George had just come from court. Danica Burdick's progress effectively squashed any kind of legal inroads Toby had made to having her taken off all life support. George was relieved, despite his client's outrage over the situation.

George sighed and took a deep draw of his Coke.

Pete came over with his salad and plopped down across from George. There was always the formality, "Is anybody sitting here today, George?"

"No. How is Detective Pete Morse today?" George asked amiably, despite the lines of exhaustion written across his face.

"Well I'm certainly better than you, George. It's only mid-January and we're starting to thaw a little. I just booked a late February vacation to Vegas with the wife. It's our anniversary. No kids allowed." He munched his greens and continued. "You look plum worn out. What's eating at you, besides your blessedly junk-filled diet?"

George sighed again and sucked out more of his Coke, wishing he'd brought his flask after all. "Danica Burdick is getting better. Her lawyer successfully filed an injunction on the withdrawal of her feeding tube. Maybe now you can leave my client and me alone."

"How is Toby, anyway?" Pete asked, his good mood bolstered even further by the news that Danica and Jimmy were getting a reprieve.

"He's pissing mad, that's for sure," George replied. "I know I rankled you in court about figuring out his motive for shutting off life support, but I'm still stymied by the whole thing. He's taking this awfully personally."

"Oh, I've figured that one out, only about a week too late. According to a source close to the Brownings, Toby found an old life insurance policy on Danica. I'm not sure how much it was worth, but he was telling anyone who would listen how life was going to be outside the trailer park."

"Hmm." George pondered that for a second and took a bite of his bacon burger. He swallowed. "I wonder why he never said anything to me about it."

"George, you're a good guy. Despite all of the funny jokes we make about lawyers around here, you do have a few scruples. Would you honestly have worked so hard to have that woman taken off life support if you'd known Toby's real reason?"

"No, I wouldn't have taken the case. Pop Dixon and I used to be good friends. It has nearly doubled me over with stress every time I've had to sue for custody. I would never have taken his daughter's life if I had known it was over money," George admitted.

They sat companionably and ate their meals. George rarely had dessert, but he saw a slice of German chocolate cake in the dairy case that he had to have. He invited Pete to have a piece too over coffee. Pete accepted.

As they dug in, George asked, "So are you going to arrest him?"

"Who? Toby?" Pete inquired innocently.

"Yes, Toby. You have a motive and circumstantial evidence on the respirator case. Are you going to pursue getting him prosecuted?"

"Oh no, George, I've got much bigger things in mind for Toby Browning. And believe me. He's going to need you plenty when the time comes."

George said nothing in reply. He simply continued to shovel the cake home until his plate was clean. He feigned disappointment with his actions and his expression, but inside he was doing a little jig and thinking, 'You go, Pete Morse. It's about time Toby Browning got what was coming to him.'

Pete left Rico's and took his cruiser to Sibby, driving straight past The Mercantile, Wren's, and Bob's and taking the back road to Jimmy and Danica Burdick's place. He hoped Jimmy went straight home after court, because Pete wanted to see him.

Seth Browning answered the door. He looked noticeably happier than the last time Pete had seen him, which was during the respirator fiasco. "Hi, Son," Pete said. "Is Jimmy home?"

Seth turned and called into the house, "Jimmy! It's that Detective from the hospital!"

With the enthusiasm of youth, Seth bounded back from the cold outside air through the laundry room, passing Jimmy as he fled.

"Whoa, Seth. You're supposed to invite the good guys in," Jimmy laughed.

"Lorna and me have got a game of *Wii Golf* going. I've

gotta get back and take my turn, 'cause I'm about to get a birdie!" Seth yelled breathlessly from somewhere in the interior of the house.

"He looks great, Jimmy," Pete commented. "The good news about Danica must be catching."

Jimmy smiled. His posture reflected the first real hope he'd had in a while. "She hasn't opened her eyes yet, but her response to stimuli increases daily. As soon as Mom gets here, I'm back there to make sure I'm around when she opens those hazel eyes of hers."

"So what caused the change?" Pete asked, curious.

"Milo did it, Pete. That's the only explanation I have for her sudden change. We brought him in to breastfeed with his mom one last time before we tried a new medication and the coolest thing happened. She wrapped her arms around him and wouldn't let him go! We got special permission from the nurses to leave Milo there at the hospital, as long as one of us is always there with him. It's Liz's shift right now, but like I said, I'm going to relieve her soon.

"Danny has been rolling over, moving her arms and legs, and sometimes even mumbling, like she's just in a really deep sleep. But she's nursing Milo like a champ whenever he's got the desire," Jimmy shared.

"That's awesome, Jimmy. Really." Pete marveled at the change in his friend. Hope really was better than any drug he could think of.

"So, Pete, what brings you out to the wilds of Sibby?"

"I heard today about the improvement Danica was making and I wanted to congratulate you. I also wanted to tell you that I finally found out yesterday why Toby was fighting so hard to let Danica die."

"Oh yeah?" Jimmy frowned with concentration.

"It was about life insurance, on Danica." He watched

the fury instantly wash over Jimmy's face. "Now, Jimmy, I knew when I told you that you were going to be mad enough to strangle the man with your bare hands. I want you to let me handle this. I think I can find out more and really make Toby pay."

"Who told you?" Jimmy maintained his calm.

"I have an informant who's tried to get close to the Brownings. Now she's being threatened by them, so she's refusing to continue, for her childrens' sake."

"That filthy bastard..." Jimmy began.

"But she's learned a lot, Jimmy. Apparently there are only a few people Ashley and Toby trust and one of them has awfully loose lips. I'm getting names, locations, and information just from the few short times these two gals were together." Pete looked hard at Jimmy. "Do you trust me?"

"For the kids' sake, I have to, Pete. Danica would kill me if I got in any kind of trouble over Toby," Jimmy admitted.

"It won't be long, I swear. You just keep taking care of your wife and your kids and this will pan out..." Pete's radio resounded on his belt. He reached to turn it down, then, listening, turned it up so they both could hear.

"Attention Fire Districts Two, Three, and Five, there is a structure fire at 303 ALBA Drive in Rickton, mobile home fire, fully engulfed, possible casualties from smoke inhalation. All units please respond."

Jimmy's eyes met Pete's. "That's the trailer park." Jimmy breathed a sigh of relief that he had Seth and Lorna.

"I've gotta go," Pete rushed back to his cruiser. The siren and lights blared as he tore out of Jimmy's place.

Chapter Thirty-three

There were several reasons Pete Morse had gone into law enforcement. First of all, he was pretty sure he'd be good at it, since following rules had always been his fervent desire and his forte. Second, he was young and he had a family to support—law enforcement didn't require an extensive education.

Lastly, he'd been born to peace-touting beatniks with a penchant for bending the law and indulging regularly in the delights of marijuana and acid. Pete's parents had taken their two kids along for most of the fun, and Pete was only nine when he went to his first underground 'sweat lodge,' which was really a bona fide pot-fest. He and his sister grew up in a 'free love' commune, and he hadn't seen her since she ran away at the age of fourteen to escape the melee.

Pete was on his own after the age of twelve. It was no wonder to him that he grew up so fast and that he and Izzy made the mistakes they did. He chalked it up to poor role models. He had escaped it though, and made sure that his own life was much more on the straight and narrow. There were a few side effects of such a childhood that Pete had never shaken—for one, he could smell burning cannabis a mile away.

So when he stepped out of the police cruiser to see two of Ashley Browning's trailers engulfed and the air smelled like a thousand joints lit in a church vestibule, Pete suddenly understood the gravity of this fire. It took one glance at gawking neighbors doubled over in hysterics and his own suddenly euphoric mood, to make him understand that the entire neighborhood was about to get stoned and that the evidence was getting destroyed in the process.

Pete immediately sought out the fire chief and realized that the firemen had already donned respirators with their gear. He should have known the chief would recognize the smell too. Pete had a gas mask with his gear in the trunk, so he put it on.

Toby and Ashley Browning pulled down ALBA Drive (named for Ashley Lynn Browning's Albatross—the legal name of her trailer court) in Toby's Camaro. They exited aghast at the horror of the burning trailers, but stayed put next to the car. The firefighters struggled mightily to contain the fire and not lose the whole park. Pete looked for occupants of the trailers to make sure everyone was out safe.

He approached Toby and Ashley because, as renters, they would know how many people to account for.

"Can you two please help us figure out how many people might be in those trailers? We need to get a head count." Pete said, all business, his other troubles with Toby aside. There might be innocent lives at stake.

"Just Shelby," Ashley replied, her icy eyes reflecting the horrible flames. "That's her trailer there," she said and pointed at the most fully engulfed of the two structures.

"Do you mean to tell me that with the fifteen trailers that are here, that you only have one renter?" Pete quizzed, his suspicions receiving grim confirmation.

"Being a landlord is a miserable business, Detective. We haven't bothered with tenants for years," Ashley said dully and waved her pearly pink nails in the air. Her faux fur sleeves flopped around her arms as she gestured.

Toby merely stood by and licked his lips nervously. Pete came around in front of them, between them and their view of the fires. His masked voice sounded hollow and intimidating to his own ears. "Alright, then, since we know that there is no one else to evacuate, and I've got a pretty good idea by the air quality, that I know how you've been paying for designer clothes and manicures, you two are under arrest. I have a police cruiser right over there where you can just sit and watch in perfect safety."

Toby started to protest. He shoved his chest forward and tried to get nose to nose with Pete. But his resolve crumbled as the air went to his head and he guffawed with all of the grace of a hyena. Ashley frowned in distaste and then a giggle bubbled up from her throat and she lost it too.

Pete cuffed them both and put them in the back of his car. Then he got on the radio. "This is Detective Morse with two suspects in custody at the ALBA Drive fire. I'm bringing them into the station for questioning. Can you please have Sheriff Posey on hand to meet me?"

"*Roger that, Detective,*" came from the radio.

"Sheriff Posey, is that you?" Pete asked in surprise. His boss wasn't usually one to man the radio. In fact, Pete was sure the man himself would have been en route to the fire by now.

"*It's me, Pete. There is a woman here who says she needs to speak with you directly. Says she might have something to do with the fire out there. Why don't you bring those suspects on in and we'll all have a little chat.*"

"Roger, Sheriff. I'll be there in less than ten minutes." Pete put his radio back on his belt and got in the front of the cruiser. He took off his gas mask and waved back to his passengers who were still in the throes of a giggling fit. He knew they would never find it so funny later.

Pete put the car in gear and accelerated. He got as far as the stop sign leading from ALBA Drive to the State highway and was waiting for an oncoming car to pass when he felt, rather than saw the explosion. The trailer park erupted into a mass of flames and confusion. The percussion was strong enough to lift the back end of Pete's cruiser. Pete, Ashley, and Toby all turned around to witness a plume the size of a four-story building rise into the air.

All Pete could do, as he turned and pulled onto the highway was pray for the firefighters, and hope to God that Toby and Ashley Browning would be forced to reckon with the havoc they had just caused.

Chapter Thirty-four

Shelby Lowe was a mess. There was a mirrored window in the holding room and she couldn't help but catch her reflection. Her cream pantsuit smelled of gasoline. Streaks of potting soil and fuel covered the lower half of her jacket and her pants. Her platinum hair was curled into a French knot that had all but come unbound as shocks of hair pointed every which direction. Carefully applied makeup had smeared and run, lending her eyes a zombie-like appearance.

Shelby felt a little like a zombie. Why she had put on her best outfit and makeup before a shoot-out with the apocalypse, she didn't know. She just figured if she was going to put it good to Ashley and Toby Browning, she'd better look smashing doing it. Besides, if they gave her time to clean up beforehand, her mug shots would be much prettier than if she'd worn her warm-up suit, which was what she was wearing when Ashley confronted her and told her to move out.

Shelby was going to do it anyway. Moving out was no problem. Shelby had never felt good about pandering to Ashley. She had nightmares for weeks when she first moved in of being caught with the pot plants in her house. She'd been raised by a preacher, taught right from wrong, until sheer greed and stupidity had gotten the best of her when she started doing Ashley's bidding. So Shelby packed her bags, set them by the front door and called her new good friend, Connie May West, to see if she could stay with her for a spell.

Connie May had apologized profusely, so very sorry that she couldn't help Shelby out, because they really had hit it off. She admitted that she'd invite Shelby into her home in a heartbeat if it weren't for the threat to her children. Her children were her whole world. Connie May had moved away from everybody and everything they had ever known clear out west to the wilds of Washington, for the good of her children. So, no, Shelby could not stay with her.

Why, she wanted to know, would it be threatening to Connie May's children if Shelby stayed with her? After all, Shelby saw the kids every day at school. The kids loved her, treated her like a favorite aunt and a confidante. Even Seth Browning thought highly of Ms. Lowe.

Well, as it turned out, Toby Browning had made it very clear that he would put Connie May's children in jeopardy should Connie May ever hang out with Shelby again.

At this news, Shelby positively flipped her lid. How could Toby, or Ashley for that matter, see fit to exert such control over Shelby's life or her friends'? By the time she'd put her stuff in her car, with no place to go, Shelby was in a fit of fury like none she'd ever felt. Still, she probably would have driven away, found a hotel or something, and figured it all out, but then she spotted a gas can leaning against Toby's trailer.

Her crime almost committed itself, such a fugue she was in as she did the rest. First, she grabbed her suit from the hanger in her car and her make-up bag, hefting those along with the five-gallon gasoline can back to her trailer. She got dressed and made up, doused every blooming marijuana plant in the trailer with gasoline, then she put on her boots and made her way across the way to Toby's trailer and did the same thing there. She found a pack of cigarettes and a box of matches on Toby's kitchen counter, and reserving one of each, Shelby lit the whole pack of matches at Toby's doorway and threw them over her shoulder to the whooshing sound of flame meeting fuel. She returned to her trailer and stood on her front porch. Shelby struck the last match against her shoe, lit the cigarette and enjoyed a small indulgence into a habit that she had kicked long ago. Then she opened the door and tossed the lit cigarette inside. Again, a satisfying whoosh. Toby's trailer was already toast by the time Shelby pulled away.

Shelby drove straight to the Rickton precinct of the County Sheriff's office and turned herself in. It was Connie May West who held her hand while she waited for the Sheriff, and then Detective Pete Morse, to arrive at the station. Connie stayed with her through giving her statement and then being booked into the jail for the crime of arson.

Shelby made her one phone call to Victor, who, in turn, called George Stevens. George readily accepted Shelby's case, knowing full well that it would be a conflict of interest for Ashley Browning, who was also getting booked that day. The way George figured it, if Shelby had the balls to light up the whole Browning trailer park in retribution for the actions of Ashley and Toby Browning, he could at least think beyond his pants long enough to give Ashley Browning the lashing she deserved.

It was sheerly by the grace of God that no one was hurt when the Meth lab exploded at the Browning place. The firefighters had temporarily retreated when the fire started to spread to Ashley's trailer, which unbeknownst to them, sat atop a five-year old basement filled with every amenity a crystal meth producer could possibly want. When the fire was finally out later that evening, just ten trailers were left standing. Five were filled with enough marijuana plants to supply the whole County. The remainder of the trailers had become storage for the ingredients and the byproducts of a full-scale Meth operation.

Toby and Ashley Browning were up to their asses in trouble; and there was not one person in their rather wide swath who felt bad about it, their lawyer included. Oh sure, the drug users and dealers were going to see a serious dent in their supplies, but Toby had alienated enough of them that Connie May had a pile-up of people coming in to make statements once the word got out that Toby had been busted. Apparently, the baddies were one step ahead of being outed by Toby when they lined up to help the prosecution, or so the theory went, anyway.

By midnight, Pete Morse had interviewed more than twenty witnesses and put three people in the lock-up. He was exhausted, ready to go home, lay his head down on his pillow, and put the day to rest. He walked out into the lobby to see Connie May still at her desk. Jimmy Burdick was standing with her, carrying on a low conversation.

"Connie May, don't you have kids to get home to?" Pete asked, sorry that his clerk had stayed so late.

"Oh, don't ya worry none, Detective Pete. My babysitter's a real angel. She's got it handled. Jimmy here's been waitin' t' see ya too."

"Thanks, Connie May. You can go on home now," Pete offered. "You did real well today, Connie May. If it weren't for you, Shelby Lowe might never have grown a conscience; and the biggest drug operation this County has ever seen might have gone on running forever."

"Yer jes' sayin' that, Pete." Connie May blushed, pleased that she had been able to help her favorite detective after all.

Pete gave her a hearty hug and sent her on her way home. He turned his attention to Jimmy.

"So the kids' dad is going to go to jail for a good long time, Jimmy. Is that why you're here? For Toby or the kids?" Pete asked.

"Nope. I knew you'd crack this one, Pete." Jimmy remained serious. "I came to thank you. I also came by to tell you that Danny opened her eyes today. She's not talking much yet, but she gave me a smile that could light New York City. She knew me and she didn't want to let go of Milo for anything."

"And so the revelations continue. Is it a full moon or something?" Pete asked, looking outside the front window of the station for the answer.

"Might be," Jimmy admitted. "You couldn't see it through the clouds, though. There's another doozy of a snowstorm coming."

"Aw, shoot, just when I thought the big thaw was coming in time for my Vegas vacation."

Jimmy and Pete laughed at this.

"There's really only one mystery left to solve before I leave town," Pete mentioned, not wanting to spoil the good mood.

"Yeah," Jimmy nodded. "We still don't know who hit Danny that day in December. Do you really think it matters?"

"It was a crime, Jimmy. And my job is to solve crimes. We've still got the DMV checking some sales records for us. We'll get to the bottom of it eventually. In the meantime, I'm sure Danica has nothing to worry about. She wouldn't know that car from any other. She was on the wrong side of it to identify it."

"But Pop wasn't," Jimmy commented. "But then, who would ever mess with Pop? He's the toughest, rifle-toting business owner this side of the Rockies."

Pete laughed. "Isn't that the truth?"

"Got time for a beer, Pete?"

"I sure do, Jimmy. I'm off duty. Let's go shoot a game of pool."

Chapter Thirty-five

The Mercantile wasn't busy the next morning, because patrons hardly dared test out the snow-covered streets just to buy tack or clothing. Mom and Pop were like kids, flitting from place to place, chattering like sparrows, their steps and their hearts lighter for the first time in more than a month. Steve was going to mind the store while the two of them went to visit Danica.

When Steve finally walked through the rear door, he was hardly able to un-bend his fingers after he gripped the steering wheel like a lifeline for the three miles to work. His winter jacket shone with the remnants of fresh snowflakes and he'd only been parked a short walk away. Mom walked straight up to him; and with her characteristic sweetness, cradled Steve's cheeks in her hands and planted a kiss right on his mouth.

"Bless you for making that harrowing trip so we could go see our girl." Marcia said.

Steve blushed to his toes. "Oh, it was nothing, Mom. It was my day to work anyway."

"Yes, but far better men than you have called in for a snow day when the weather is this foul," she said, holding out her arm for Steve's outer jacket so she could hang it up to dry near the heater.

"Well I, for one, am just as excited to see Danica as you guys are. I can't believe she's awake." Steve marveled.

Pop chimed in, joining them. "If you didn't believe in

miracles before, it would be pretty hard to refute this one."

Steve and Mom bobbed their heads in complete agreement.

"I'd like to go see her tonight, after my shift ends," Steve said. "Liz already said she'd go with me. She's minding Wren's today, because I guess Glenna has doctors' appointments."

Mom frowned at that news. "I hope it's just routine."

"You know, I'm not sure. Something strange is afoot there. Glenna hasn't been herself since Liz and I got back from Seattle." Steve changed from his winter boots to a pair of lace-up ropers he kept at the store.

"Mom and I will be checking on her just as soon as we get a visit with our Danica—that you can be sure of." Pop promised.

"I'd appreciate that. I'm just finally getting Liz back on track. She'd be a mess again if anything happened to Glenna. Liz is going to medical school, did you know that?"

"Why, no I didn't!" Mom touched Steve's shoulder. "That's super. But then, how will the two of you stay together if she goes away to Nashville?"

"Actually, I think Nashville might be right up my alley. I've been writing songs since I can remember, and the only place they ever got sung was in a cow pasture or on the back of a horse."

"Steve Oaks, you are a surprise. So that means you're going to leave us too, then?" Mom lamented.

Pop watched this all transpire with his newly finite wisdom. Before Danica's accident, he probably would have yelled and postured, demanded that Steve give up any such hullabaloo and stay at The Mercantile for the rest of his life. Then after all of that, when Steve decided to leave with Liz anyway, Pop would have not so kindly asked him to leave right away and not to let the door hit him in the keester on the way out.

Now, though, he realized that life was too short. Pop had given Danica too much grief about quitting the store to take care of Milo. His expectations had always been much too high for his only offspring. She was just a mom with a family, and Liz and Steve were only young people trying to figure out a new life. Love was always at the center of these predicaments. What were loyalty and the drudgery of an everyday retail job, but just a drop in the bucket of life anyway? Pop could dole out misery born of anger, or he could just be happy for these young folks, as he knew Marcia would be.

Deciding on the latter, Pop invited Steve to warm himself by the furnace while Mom got him some hot chocolate. It wasn't going to be a busy retail day anyway, so Pop asked Steve if he'd like to borrow a book from the shelf upstairs to keep him company.

They got Steve and the store settled, and Mom and Pop bundled themselves into the car to drive to Rickton Community Hospital. Mom looked hard at Pop as he turned over the engine.

"What?" Pop asked, uncomfortable with his wife's scrutiny.

"If I didn't know better, I'd think you've become a bit more of a softy, Pop Dixon."

"Yeah well, whatever you do, don't tell Danica. She won't know what to do with me."

Mom laughed, her heart full with love for the man next to her and the knowledge that he and her daughter would actually get the chance to discover his newfound grace.

Danica was propped up in her bed playing with Milo when Mom and Pop walked into her hospital room. She'd been moved that morning from the ICU and a crib for Milo fit in the room with her. They placed the bed in a corner so that Milo could play on the inside of the bed, without falling off the edge. Danica was still physically weak from weeks without putting weight on her limbs; and her femur still needed to heal from her surgery, but the nurses gladly helped her with the baby. Milo was a delight and they couldn't bear to separate mother and baby when that bond had obviously been so vital to Danica's recovery.

Danica looked up at her parents and beamed. Her words were still hesitant and her voice still scratchy, but her sentence was clear as a bell. "Hi Mom and Dad."

She looked back at Milo. "He got bigger."

Mom and Pop each gave her a big hug, earning smiles from Milo. Danica examined each of their faces in turn.

"Mom, don't cry." Danica ordered.

"I can't help it, Danica, sweetie. I wasn't sure I'd ever see you open your eyes again. When Jimmy called late last night and said you were awake, I could scarcely believe it. Seeing you this way, well, I'm pretty sure we're adding those years back to my life I lost when you had your accident."

Danica frowned. "Don't remember what happened." She said tentatively.

"Thank God you don't," Pop replied. "We'll remember enough to last forever. I'm just so grateful to have you back with us."

They sat for a time and Mom held Milo, then Pop played peek-a-boo with him through the crib. Danica began to look strained and tired.

"You need your rest, honey," Mom noted. "Pop and I are going to have lunch in the cafeteria. Why don't we take Milo with us and see if there's anything mushy he can have down there. You should get a nap before the parade of people who've wanted to see you crashes down your door."

Danica nodded gratefully. Then she turned to Pop. "Mom, take Milo? I need Dad for a minute."

Pop walked to Danica's bedside and took her hand.

"You see what happened, Dad?" She asked as if she feared the answer.

"I saw the whole thing, Danica. Suffice it to say that it was awful watching you go through all of that. You are one lucky young woman to be here today."

"Will you tell me?" She asked tearfully.

"Someday I will, Danica. I know how you must feel, like nearly two months of your life are a complete blank. You're exhausted and you're in pain. You want to know why, don't you?"

Danica nodded, tears still brimming her almond eyes. Pop couldn't help but think that she looked just like the first time she'd ridden without training wheels on her bicycle and she had crashed and burned. Her expression was a mixture of disappointment and trust.

"It was an accident, Danica, pure and simple. It was slick outside and you fell and there was a car…"

Danica closed her eyes in understanding.

"It was nobody's fault." Pop soothed, knowing full well that, responsible or not, the driver of the car still hadn't owned up to his part in the tragedy. He decided to change the subject before he got his blood pressure up again.

"I don't think I told you often enough before this happened Danica—I love you and I'm proud of the fine young woman you've become. You have wonderful kids and your husband loves you more than life itself. What a blessing you are." Pop emphasized the last with a kiss to Danica's forehead.

"Thanks, Dad. Love you, too," Danica replied tiredly.

"Now get some rest. Mom and I will come back later after you've had a long nap."

Mom and Pop were having lunch in the cafeteria with Milo when Jimmy walked in looking refreshed, like he'd finally slept for the first time in a month. Each of them recognized the change, since they'd felt it themselves. Jimmy took his measure of mashed potatoes and turkey gravy and slapped a side of green beans onto the mauve tray. He joined Mom and Pop at their regular table.

"I'll sure be glad when we can abandon this mass-produced hospital fare," Jimmy commented as he sat down. "Hey, Buddy!" He said to a grinning baby Milo.

Mom smiled also and murmured in agreement. "Still," she said, "These people have seen to it that we're nourished every day. We might have starved otherwise."

"Oh I could never have starved with all the casseroles and pots of coffee you made for me and the kids," Jimmy said, teasing Marcia, appreciation high in his eyes.

"If Danica is to be believed, it's a darn good thing I cooked for you too. According to her, you're challenged to boil a pot of water. I didn't want my grandchildren looking like starved little orphans." Mom teased back. Then she realized what she had said.

Back-peddling, she said, "They wouldn't really have been orphans, though, Jimmy. Even with Toby in jail, they would always have had you."

"Thank God for that," Pop emphasized.

Jimmy cleared his throat. "Look, guys, I know we've had some differences on Danny's treatment..."

Pop interrupted. "Jimmy, you must realize this, first of all: I know you love my daughter and you've proven it over and over during this difficult time. As far as I'm concerned, you and your baby boy are the only reason she came back to us. Thank you, Son."

Jimmy choked up and, at a loss for words, took a bite of

his mashed potatoes. Mom simply patted his free hand, in total agreement with her husband.

"So what's next?" Mom asked. "When do you have to go back to work, Jimmy?"

"I've never been so thankful for my partnership with my brother. He's pretty much picked up where I left off with the business by sending one of his senior foremen to stay in Lewville for a few months. He couldn't pay me more than I had saved up for vacation, though, so I've cut into our savings almost totally just to live on."

Mom and Pop nodded their understanding.

"Do you need any help with money, Jimmy? Mom and I have savings too." Pop offered.

"No. I think I have enough to get us by until Danny can come home. Doc thought it might be a few more weeks. I might need some help at home for her when she gets there, though, so I can go back to work."

"I'd be happy to help Danica at home," Mom offered.

"That's a relief. She'd like that much better than having some nurse she doesn't know." Jimmy said. "As for today, I can stay until two and then I've got to go get Lorna and Seth from school so they can come see Danny too. I would have kept them out, but Seth had a big math test to take."

"I'll go get them, Jimmy," Mom volunteered. "I've got a few things to do with the books back at the store. I'll be able to just skip over there to the school—less driving that way, since I'll already be in Sibby. The three of us can come on back when it looks like the snow is letting up a little. You and Pop can stay here with Danica and Milo."

"That's generous of you," Jimmy said, accepting her offer. "I just hope that snow lets up. If it doesn't, I'll bring Pop back before it gets too dark and bring the kids this evening after dinner."

"Okay, then, it's settled." Mom said and the three of

them finished their meal companionably, taking turns staring out the metal framed window into the flurry of snowflakes and drifts of snow.

Mom looked back at Milo, who'd painted mashed potatoes all over his high chair and himself. She laughed. "Whew, look at you. I'll get him cleaned up, Jimmy."

"Don't worry about it, Mom. I'll hose him off. Let's let him finish first." Jimmy said.

"I'm going to be off then," said Mom.

"Mom, you be real careful on these roads," Pop said as she rose to leave.

"Oh, Pop. You know I've been driving these winters long enough to know what to do. I'll take it easy." Mom promised.

Pop believed her. Why, then couldn't he fight the unease that rankled him as he watched Marcia walk gracefully out the door of the hospital into the storm?

Slippery   Kimberly Ann Freel

Chapter Thirty-six

Lou Jacobs was at The Mercantile when Marcia returned, apparently the only customer they had on such a gloomy day. He chatted jovially with Steve. Lou had brought coffee from Bob's Hardware again and, Marcia noticed, fresh scones from Wren's Market.

"Well, hello Mr. Jacobs," she said warmly. "I can't believe you've braved the storm just to bring us goodies again."

"I had hoped that Pop would be here too," Lou said. "By the way, please call me Lou. I've already talked Steve, here, into doing it."

"That's right, Lou," Steve admitted, anxious to leave the pompous little man in front of him and go back to marking down flannels in preparation for Spring. Even the dry western novel he had picked out was better than getting stuck talking to Lou. "Hey, Mom. I'm glad to see you made it back, but where's Pop?"

"I'm going back to get him in about an hour and a half, after the kids are through with school, so we can all go see Danica together. In the meantime, I've got some charge accounts to go over and bill out. That should keep me busy for a while."

"Don't let me keep you," Lou offered. "I just brought some of Glenna's scrumptious blueberry scones and coffee, thinking you two might enjoy them." Meaning her and Pop, Mom deduced.

"It was nice of you to drop in, Lou, but I'm afraid I'm not much use to you without Pop."

"Right, right. Well, we're neighbors now," Lou said cordially. "I'm hoping to get to know you better, too, Mrs. Dixon."

"I'm Marcia. Everyone else calls me that or Mom. You pick."

"Well, then, Marcia. It has been a pleasure. Steve, you get back to those flannels. I'll be seeing you all very soon," Lou bid them goodbye and the door chimed as he left.

Why did that harmless little man give her the creeps, Marcia wondered. "I'm going up to the office. Holler if you need anything," she said, climbing the stairs.

The office was a loft half a story off the rest of the downstairs. The store itself had twenty-two foot ceilings, so the original owners had built a half-staircase leading to Marcia's alcove at the back of the store. It was tiny, just eight by eight feet, yet every important document about The Mercantile and Mom and Pop's finances was housed in that space. For that reason, Mom always locked up when leaving. She always left the door unlocked when she was inside, though, in case Pop or Steve needed to reach her.

Her heart and mind still light from the ministrations of the morning with her recovering daughter, Marcia set to work pulling out charge tickets from some of their oldest customers. There were natives of Sibby who had charged their goods at the store since before Mom and Pop's time and the Dixons were only too happy to accommodate the same terms when they took over the business. Most customers were excellent about paying their bills on time every month. There were a few, though, that Marcia had to repeatedly invoice. She frowned now as she realized there were at least five accounts that were more than two months past due.

Taking out her calculator, Mom started to add up the figures from the tickets to re-invoice the overdue accounts. Concentrating, she didn't hear the door to the office open and she didn't look up until she heard a creak on the floorboard behind her.

"Steve, what…" She stopped. It wasn't Steve.

"Mr. Jacobs." A shudder went through Marcia, yet she chose to remain cool. "What can I help you with?"

"Lou. Please call me Lou. We need to talk, Marcia."

"H-how did you get in here?" Mom asked, trying mightily to keep the tremor from her voice, unease bubbling to the surface.

"You didn't lock the back door of the store. I didn't want Steve being alarmed when I approached you. After all, I'm sure we can talk about things civilly," Lou said, his beady blue eyes taking on a maniacal gleam.

"I don't know what there is to talk about," Mom reiterated. "Pop isn't here and he and I are equal partners in The Mercantile. I'm going to ask you to leave now, and return when Pop is here to join us."

"I've tried to talk to Pop," Lou said angrily, pulling his mackinaw cap off his purely white hair. His skin was fast turning the beet color Marcia had come to recognize as a sign of his discomfort. "Pop isn't being reasonable. You, on the other hand, have the power to reason with him. He's your husband, and I believe you could talk him in to partnering with me."

"Why would I do that?" Mom asked, trying with all of her might to figure a way to alert Steve to Lou's presence. "Pop and I are partners. We've never had any desire to let anyone else invest. We're solid without outside interference."

"See, now you sound just like him. Marcia, Marcia. We're going to have to try this a different way," Lou's face pinched distastefully and he reached inside of his wool overcoat.

Marcia's blood ran cold as she suddenly stared down the barrel of a .45 caliber Magnum pistol.

"Now, Marcia. Let's try again," Lou said with increasing confidence, as he gently closed and locked the office door.

Chapter Thirty-seven

Pop and Jimmy spent the early afternoon playing chess in the family waiting room of Rickton Community Hospital. Danica was taking a long nap, and the nurses had suspended even the taking of vital signs until she woke up. Milo had taken Danica's cue and settled in for a nap himself. He'd taken a liking to his crib since Danica had been away, sleeping sounder when his Mom and Dad weren't around to roll over and disturb him.

It was three o'clock and Jimmy was preparing to rouse Milo so he would sleep that night. Jimmy's cell phone rang unexpectedly, and Pop glared at the phone. He had always eschewed the disruptive things himself. Of course, Jimmy had kids and a mobile type of job. Pop supposed that such a man should probably have a phone on him at all times.

Jimmy flipped the phone open. "Hello, Jimmy speaking."

"Mr. Burdick? It's Ronald First. Normally, Miss Lowe would be calling, but, well…"

"Yes, I know about Shelby. Go on," Jimmy prodded.

"Nobody has picked up your children yet. They're the last kids here and the buses are already on their way. They said you would be picking them up. I know you've had some tough circumstances, but it's fierce weather out there. Is everyone all right? Do you know when you'll be coming to get them?"

Jimmy looked hard at Pop, who recognized the alarm

there. "My mother-in-law, Marcia Dixon, was supposed to pick them up. Are you sure there's no sign of her?"

Pop got to his feet. As much as he hated blasted cell phones, Mom always kept hers with her. Why wouldn't she call if she couldn't make it to the school?

'Unless she couldn't call,' was Pop's next thought. The blizzard outside had even enveloped the cars in the parking lot. He looked from the window back at Jimmy.

"Thanks, Mr. First. It'll take me about twenty minutes to get there in this weather, but I appreciate you waiting for me." He flipped the phone shut and looked back at Pop.

"I'm sure there's a reasonable explanation, Pop. Let's not panic. I'll let the nurses know that they need to wake Milo. You use my cell phone to call the store. By the time I get back from the nurse's station, we'll have this all worked out."

Pop nodded and took the phone. He dialed the store. Steve answered. "The Mercantile."

"Steve, Pop here. Is Mom there?"

"I haven't seen her since she went up to the office. I assumed she had gone to get Seth and Lorna by now."

"You didn't see her leave, though?" Pop asked, every fiber of his body keen on Steve's words. Something was amiss.

"Sometimes she goes out the back, but you're right, Pop. She does usually say good-bye. I'm sorry I wasn't paying more attention."

"That's okay, Steve, but I need you to take the cordless and check the office for me, please. She hasn't shown up to get the kids." Pop could hear Steve switch over to the cordless phone and walk toward the back of the store. Pop could barely still his breathing as he waited to hear what was happening at the store.

"The door is locked, so she must have left," Steve

deduced. "She never locks it when she's inside."

"Can you please see if her car is out back?"

Pop could hear the winter wind whistling in the cordless phone. "That's odd. Her car is still here. Maybe she went up to the apartment. Should I go up and check?" Steve offered.

"Yes, absolutely. Don't bother knocking. Please just find her safe and sound. If you startle her, tell her I sent you. Steve, one more thing before I hang up: Do you see any footprints out there?"

"I'm afraid the snow would have filled any in by now, Pop. It's a whale of a storm we're having."

"Okay, well Jimmy's cell number is programmed into that phone. I want you to check upstairs and call me back. Jimmy and I are on our way."

The grim look on Pop's face did nothing to allay Jimmy's concern as Pop handed him back the phone.

"We need to get to Sibby," was Pop's terse order as he headed for the exit.

The kids were none the worse for wear for having to wait. Mr. First had let them wait in one of the classrooms where they were allowed to play computer games. It took Jimmy and Pop closer to twenty-five minutes to get to the school. The roads were unbelievably icy as the snow melted and compacted on the roadways. The visibility was worse than the thickest fog Jimmy had ever encountered.

By the time they reached Sibby, Jimmy and Pop were practically sitting on the dash trying to keep their eyes peeled through all of the snow.

Pop loaded the kids impatiently into the jump seat of Jimmy's truck. If he could have thrown them in without actually stopping, he would have. Something was terribly wrong at the store. Pop felt it in his bones.

"You can just drop me off at The Mercantile, Jimmy, and take the kids home. I'm sure Mom and Steve are having a good laugh about the whole mishap by now," Pop said. 'Except for that Steve hasn't called me back yet,' Pop thought.

Jimmy sensed the scarcely concealed panic in Pop's words. This was a man who loved his family above all else. Pop had finally gotten his daughter back. Jimmy knew Pop couldn't bear it if something happened to Mom.

"No way, Pop. I'm going too." Jimmy challenged.

"Okay, but only if you take the kids to Wren's first. If anything is amiss at the store, I don't want them in the middle of it." Pop's mind's eye imagined Mom collapsed, hurt, or, God forbid, dead somewhere in the building. The kids couldn't be allowed to see any of that.

Jimmy pulled up in front of Wren's. Liz saw them through the window and greeted Seth and Lorna at the door. Jimmy went with them and explained what was going on to Liz in low tones, so that Seth and Lorna wouldn't be alarmed. Jimmy jumped back in the truck.

"That's odd." Pop said as Jimmy shook the snow off his head.

"What's that?" Jimmy asked.

"The store lights are off. We don't close for another two hours. Why would Steve have shut down the store?"

Jimmy and Pop exchanged concerned looks.

Pop was going to get to the bottom of this. "Jimmy, you wait here. I'm going to check the front door."

Jimmy waited while Pop did so. It was locked. Pop jumped back in the truck.

"I have my keys on me, but they don't unlock the deadbolt on the front door. That has to be locked from the inside, which it is. Drive me around to the back."

Jimmy did as he was told and exited the truck with Pop.

The men unlocked the back door. The scene before them made their blood run cold. There in the back room sat Mom and Steve, their hands bound with pantyhose, their mouths gagged with duct tape. In front of them, with a stainless steel pistol, stood Lou Jacobs, looking calm and collected. Steve was unconscious. His head lolled forward on his chest. Mom, however, was not so lucky. Her eyes were wild with terror, and now fear for Pop and Jimmy. The two of them froze.

Lou turned the gun toward them, his white hair flying, his eyes wild—insanity personified. "Welcome, gentlemen. Please join us. I had hoped to end this without violence, Pop. But, as you can see, your good guy, Steve, got in my way when he insisted on getting a key and unlocking the office."

"Is he…" Pop squeaked and kept his hands visible. Glenna and Liz would never forgive him.

"Oh, he's alive. He's just got a nasty bump on his head. Marcia did a brilliant job of tying him up, though, don't you think?"

Tears began to fall from Mom's eyes. Pop was helpless to comfort her. He tried reasoning with Lou. "Look, Lou, I don't know what it is you want, but I'm sure we can work this out without anybody getting more seriously hurt. You want the store, is that it?"

"I do wish you had listened to me when I inquired about the store before. The Mercantile is the pinnacle of my theme town, Pop. I must have it. I own every other piece of real estate on this main street, including Wren's. I need this business, affordably and reasonably. You could have helped me with that, but you continually refused to listen."

"I'll give you the store if you let us go." Pop offered, shaken that even Glenna had given in to Lou's master plan.

"Sure, now that I have you cornered and at gunpoint, now you want to be reasonable. That won't work for me, Pop, because you'll simply have me arrested and then all will be lost, won't it? No. It's not that simple. I must think."

Lou began to pace, the war in his mind evident as he alternately nodded and shook his head.

The cordless phone rang on the floor next to Steve. Everybody in the room jumped.

Lou pointed the gun at Jimmy. "You answer that. Not a word, though, or a false move, or I will shoot you and the rest of your friends."

Jimmy followed instructions again and answered the phone. "The Mercantile."

"Jimmy? What are you doing there? It's Pete Morse. Listen, I've got news for Pop."

Jimmy said nothing, just listened and allowed Pete to continue.

"Anyway, when I got on shift late this afternoon, I finally got my report back from the licensing people. The sedan we were looking into, the one that Victor Billings recently purchased went through a dealer and an auction, but we've finally traced the original owner. His name is Louis Jacobs. Do you know him?"

Jimmy closed his eyes and shook his head silently. This was the man who had hit Danny, the man who held them all at gunpoint now, the man who had most definitely lost his mind. He tried to think.

"Jimmy?" Pete asked.

"I'm here, Pete. Just a minute, I'm putting him on speakerphone." Jimmy hit the speaker button on the handset.

Lou turned beet red as he was caught off-guard. "Who's Pete?" he asked in confusion.

"*Louis Jacobs?*" Pete asked, as confused as Lou was.

Jimmy knew that Lou didn't realize Pete was privy to his guilt in Danica's accident.

"Yeah, Lou's at the store with all of us. I guess he's a friend of Mom and Pop's, so he decided to visit The Mercantile today. Listen, Pete. We've got to go. I'll see you soon, okay?" Jimmy hung up before Lou could grab the phone away.

Lou's tone was acid. "*Who* is *Pete?*"

Jimmy thought fast. It was critical that Lou not know it was a police officer that had been calling. "Pete is Glenna Stone's brother-in-law," Jimmy lied. "He called to tell Mom and Pop that you bought the store from her." He feigned innocence. "I didn't think you'd like me to share more with him, considering the circumstances."

Pop concealed a nervous grin. Lord help him, this was the worst possible situation they could all be in, but he couldn't believe the whopper good ol' Jimmy Burdick had just told, straight-faced and sincere-like. He silently prayed that Jimmy's ploy would work, and fast.

Chapter Thirty-eight

Pete Morse hung up the phone at his desk at the station and looked out his porthole-type window. He knew Jimmy was being cryptic. Louis Jacobs was at The Mercantile—that Pete was sure of. What he couldn't fathom was why Jimmy couldn't elaborate, nor why he didn't react more strongly to the news that Mr. Jacobs was Danica's assailant. He did know this: Louis Jacobs had to be arrested. Pete had his location, and given the strange nature of the circumstances, Pete was taking back-up.

He looked outside again. The question was: How many cruisers did he risk in the worst snowstorm of the winter?

He deferred to Sheriff Posey who allocated him three men, plus himself. Pete led the way in his cruiser, taking one of the patrolmen with him. The other two followed in a Blazer. They tiptoed down the highway to Sibby, taking nearly a half-hour to get there. They turned off their sirens when they reached town and did a drive-by of The Mercantile first. It looked closed, which was odd, since it was only five in the afternoon. Pop usually didn't close until after six. Wren's still shone bright, so Pete pulled in front of the store. Glenna Stone's daughter Liz, greeted them at the door.

"Thank God you're here. I already called 911 to have them send a car around and they said you were on your way. Something is wrong. My boyfriend, Steve, is supposed to still be working across the street and they haven't had their lights on for almost two hours. Plus, I told Jimmy Burdick that I'd watch his two kids while he and Pop checked things out almost an hour ago, and I haven't heard from them either. Something is definitely wrong over there." Liz was frantic, worried about Steve, and Danica's family.

"Do you know a man named Louis Jacobs?" Pete asked.

"*I* do." It was Glenna. She'd come from the back of the store to see what was going on.

"Would he have any reason to bother Pop Dixon?" Pete inquired.

"He promised me that he wouldn't bother Pop…" Glenna began.

"Mom?" Liz was perplexed.

"Louis Jacobs has been buying up all of the properties in Sibby to make it into some sort of tourist destination." Glenna looked guiltily at Liz. "I sold Wren's to him last week."

"You *what*?" Liz shouted.

Pete cleared his throat. "It sounds like you ladies have a lot of talking to do, but I need to first know from you, Mrs. Stone, if you think Mr. Jacobs might be capable of using force to get what he wants."

"I honestly don't know what he's capable of, but my gut tells me you need to be careful," Glenna warned.

"My innards tell me the same," Pete admitted. "Do you know any way into the store besides the front door?"

"There's the back, but that's the way the guys went in," Liz replied. "It could be trouble. Danica and I used to sneak in and out via the fire escape that goes to the second and third floors." She watched Glenna roll her eyes. "It might be kind of treacherous in this weather, but I can show you how to draw it down to ground level." Liz began to put on her coat, boots, and snow gear.

Seth came bouncing out of the back room, covered with flour from his baking ministrations. "What's goin' on?" He asked, taking in the serious expressions of Liz and Glenna, and the uniformed police officer. His dad had caused enough trouble. What could possibly be wrong now?

"Do me a favor, Seth. Get your sister and head out to my car," Glenna requested, knowing that distraction was the best tactic with these kids. "We need to go see your mom. I'm sure Danica is wondering where her favorite munchkins are today."

"Yeah," Seth said. "We wanna see her too!"

Liz hugged her mom. "You're brilliant. Just promise me that you'll be careful out there."

"Oh, we should be fine as long as all the other idiots are off the road. If it's as bad as I think it is, though, I wouldn't expect us to come home tonight. I'll pack provisions for all of us to stay overnight at the hospital. Good luck, Detective Morse."

Not wanting to delay any longer, Pete and Liz and the other three officers made their way through the blur of snow to The Mercantile building.

The apartment was abandoned, so the five of them walked slowly down the stairs and fanned out into the store. Pete gestured to Liz to stay put behind the register and she complied.

The air tasted stale in the overheated building. Pete longed for the cleansing of the snowstorm as he smelled his fear mixed with the stench of used cardboard and new clothing. Weapons drawn, the four officers continued toward the back of the store, where they could hear just one voice.

The male voice was ranting: "It would have been so simple. One three-story building as the one-stop shop in an old-west themed town—museum, general store, souvenirs, and café. This gorgeous old building would have housed all of it. I could have had the funding too, after my investors knew I had the whole town secured. But you held out, wouldn't listen to reason. They've threatened to pull their money. I've got to have it. The Mercantile will make or break me."

Lighting from the back room cast it as if the people there were on stage. It also allowed Pete and his men to see each other in the otherwise darkened store.

Pete climbed the first two stairs toward the office where he could see the man pacing back and forth in the back room, gun in his hand, flailing it around to emphasize his words. Pete gestured to the other men to get closer to where the Dixons, Jimmy, and Steve watched, unwilling to move lest Lou Jacobs decided to fire his gun. It looked like Steve and Mrs. Dixon were bound to chairs. The other men were standing with their hands visible, closer to the door.

Rather than jump the lunatic and risk his gun going off, Pete gave the hand signal for all of the men to aim their weapons. He did the same. In his best, authoritative voice, he yelled: "Louis Jacobs, you are under arrest. Slowly lower your weapon to the floor and then stand up with your hands in the air."

Lou stopped and swung around, weapon still in hand. "Drop it!" Pete yelled at the top of his lungs. Lou swung Pete's direction, still hanging onto the pistol. Pete, by pure reflex, did the one thing he never thought he'd have to do when he went to work for a rural police department, and he fired his weapon, ONCE, TWICE. As the assailant fell, Pete lowered his gun and dropped it gently on the stair in front of him.

Chapter Thirty-nine

Jimmy and Pop watched Lou Jacobs take his fatal fall to the floor. Pete's shots had gone to the right shoulder and left knee, knocking Lou off his feet and onto the floor where his head met the shale edging at the base of the furnace, killing him instantly. Bulging eyes stared vacantly ahead in macabre surprise.

Pop kicked the weapon away from Lou's grasp anyway; and he and Jimmy went immediately to ungag and untie Mom and Steve, who had regained consciousness only moments before the shooting. Liz raced to Steve and cradled his head gently in her arms.

Pop helped Mom out of her chair and planted a kiss on her swollen mouth. She collapsed in a fit of relieved tears. She kept her gaze averted from the obviously deceased Lou Jacobs.

Jimmy went over to his friend, Pete, who looked stricken after pulling the trigger. "You did good, Pete. He would have killed us all, maybe even himself. The man was sick."

"I know. Still, if he had dropped the gun, I wouldn't have had to shoot him."

"You didn't kill him, you know." Another officer offered.

"Then how come he's dead?" Pete asked dully.

"He just fell wrong," was the reply.

Pop chimed in. "Pete Morse, that was as fine an example

of marksmanship as I've seen, and believe me, I know. You wounded him so that he couldn't fire his weapon or run. That's what you were supposed to do. You couldn't have foreseen that Mom and I would have put that nasty shale base on the furnace to shore it up further off the floor or that Lou would fall that direction."

Jimmy, Pete, Liz, Steve, and Mom and Pop filed out of the back room while the other officers called for the coroner and reported back to the Sheriff. Pop flipped on more of the store lights.

"Looks like you solved the last of your mysteries, Pete." Jimmy offered.

"What does he mean?" Pop asked.

"That phone call? The one that saved our behinds? Well, that was Pete calling to tell you that Lou Jacobs was the man who ran over Danica with his car." Jimmy spilled.

Mom and Pop let out a collective gasp.

"Then I am doubly grateful that you made him pay for what he did, Pete. You didn't wound that man any worse than he wounded Danica. He just paid the bigger price." Pop reasoned.

Pete shook his head, emotionally exhausted. "I really need that vacation."

"Shoot, Pete. Take two weeks off. I'll send you anywhere you want to go," Pop offered.

"That sounds great, Pop. Do I get to go too?" Steve deadpanned, his head in his hand. They all laughed in relief, as they heard the ambulances descend on the quiet town of Sibby, Washington.

Slippery

Epilogue

It was two months later and the great thaw had finally come to North Eastern Washington State. Crocuses were poking their waxy leaves tentatively from the soil, and geese were flying in droves back to their Northern nesting grounds. Mom picked out new pots to put in front of The Mercantile for her annuals. She realized happily that she needed to pick out pots for Wren's this year too.

George Stevens and his wife, Loretta, pulled up in front of the store. Pop acknowledged George, but stopped short of welcoming him. Mom, happy to see her old friend, invited Loretta upstairs for coffee while the two gentlemen talked.

"Well, George, to what do I owe this pleasure?" Pop quizzed.

"I've come to give you an apology, years overdue." George admitted.

"Is that right?" Pop asked.

"That's right. I'm sorry for the pain my former clients have caused you over the years. I should never have fallen for Ashley and Toby's wiles."

"I noticed you didn't represent them in the drug cases." Pop said.

"Are you kidding? If I'd had any idea just how sleazy they were, I would have had nothing to do with them."

"Sure. Okay, well, apology accepted."

"I have other good news for you," George offered. "It's

about Danica. How is she doing, by the way?"

"She's wonderful. She's in physical therapy learning how to walk with the metal rod in her leg and she's still reliant on crutches until she masters it, but she's home and we're all so grateful for that." Pop shared.

"How about the kids? How are they handling their father and grandmother going to jail?"

"Seth and Lorna are fantastic since they have their mom home. It's not like Toby was a great influence on them anyway. The kids' life has always been most stable and happy at home with Danica and Jimmy."

"Are Danica and Jimmy doing okay with hospital bills and such?" George asked, though Pop found this intrusion unsettling.

"They've got a bit of a hole to dig out of, thanks to grief from Danica's medical insurance company, but they'll be okay. Jimmy's brother is sending as much work as possible his way. Why do you ask?"

"I was the attorney of record for Louis Jacobs as well."

"Well *that* figures," Pop quipped.

"Yeah. Yeah. A man has to earn a living, right? That's why you've gone and bought Glenna Stone's place too, isn't it?"

"I bought Wren's because Glenna found out she has rheumatoid arthritis, a condition that Liz stands to inherit too, and she can no longer handle the baking. I've hired a baker and a manager; and I'm going to hold onto the store, should Liz ever come back to Sibby and desire to take on a business that has been in her family for four generations. If she did so, I would sell it back to her. In the meantime, it's been a profitable business, so it's a good deal, yes." Pop agreed.

"I think that's noble of you, to say the least. That aside, though, I need to tell you another reason I'm here."

"Of course," Pop agreed.

"Lou Jacobs has been proven to be the man responsible for striking Danica with his car. My understanding is that it was an accident, but because Lou drove away, his insurance company was never aware of it. It turns out that his auto insurance company is responsible for Danica's medical expenses. They've heard about the entire fiasco; and in lieu of a lawsuit from Danica's health insurance company, they've already come forward with a settlement offer."

"Really? Does Danica know about this?"

"She does. Jimmy wouldn't let me past the front door, what with my role in Toby's custody cases, but he promised to pass the word on to her. I came straight from there because Jimmy thought you might like to hear about the offer also."

"Good, old Jimmy. You know, they've been saving up ever since they got married to make their house bigger for the kids. They had to use all of that money and then some to cover Jimmy's time off work and Danica's bills. This should make them very happy." Pop admitted.

"Oh, this will make them more than happy. As far as the folks in Sibby are concerned, the amount of money I'm talking about will make them rather rich."

Pop's face lit with genuine gladness for his daughter. It was about time the Burdicks got a break.

"At any rate, Pop. I wanted to have this all out with you because you and I used to be pretty good friends. I'm wondering if there might be a little part of you that misses that friendship like I do."

Pop pondered this for a minute. "Maybe so, George. Maybe so. Why don't we go and join the ladies upstairs for coffee and we'll just see about that, won't we?"

George nodded, felt for the flask in his pocket, and decided to leave it there.

Pop turned to his new assistant. Steve and Liz had left for Nashville the minute the roads cleared. Liz was accepted to start medical school during the Spring Quarter at Vanderbilt.

Pop hired Shelby Lowe and offered to sign off her hours as community service until she met her requirements from the court, and while she still wore an ankle monitor that confined her to her home and work. She was staying at Glenna's in Liz's old room. Shelby was proving to work out so well at the store, that Pop planned to hire her full time when all was said and done.

Shelby became an unlikely ally by turning Toby and Ashley Browning's drug operation to smoke. Pop figured, in a way, they owed her. Besides, Pete Morse's good friend, Connie May West, had given Shelby a glowing recommendation.

Shelby nodded as Pop asked her to mind the store. Pop reminded her of her preacher father—righteous, but gentle too, a man to look up to. With he and Mom behind her, she felt the good girl inside of her unfurling once again and she was grateful.

It did Shelby's heart good to know there were still decent people in the world like the Dixons and the Burdicks. She thought, as she wiped down the shiny wooden countertop of The Mercantile, that a happy ending for all of them couldn't be more deserved.

Danica relaxed on the porch swing and admired the lawn, who's green shoots stretched in the early spring sunshine, a promise of the long, lazy, summer days just around the corner. The dogs were flaked out under the birch tree. The kids were in school, but they would be out again in a week for Spring Break. Danica looked forward to uninterrupted family time, a chance to get to know Seth and Lorna again and try to make up for the time they'd lost.

Milo lay kitted out in a fleece suit on a quilt next to Danica. He was getting a morning nap after nursing himself to sleep. Jimmy was on his way to work in Lewville. She rubbed Milo's back thoughtfully. Maybe she would join him and just lean back and close her eyes…

The swing swayed and Danica's awareness softened. She still remembered some of the dreams and feelings from what she called her 'time away.' The to- and fro- of the swing reminded her of her lakebed. The only difference was that now she could will herself to wake up, to remember the laughter of each of her children, and to feel her husband's touch and watch her son's gentle breathing.

Danica had allowed stress over their financial burden to harden her resolve to feel better, walk better, and work away any evidence of the accident that had nearly shattered their lives. The sheer effort of her determination exhausted her. Now, according to Jimmy, they weren't going to have to worry about money. She embraced this knowledge and let peace and gratitude be the feelings for the day. Thus, the porch swing invited her, soothed her and her baby boy.

She wasn't sure, thinking back, what defined her most. It felt like she had lived three lifetimes: First, the lot of a teenage mother in an unhappy marriage; second, the blissful housewife with an adoring husband and a new baby; and third, the victim of a tragic accident, who'd held the hand of death and emerged stronger than ever. It was ironic that her birthday in May would only see her at the ripe old age of twenty-six. What else could the long life ahead possibly hold for her?

Maybe she would do like Liz and initiate a support group: In Liz's case, it was a victims of rape support group; in Danica's it would be for people with near-death experiences. Or perhaps she would volunteer to work a few days a week at Wren's and learn how to bake, a skill that had yet evaded her. Better yet, she could plan the remodel of the Burdick home, and become a carpenter, painter, and decorator. Then, of course, there was always the acting thing. Danica opened her eyes, energized now. Why couldn't she do it all?

She would start with chucking the crutches, she decided. She rose carefully, so as not to upset Milo, and took a few tentative steps toward the door of the house. Danica moved proud and tall, the shooting pains in her leg tolerable and just a not-so-subtle reminder of her ordeal. She shoved the discomfort aside. This was her second chance at life. She wouldn't dream of wasting it. Danica had a lot to do.

About the Author

Kimberly Ann Freel lives in North Central Washington State on a ranch with her husband, four children, two horses, two ponies, a black Labradog, and one sweet, cross-eyed cat. *Slippery* is her fourth novel.

Please visit *www.kimfreel.com* to learn about Kimberly's latest writing endeavors and to read witty and practical insights on time management for creative people.

For more information about *CMP Publishing Group, LLC*, be sure to visit *www.cmppg.com*!

www.ingramcontent.com/pod-product-compliance
Lightning Source LLC
LaVergne TN
LVHW040735250326
834688LV00031B/304